Readers love *Truth Will Out*
by K.C. WELLS

"…an enjoyable, feel good cozy mystery. Great for a trip, or a rainy fall afternoon where you can curl up with your furry four-legged buddy and a cuppa something hot. I'm looking forward to the next in the series."

—Gay Book Reviews

"I loved it and cannot wait for the next one, and I highly recommend it!"

—The Novel Approach

"*Truth Will Out* is a rather quintessential British mystery…. I look forward to more adventures in Merrychurch."

—Joyfully Jay

By K.C. WELLS

Published by DREAMSPINNER PRESS
www.dreamspinnerpress.com

Roots of Evil

K.C. Wells

DREAMSPINNER PRESS

Published by
DREAMSPINNER PRESS

5032 Capital Circle SW, Suite 2, PMB# 279,
Tallahassee, FL 32305-7886 USA
www.dreamspinnerpress.com

Roots of Evil

Cover Art

Mass Market Paperback ISBN: 978-1-64108-164-1
Trade Paperback ISBN: 978-1-64405-271-6
Digital ISBN: 978-1-64405-270-9
Library of Congress Control Number: 2019904444
Mass Market Paperback published January 2020
v. 1.0

Printed in the United States of America
∞
This paper meets the requirements of
ANSI/NISO Z39.48-1992 (Permanence of Paper).

In memory of my father, Peter Jones. I'm glad we got to discuss this one.

Dear Reader, if you get the feeling that someone is reading over your shoulder, but there's no one there? Don't panic—it's just my dad. He's checking my grammar. ;-)

ACKNOWLEDGMENTS

AS ALWAYS, thank you to my beta team. Your eyes see so much.

But special thanks to my husband, Andrew. There is so much of you in this book—your ideas for the plot, dialogue, intrigue, humor…. I couldn't have written this one without you.

CHAPTER ONE

Saturday, November 4, 2017

JONATHON DE Mountford circled the bonfire, unable to keep his grin at bay. "This is going to be great." The pile of wood and other combustible items had been growing steadily since before Halloween, after he'd announced a Bonfire Night party to be held at the manor. Every day had seen more added to its height, and he'd watched its progress with glee. "Only six hours to go!" He came to a halt at Mike's side, admiring the view.

"You're nothing but a big kid at heart, aren't you?" Mike Tattersall gave him a playful nudge with his elbow. "Look at you, all excited about setting fire to a pile of... crap."

Jonathon narrowed his gaze. "Crap? *Crap*?" He caught the twinkle in Mike's eye. "Don't give me that. You're just as big a kid. I saw you drooling over the list of fireworks." He gave Mike a smug smile. "And don't tell me you were merely checking in the interests of public safety. That *was* you, wasn't it? 'Ooh, Catherine wheels! Cool.'"

Mike aimed a mock glare in his direction. "Which only goes to confirm my suspicions. *You* have ears like a shit-house rat."

Jonathon let out an exaggerated sigh. "I guess the honeymoon is definitely over."

Mike snorted. "Sweetheart, the honeymoon was over the first morning you rolled onto your side, snuggled up against me, and farted."

Jonathon gave him the sweetest smile he could muster. "How does the saying go? 'If you can't beat 'em, join 'em'? Because that's all *I* was doing."

Mike held up his hands. "Okay, okay, so we're both as bad as the other." He gazed at the towering pile. "It's very impressive. I can't believe how much stuff people have brought."

It had been Jonathon's idea to provide the firework display, but rather than make it a lord-of-the-manor thing, he'd wanted to involve the whole village. Between Mike (in the pub), Rachel Meadow (in her tea shop), and Mike's sister, Sue (everywhere else), they'd gotten word out that villagers were to bring the components of the bonfire. It began as a trickle but had soon swelled into a steady stream of people carrying whatever they could lay their hands on.

Only, it hadn't stopped there. Paul Drake, a local pig farmer, announced that he was going to supply a hog roast. Rachel came up with the idea of providing tea, coffee, and hot chocolate. Mike was planning a beer and mulled wine stall, and the Women's Institute stepped in to say they'd provide baked potatoes, hot dogs, and burgers. The Merrychurch brass band agreeing to play was the icing on the cake.

It was going to be a fantastic event, and Jonathon couldn't wait. The bonfire had surpassed his initial expectations, and it warmed his heart to see the village pulling together. Everything was in place to make it an evening to remember.

"At least the rain held off," Jonathon commented. There had been indications that a shower was possible, but the skies remained clear. "Not that it would have mattered. We'd simply have moved the event to tomorrow night."

Mike coughed. "Er, no, we couldn't. Remember? We'd have had all the ladies on the Parish Council on our backs. Why do you think I suggested holding it on the fourth instead of the fifth?"

"I did wonder about that." Mike had assured him this was the way it had to be, and Jonathon had acquiesced.

"It's always been this way. Celebrating Guy Fawkes' Night on a Sunday is generally frowned upon. Seeing as we *are* remembering a plot to blow up the Houses of Parliament." Mike affected a cut-glass accent. "Not quite the done thing, eh?"

Jonathon sighed. "I wouldn't know. I never went to bonfire parties when I was younger." He gazed around the grounds. "Maybe this is my way of making up for what I missed."

"Then we're gonna make this one memorable. Did I tell you?" Mike grinned. "Sue is doing a bobbing-for-apples stand with Andrew. That should be a laugh. And Doris from the village shop is doing a raffle, all proceeds going to charity. She says she's been asking for donations for the last week, and so far people have been really generous. Doris did want me to remind you. Apparently you're contributing a grand prize."

Jonathon nodded. "I've been putting together a hamper. It's full of local produce, including a lot of fresh meat from the farms on the estate. I spent three days last week going around and asking if local businesses wanted to contribute. I'm adding a couple of bottles of champagne and those handmade chocolates I picked up in London, to make it a bit special. By the time I'm finished, there won't be room to add a chocolate drop." He peered at Mike. "Is everything ready for your stall?"

"Right down to the oranges and cinnamon sticks for the mulled wine. The pub won't be open tonight. I don't see the point—everyone will be here."

Jonathon was keeping his fingers crossed. The summer fete had been organized by Melinda Talbot, the vicar's wife, but this was *his* baby, the first event he'd arranged in the village, and he wanted it to be a success. Slowly but surely, he was getting to know the villagers, but there were still so many he hadn't met yet, including his own tenants. Hardly surprising, seeing as he'd not been in the village all that long. That was another reason for holding the bonfire party—a chance to get to know more of Merrychurch's inhabitants.

It'll be fine. As long as we don't set fire to anyone.

"THAT GUY Fawkes is amazing," Melinda exclaimed, her thin, gloved hands wrapped around a polystyrene cup of mulled wine. "I must admit, it made my heart jump when they threw it onto the bonfire. It's so realistic."

"Do you think the event is a success?" Jonathon peered anxiously around them. With twenty or so minutes to go until the fireworks began at nine o'clock, it seemed like most of the village had turned out. Graham Billings, the local constable, had roped off the bonfire so no one could get too close, and had checked it several times before Jonathon lit it, to make sure no animals had gotten into it. He was presently engaged in strolling around its perimeter, giving stern glances at kids who were trying to set off fireworks on their own. Everyone was standing around the blaze, talking and laughing, their faces glowing in the firelight.

Melinda patted his arm. "Relax, Jonathon. You've done really well, especially considering how little time you've had to pull this all together." She laid her hand on his cheek. "Dominic would be very proud of you, to see you settling in like this."

That remark was enough to send warmth surging through him. The cheers that had filled the air when he'd lit the bonfire had been gratifying.

The Merrychurch brass band launched into "Light My Fire," and everyone around them laughed and applauded enthusiastically. They'd already played "Fire" by Arthur Brown, and "Play with Fire" by the Rolling Stones. Someone in the band obviously had a sense of humor. Not only that, but it showed a lot of commitment: there hadn't been all *that* much time to learn the pieces.

Jonathon glanced around. "Where's Lloyd? Didn't he come with you?"

Melinda sighed. "He sends his apologies, but he has to finish his sermon. And then there's Jinx. That cat is scared to death every Bonfire Night. I looked in on Lloyd before I came out this evening, and Jinx was tucked in behind him on his chair. It can't have been comfortable, but Lloyd said he didn't have the heart to move him."

Mike appeared at Jonathon's side, bringing him a cup of mulled wine. "No luck finding him a curate?"

Melinda shook her head. "It appears no one wants to be the curate of a small village where nothing happens."

Mike chuckled. "Merrychurch is hardly that, especially after this summer."

Melinda glared at him. "Do *not* remind me, please. The number of people who stop me in the street—almost three months later, mind you—and ask if I'm sure I had no inkling that Sebastian was capable of murder…." She shivered.

Jonathon put his arm around her. "Ignore them. None of us had any idea, okay? How could we?"

Melinda gave him a grateful smile. "Not exactly an auspicious start to your life in the village."

Jonathon was doing his best to put it behind him, but living at the manor house wasn't easy. There were so many memories of Dominic. Although the study was a beautiful room, Jonathon hardly ever went in there. The marble would always bear the stain of his uncle's blood. Instead, he'd decided to live mainly in the west wing, where he'd chosen a large room to act as a photography studio, and was focusing his energies on getting it ready to use.

"This was a wonderful idea."

The loud voice plucked Jonathon from his thoughts and dropped him back into the present. A small crowd of people had gathered around him, Mike, and Melinda, but some of them were strangers to him. He recognized the speaker instantly, a distinguished-looking man in his forties.

"Thank you—" Jonathon cleared his throat. "Do I address you as Mr. Mayor?"

The mayor laughed. "That would be fine if this was a public engagement. But tonight I'm just John Barton, enjoying the village bonfire with my family." He inclined his head to the well-dressed woman on his right arm. "Have you met my wife, Debra? And this is our son, Jason."

Jonathon shook hands with Debra. "I'm pleased to meet you." He gave Jason a nod. The young man had to be in his late teens, a handsome boy with the most beautiful green eyes.

To Jonathon's surprise, Jason grasped his hand and shook it enthusiastically. "I've got your books. I think your photos are so cool."

"Thank you." It didn't matter how many times Jonathon heard remarks like that. The result was always the same: his face grew hot and he didn't know what to say next.

"Ay-up mi-duck." An elderly woman with a lined face and bright blue eyes addressed Jason with a wide smile. "Lookin' more 'andsome every time I see ya. Just like your dad."

Jason smiled politely. "Good evening, Mrs. Teedle."

Beside him, his mother stiffened momentarily but quickly recovered and gave Mrs. Teedle a polite nod, her expression impassive. Around Jonathon, others reacted similarly.

Jonathon might not have known some of the vocabulary, but there was an inflection to her voice that he recognized immediately. "I don't think we've met." He held out his hand. "Jonathon de Mountford."

"An' like Jason said, I'm Mrs. Teedle." She took his hand, cackling. "Allreet. Don't think tha's met all the tenants yet."

He cocked his head to one side. "Perhaps not, but it's obvious you've spent time in Australia."

She hooted with laughter. "Bless ya, duck. Thirty years I lived there. Don't exactly sound like a native, though, do I?"

He laughed. "Not really. It's just now and then, the way your voice rises in places...."

"I've been back twenty years, but yeah, I can still hear it now and again. Roots win out in the end. I've never managed to shift me accent." She inclined her head toward the lower part of the field, where the fireworks had been set up. "What time is kickoff? 'Cos I want to be out of here before then."

Jonathon frowned. "Oh. But the fireworks are the best part."

Mrs. Teedle shook her head. "Not for me, mi-duck." She lifted a wrinkled hand to gently pull back her gray-and-white hair, revealing her ear. "One Bonfire Night when I were a kid, a Roman candle took off when it should've stayed put and took part of me ear with it."

Jonathon peered closely. The ear had a pointed look to it. "I'm sorry."

She shrugged as she removed her hand. "It were a long time ago. An' to this day, I'm still not that keen on fireworks. This hasn't bothered me for many a year. I used to tell people I was Mr. Spock's understudy." She grinned, the lines deepening around her eyes.

Mike snickered. "Have you bought a raffle ticket yet, Mrs. Teedle? There are some great prizes."

Mrs. Teedle let out another hoot of laughter. "Bless ya, mi-duck, that's why I came. I've donated some of me jams as one of the prizes." She peered intently at Jonathon. "But seeing as you're me landlord, I guess it would be polite to buy a ticket. Besides, I saw the champagne bottles just now, stickin' out of that hamper. Always was partial to a bit of bubbly."

Mike dug out the envelope containing the tickets from his jacket pocket. "I've only got a couple left anyway. You never know—one could be the winning ticket."

Mrs. Teedle fished in her pocket and brought out a pound coin. "There ya go. Me last bit of change." She peered at the pink ticket. "Well, gerra move-on an' write me name on your copy. I'm not gonna 'ang about 'ere. I may be British born and bred, but these old bones have got a bit nesh in me old age. I'm off to my warm bed."

Mike scribbled her name on the duplicate ticket. "All done. Good luck."

Mrs. Teedle regarded him with bright eyes. "I've always believed you make your own luck." Her grin widened. "An' I've always been a jammy sod." She acknowledged Jonathon with a brief nod. "Pleased to meet the lord of the manor at last. Good night, ladies an' gents." And with that, she shuffled away from the small gathering.

Jonathon had to smile. "Is she what you'd call a village character?" Mrs. Teedle was maybe in her seventies or eighties, dressed in black, but she moved fairly sprightly for her age.

Melinda cleared her throat. "That's one way of describing her. In less charitable times, she'd have been called the village witch."

He blinked. "Seriously?"

"Witch is right." A woman next to Melinda stared after Mrs. Teedle with her eyes narrowed to slits. "All those potions of hers… you don't know what you're getting half the time." She tossed back a mane of long blond hair.

The man next to her rolled his eyes. "For God's sake, Dawn, let it drop, will you? It's been three years."

Dawn glared at him. "Yeah? And where would I be now if she hadn't stuck her oar in?"

"You don't know that," the man said softly. He pulled gently on her arm. "Come on. I'll buy you another roast pork sandwich."

Grumbling, she allowed him to lead her toward Paul Drake's hog roast stand.

Jonathon's head was still reeling. "But… she's not really a witch… is she?"

Jason laughed. "She's this old biddy who lives in a cottage at the edge of the forest. Sure, you hear lots of stories about her, but I've known her all my life. People are always gonna have shit to say about someone, right? Especially someone who's a bit mysterious and minds their own business."

His father gazed at him with affection. "And *some* people always see the good in others."

Jason's face flushed, and he coughed. "Is it time for fireworks yet?"

Jonathon laughed. "I think that was a hint." He addressed those people standing around him. "If you'll excuse me, I have to go press a switch."

"And I'm gonna go with him to make sure he doesn't blow himself up," Mike added with a wink. That got a laugh from the small crowd.

"I'll get Graham to tell everyone," Melinda called out as they walked toward the bottom of the field, where a control box had been set up. Everything would begin with the press of one button.

When they got there, Jonathon paused and looked back. The facade of the manor house was lit by several lanterns, which cast eerie shadows over the stone front-age. The bonfire still burned, its flames reaching high into the sky. It would be a few hours before it would extinguish itself.

Mike nudged him. "Ready to set fire to about a thousand pounds-worth of fireworks?"

Jonathon chuckled. "To get everyone together like this, virtually the whole village? It was worth every penny." He stood still, listening to Graham's strident announcement via a megaphone. Suddenly the air was filled with voices as the countdown began.

"Five… four… three… two… *one!*"

And with that, Jonathon pressed the switch, then hurried back up the field to get a better view, accompanied by a chorus of *ooh*s and *aah*s. The night sky was filled with showers of colored light, set against a soundtrack of whizzes, cracks, whistles, and bangs. Jonathon watched the display with joy, Mike's hand curled around his.

Yeah. Worth every penny.

CHAPTER TWO

JONATHON ROLLED over in bed, smiling to himself to find Mike still there, on his side facing the window, obviously fast asleep. It wasn't as if Mike shared Jonathon's bed every night, not that Jonathon would mind *that* in the slightest, but Jonathon loved those nights when he heard the crunch of gravel outside as Mike drove his 4x4 onto the drive, and a thrill of anticipation rippled through him.

I love it when he stays the night.

Jonathon hadn't had many relationships in his life thus far, and he knew it was still early days. The signs were good, however, in spite of the reception Mike had received from Jonathon's father—enough to cause frostbite in the middle of August. Thankfully, Thomas de Mountford's career kept him busy enough that visits to Merrychurch would be few and far between.

Jonathon shifted across the bed, wrapped his arm around Mike's waist, and planted gentle kisses across his shoulders.

Mike stirred slightly, and a soft noise of appreciation gladdened Jonathon's heart. "Morning."

Jonathon kissed Mike's neck, loving the shiver that shuddered through his body. "It's only seven. We have plenty of time."

Suddenly, Mike moved, pushing Jonathon onto his back and rolling on top of him. He gazed into Jonathon's eyes, his lips twitching. "Time for what?"

Jonathon let out a contented, drawn-out sigh. "Whatever you want."

Mike's equally happy sigh was music to his ears. "I like the sound of that." He drew the sheets over their heads and tugged Jonathon farther down the bed, the two of them lost in a cocoon of soft cotton, a padded mattress, and kisses that promised much more to come.

Jonathon loved his mornings.

"THERE'S MORE toast if you want it, sir," Janet said as she cleared away the plates from the dining table. "And Ivy's just brewed another pot of coffee, seeing as Mr. Tattersall is here." Her pink cheeks glowed.

Jonathon gazed at her in silence for a moment, then smiled. "Yes to both, please, Janet."

She nodded and disappeared from the room.

Jonathon sighed. "It's not much to ask, is it? I'm Jonathon. You're Mike." Janet had been with him a month and didn't appear to have gotten the message.

Mike's eyes twinkled. "It's not gonna happen. She's your housekeeper. You're always going to be *sir*."

"I'm still not convinced I need a housekeeper," Jonathon grumbled.

Mike laughed. "At least this way I know someone is looking after you, making sure you eat, seeing to the laundry, et cetera, when I'm not around." He chuckled. "You need a keeper."

Jonathon straightened in his chair. "I managed to look after myself just fine in—"

"Yeah, yeah, I know. You've traveled all around the world. Well, Mr. Explorer, you're home now. You're not staying in a shantytown or a tent or God knows what. You have a manor house to think about. And even though you may only live in part of it, the place still needs looking after and cleaning. As do you. So either like it or lump it, Mr. Lord of the Manor." Mike folded his arms across his chest and stared at Jonathon as if daring him to reply.

Jonathon knew better. He let out another sigh. "When I was a kid, we had a cook, a housekeeper, and a gardener. That's how I grew up. So maybe I simply need to get used to that kind of life again."

Mike's smile spoke of approval. "Exactly. And Ivy's more forthright than Janet. She's not shy about telling you what she thinks, is she?"

That made Jonathon laugh. Ivy was a middle-aged woman whose children had all grown up and left the nest. Her husband was away a lot on business, and she'd needed something to do. Cooking for Jonathon provided that. And he had to admit, her culinary skills were amazing. He'd never eaten so well.

"Ivy's great. They both are."

Before Jonathon had taken them on, one of the first topics he'd brought up had been the subject of Mike. The last thing he wanted was people working for him who would not be comfortable with the reality of a gay employer. As it was, he couldn't have wished for better staff. Ivy's older brother was gay, a fact she'd shared almost instantly, and Janet's face had flushed when she announced she was more than happy to work for him. That only left old Ben Threadwell, who worked in the gardens. He'd given Mike an odd glance or two at first, but that had been it.

Janet entered the dining room with a pot of coffee and a replenished toast rack. "Can I just say what a great time I had last night, sir? That bonfire was wonderful, and I've never seen so many fireworks. *And* I won a prize in the raffle." She beamed. "There was this lovely, soft rainbow scarf and gloves. That'll do me a treat this winter."

Mike smiled broadly. "Aw. My sister knitted those."

Jonathon had been delighted by how many tickets they'd sold. All the prizes had been collected, with the exception of the hamper. "You've both reminded me. I have to inform the winner of the grand prize today."

"Who won it?"

Jonathon grinned. "The village witch, apparently." He straightened his features. "Sorry. That was how she was described to me last night. It conjured up images of her crouching beside a cauldron, stirring a boiling liquid...."

To his surprise, Janet pursed her lips. "You may think it's a joke, sir, but trust me, there's no smoke without fire. The stories I could tell you about that Mrs. Teedle...." She drew herself up to her full height of five feet. "But I'm not one to speak ill of people behind their backs." And with that, she marched out of the room.

Jonathon stared at the closed door. "Wow. I think I touched a nerve." He glanced across at Mike. "What do *you* know about Mrs. Teedle?"

Mike snickered. "You keep forgetting, I've not been here all that long, not much more than a year. I've seen her once or twice in the village, but that's all. She doesn't come to the pub, and she hadn't popped up on my radar." He shrugged. "Maybe it's like young Jason said last night—she's just a harmless old lady who likes to live alone."

"And is that what Sue says?" Jonathon asked with a grin.

Mike speared him with a look. "Seeing as my sister has an opinion on everything and everyone in this village, of *course* she has something to say. She thinks Mrs. Teedle is a creepy old lady, but most of that is based on where she lives."

Now Jonathon was intrigued. "And where is that?"

"You know the forest that starts right at the outer edge of the village? Not far from Ben's place? She has a house there, just along the path that leads into the forest."

"What—*in* the forest?" Jonathon gave an exaggerated shiver. "I'm with Sue, then. That sounds spooky."

Mike bit his lip. "Well, you get to see for yourself today. As she left before the raffle was drawn, it's *your* duty to deliver the prize to her. And she *is* one of your tenants, after all." When Jonathon blinked, Mike nodded deliberately. "Her house belongs to the estate. She did say so last night. You're her landlord." He smiled. "I guess you've had so much on your plate since you moved here that you haven't come to terms with it all yet. *Now* maybe you understand why I keep saying you need to add an estate manager to your staff. Right now you can't keep track of it all."

Mike had a point. "Maybe you're right." Jonathon gazed at the table, covered in its snow-white cloth. "I'll go see Mrs. Teedle later this morning."

"And why not now?"

Jonathon snickered. "Not when we still have toast and fresh coffee."

MIKE PARKED the 4x4 in a lay-by at the edge of the forest and switched off the engine. "Okay, grab the hamper and let's get this done." He opened the door and climbed out.

Jonathon chuckled. "No one said you had to come with me, you know."

Mike shrugged. "I was around. It made sense. Abi's opening the pub." He grinned. "And besides, what else am I going to do on a Sunday afternoon?" Jonathon coughed, and Mike aimed a mock glare in his direction. "Besides that." He pointed to the path that disappeared into the forest. "That way." Mike shivered.

"I thought it was Sue who said this place was creepy."

"Forests are creepy, full stop. They're too quiet. Why do you think there's always a house in a spooky old forest in all those horror films? The stuff of nightmares."

Trying not to laugh, Jonathon carried the hamper carefully in both arms, glancing at the ground to see where he was going. "This path looks well used, though."

"Ramblers use it all the time. If you carry on along it, eventually it brings you out on the far side of your estate."

"It does?" Jonathon was having a hard time working out the topography.

Mike sighed. "I thought you'd be good at geography, Mr. Well-Seasoned Traveler. The forest is kinda laid out in a curve around the estate." He shook his head. "I'm sure somewhere in that manor house, there's an aerial photo of the hall. That would make things a lot simpler." His eyes twinkled. "I forgot—you're a visual learner, aren't you?"

Jonathon had the distinct feeling they weren't talking about geography.

"There's a well somewhere too." Mike came to a stop and pointed. "There you go. That's the place."

Jonathon stared at a dark gray stone cottage that had seen better days. The roof was covered in moss, and ivy clung to its walls, snaking itself around windows and doors, of which there were two. Ridge tiles had gone and some of the roof slates had moved, giving the cottage a sad air of neglect.

What caught his eye was the table standing by the nearest door. On it were lots of jars with brightly colored labels, and to the left was a metal box, fastened with a padlock but with a slit cut into the top. A clipboard was attached to the edge of the table, with a pencil dangling from it on a string. Jonathon put down the hamper on the solid doorstep and peered at the table.

"Ah. She said something last night about jams," he said quietly to Mike.

"Yeah. Lots of folks around here do this. They put out their jams and an honesty box." Mike pointed to the clipboard. "People can leave comments here, and there's a price list too." He picked up a jar. "This sounds lovely. Mango-and-peach jam." The colorful printed label contained a handwritten date.

Jonathon chuckled. "You couldn't just leave a box out like this in some places. It'd get stolen. And how would you know if people put in the correct amount?"

Mike patted his back. "That's why it's called an honesty box? They expect you to be honest." He gestured toward the hamper. "Okay, pick it up and let's do this. If you're good, I'll buy you some jam for your morning toast when we're done."

Jonathon hoisted the hamper into his arms. "If *I'm* good," he muttered.

Mike rapped on the aged wooden door, but there was no sound from within. He repeated the action. Still no reaction.

Jonathon snickered. "I'm beginning to have déjà vu here."

Mike said nothing but tried the heavy doorknob. The door swung inward with a loud creak. "Mrs. Teedle?" he called out.

It seemed to Jonathon that silence had fallen all around them. There was no birdsong, not even the rustle of the wind through the trees. Cold trickled its way through his body. "I'm getting a bad feeling about this."

Mike held a finger to his lips, then stepped into the cottage. Jonathon followed. They were in a large room that had the appearance of a kitchen at first. One wall was covered in shelves, and every shelf was lined with glass jars and bottles. Along the opposite wall were yet more shelves, and beneath them was a long counter, into which was set a deep Belfast sink. The surfaces on either side of it were cluttered with yet more jars, labels, bowls, mortars and pestles, a rack of knives....

"Jonathon." Mike touched his arm.

Jonathon followed Mike's gaze to.... "Oh shit."

Mrs. Teedle sat at the heavy oak kitchen table, leaning back in a chair, her eyes wide open, her mouth stuffed with what looked like gnarled roots, her cheeks bulging.

Jonathon approached her haltingly as Mike drew closer to delicately place two fingers at her neck. Not that he needed to. It was obvious she was dead. On the table in front of her was a plastic mat, on which were chopped green flower stalks. More stalks and big-lobed leaves were on the table. Beside the mat lay a pair of black gloves and a large kitchen knife, its silvery edge stained slightly with….

"Is that blood?" Jonathon took a deep breath. "Look, I have to put this down. It weighs a ton." He brushed aside some of the leaves and stalks with the edge of his hand and placed the hamper on the table before straightening his back. Something sticky clung to his hand, and he brushed it against his jeans. "What on earth is this stuff?"

Mike gaped at him. "I'll tell you what it is. This is a crime scene. So put your hands behind your back or in your pockets and touch nothing."

Jonathon scowled at him. "All I did was move some plant stuff." He peered at the plastic mat. "I'm not even sure I know what this is."

Mike rolled his eyes. "Which is why I said don't touch anything. I have to call Graham—and we have to leave. Now."

That was fine by Jonathon. "Graham is not going to believe this." He took one last look at Mrs. Teedle and shivered. "There's no way *this* can be called an accident."

Mike's expression was grave. "No. We're talking murder."

"But… who would want to murder an old lady?" Jonathon's hand itched a little. "And what the hell was she chopping?"

"Good questions that can wait until we're somewhere else, with a hot cup of coffee inside us." Mike glanced around the kitchen and shuddered. "Let's get out of here." He strode out of the cottage, with Jonathon not far behind him, still stunned.

To have one murder in the village had been unfortunate.

But two?

CHAPTER THREE

MIKE HAD to admit, Graham Billings hadn't wasted any time. Ten minutes after he'd finished the call to Merrychurch's police station—which was more of a police house—Graham had arrived at the cottage on his bike. Mike and Jonathon got out of the car and met him at the front door as he leaned his bike against the wall.

Graham gave Jonathon an amused stare. "This is getting to be a habit, you finding dead bodies."

Jonathon shivered. "Well, trust me, this was no fall. This is murder."

Graham glanced at Mike. "I know that's what you said on the phone, but really?"

Mike pointed to the cottage. "One look inside, mate. That's all you'll need."

Graham got out his notebook. "Stay here." He pushed open the door and entered.

Mike put his arm around Jonathon's shoulder. "Are you all right?"

"Not really." Jonathon gave another shiver. "This isn't like Dominic."

Mike could understand that. Finding his uncle dead of a fall had been one thing. At least Jonathon knew his death hadn't been deliberate. But this? "There's such… malice behind this. All that stuff in her mouth. Who would do that?"

Before Jonathon could reply, Graham came out of the cottage. He regarded them both sternly. "You haven't touched anything in there, have you?"

"I touched the outer doorknob," Mike said, "but nothing inside."

Graham made a note before giving Jonathon a speculative glance.

Jonathon bit his lip. "Just some of the green stuff she was chopping. When I put down the hamper." His eyes widened. "The hamper!"

"Can stay where it is for now," Graham said firmly.

"But it's got meat and—" Jonathon clammed up when Graham gave him a hard stare.

"I'm gonna call the coroner. She won't like having her Sunday ruined, but then, neither do I. But you two are not to go in there until SOCO have been over it, and that might not be until tomorrow. Doubtless they'll send the boys from Winchester." His face fell. "Yeah, that'd be right. They're not gonna let a village constable investigate a murder, are they?"

Mike groaned. "As long as they don't send Gorland, like last time."

Jonathon snorted. "It's not high-profile enough for him."

"Yeah, you're right. It'll probably be some detective from CID." Graham's expression was gloomy.

"Any ideas as to the cause of death?" Mike hadn't had time to take a good look, but the skin around her neck had appeared a little odd.

"There's blood on the back of her head, so maybe someone bashed it in. But there are other indications that need checking out too." Graham grimaced. "Why stuff her mouth full of ginger?"

"Is that what it was? I didn't get a close look." Mike had been too busy trying to get Jonathon out of there.

"There was a whole heap of ginger root on the counter. Plus it looks like there's another root shoved in there too." When Mike cast a glance toward the cottage, Graham snickered. "You'll have to wait, Sherlock, before you two can go rooting around in there— pun intended."

"What makes you think we want to do that?" Mike asked indignantly.

Graham arched his eyebrows. "Because I know you? So do me a favor and take your fella home or for a coffee or something, while I wait for the coroner. He looks like he needs some sweet tea."

Mike took one look at Jonathon's pale face and came to a decision. "Come on," he said quietly, tugging on Jonathon's arm. "Let's go to Rachel's." He gave Graham one last nod. "Keep me in the loop?"

Graham gave him a pained look. "You know I will."

Mike tried to lead Jonathon away, but he pulled out of his grasp. "I don't need mollycoddling. I'm not going to faint or some nonsense like that."

"I know that," Mike replied calmly. "But we're still going to Rachel's."

"Why?"

Mike grinned. "Because she sees and hears a lot. And I have a few questions about Mrs. Teedle."

Jonathon smiled. "Ah. We're on the case. That makes more sense. Come on, then." He reached the car first, shuffling from foot to foot as he waited for Mike to unlock it.

Mike chuckled. "God, you're an impatient sod sometimes."

Jonathon climbed in, and as Mike got behind the wheel, he leaned over and kissed Mike on the cheek. "You wouldn't have me any other way."

And wasn't that the truth? Mike liked how things were working out between them. Three months into their relationship, and although they still had a lot to learn about each other, it was clear to him that they had something good going on.

Mike couldn't wait to see how things progressed.

RACHEL BEAMED as they entered the coffee shop. "Well, if it isn't the organizer of the best bonfire party ever. Oh, and his sidekick, of course." She gestured to the empty tables. "Wherever you like, boys. As you can see, I'm swamped." She rolled her eyes. "Why I even considered opening today, I'll never know. Sundays are usually dead."

Mike chuckled. "I know why. You saw that group of ramblers in the village, the same as I did, and you thought 'hey, there's an opportunity.'"

She laughed. "Damn. You got me. What can I get you? The usual? Two coffees and a couple of slices of whatever I've got in the way of delicious cakes?"

"That sounds perfect." Mike waited until Rachel had disappeared behind the door at the rear of the shop before leaning forward. "You sure you're okay?" He kept his voice low.

Jonathon shivered. "I keep seeing her in my head. That's all. The awful way she was staring."

Mike reached across the table and covered Jonathon's hand with his. "I know."

Rachel walked over to their table, carrying two plates. "I've got your favorite," she told Jonathon, placing a slice of carrot cake in front of him.

He smiled. "Just what I need." He peered up at her. "Rachel? What do you know about Mrs. Teedle?"

Rachel grinned. "Ah, you've finally met her? She's a character, isn't she? We get on, I suppose, but that's probably because I buy her homemade jams to use here. I always try to use local produce where I can. But I think I'm in a minority." She tut-tutted. "I hear so many people complaining about her rudeness. She can be a little... brusque, but I think that's her way. Have you seen that cottage of hers?"

"This morning, when I delivered her raffle prize. I couldn't help noticing... all those jars and bottles."

Rachel gave a slow nod. "Just let me get your coffee." She disappeared again.

"You haven't shared the small but significant detail that she's no longer with us," Mike remarked dryly.

"I know. I figured I'd let her talk and find out what I could first." Jonathon shut up as Rachel returned, carrying the tall coffeepot and cream jug. She placed them in the center of the table, then pulled out a chair and joined them.

"So," she began, leaning forward conspiratorially. "The jars and bottles contain all her ingredients."

"For jam?" Mike couldn't recall much of their contents, but he didn't think that sounded likely.

Rachel burst out laughing. "Bless you, no. Mrs. Teedle makes homeopathic remedies."

"Do those things actually work?" Jonathon sounded skeptical.

Rachel shrugged. "Who knows? I always say, if we look hard enough, Nature has a cure for everything, right on our doorstep, from the common cold to cancer." She chuckled. "I have to say, sometimes when I go to collect the jams, I half expect to find her crouched beside a cauldron, stirring away at some strange-smelling brew, and then a hand floats up to the surface, like in the horror films."

Jonathon gaped. "I had the same thought this morning. Well, except for the hand part."

"Does she have many customers?" Mike didn't think she would have had a lot of business in Merrychurch.

"More than you might think. I know Nathan Driscoll, the chemist, is always complaining about her, but I put that down to him being scared of a little competition. And I know she sends her remedies to people by post too, so she must be doing something right."

"How long has she lived in the village?" Mike asked before helping himself to a forkful of rich chocolate cake.

Rachel stroked her chin. "Let me think. Jason Barton is about seventeen now, so it was a few years before then. Maybe twenty years?"

"She told us that last night," Jonathon added. "Remember? She was saying how living in Merrychurch for twenty years hasn't robbed her of her Australian accent."

Mike gazed at him proudly. "Well remembered." Then he frowned. "Why reference Jason Barton?"

Rachel chuckled. "Because she delivered him, that's why! It was during the summer fete of 2000. Debra Barton was there, already a couple of weeks overdue. Well, when her waters broke, Mrs. Teedle was amazing. She took her into the first-aid tent, gave a lot of instructions to people, and delivered the baby like she did it every day of the week. It was all the village talked about for months." She shook her head. "Probably the only positive story I've heard in relation to her."

"There have been others that weren't so positive?" Mike wished he was writing all of this down, but then he reasoned that Jonathon was likely to remember it all.

Rachel pursed her lips. "Most of the time it's just talk. I mean, she lives alone in that creepy house, she doesn't interact much with the rest of the village, and her manner is a little… cold. But yeah, there have been stories. Like the one concerning Dawn Dangerfield. A few years back, she was our Miss Merrychurch."

Jonathon smiled. "What—like a beauty queen?"

"Sure. Except she went on to win Miss Wiltshire. The next step was the national stage, and Dawn thought her chances of winning were pretty good. Until… she got this rash on her face, you see, and she went to Mrs. Teedle for a cream to treat it." Rachel grimaced. "She had an allergic reaction to something in the cream, and her whole face… erupted. It wasn't pleasant. To this day, she still blames Mrs. Teedle for her not being able to take part in the competition. So much bitterness there."

Jonathon's expression grew thoughtful. "I think we met Dawn at the bonfire."

"Yeah, well, there are more tales like that. Some of them are simply because people are stupid and don't follow instructions. But there are plenty of people who don't like her and are more than happy to tell you why." Rachel gazed around her. "I hear so much of what is said in here."

"Well, you're going to hear a lot more of it, once the news breaks," Mike said quietly.

Rachel stilled. "What news? Has something happened to her? Has she had an accident?"

Jonathon sighed. "If only." He looked Rachel in the eye. "Don't say anything yet, because Graham's only just started his investigations, but... she's been murdered."

Rachel's mouth fell open and her eyes widened. After a moment, she took a deep breath. "You think you get used to something, but no, it's still a shock. I thought when they arrested Sebastian that I'd had all my shocks for this year." She sagged into the chair. "How was she killed?"

"Not all the details are known yet," Mike admitted. "Doubtless once the coroner's report is in, word will soon spread." He wasn't about to share what they'd seen.

Rachel gave a wry smile. "Of course. This *is* Merrychurch, after all. Nothing stays a secret for long around here. Although...." Her eyes sparkled. "No one guessed about Dominic and Trevor's affair, so maybe I'm wrong. The way I describe it, you'd think secrets lurk behind every door."

The bell above the main door tinkled, and Rachel got up to greet a group of four walkers.

"Well, *someone* in Merrychurch has a secret," Jonathon said under his breath. "Unless we're proposing she was killed by a stranger who happened to be passing through or who came here deliberately to murder her."

That was when Mike realized he needed to know more about the late Naomi Teedle. Maybe the answers lay in her past.

All they had to do was root them out.

CHAPTER FOUR

FOR A Sunday night, the Hare and Hounds pub was surprisingly full. But once Jonathon had caught some of the conversations, the reason for the sudden surge became obvious.

Word had gotten around.

Paul Drake sat on his usual stool at the bar, nursing a pint. "Merrychurch used to be such a quiet little spot—before *you* arrived," he said, his eyes gleaming as he aimed an intense stare in Jonathon's direction. "Now we got dead bodies piling up all over the place."

Mike guffawed. "Hardly." He glanced toward Jonathon. "Don't listen to him."

Jonathon laughed. "It's okay. I know Paul well enough by now to spot when he's pulling my leg."

Paul gave him a nod of approval. "That's it, nipper. You've got your head screwed on all right." He gazed around the pub, shaking his head. "This is bloody weird."

"What is?" Jonathon couldn't see anything out of the ordinary, apart from the influx of drinkers.

Paul leaned across the bar, and Jonathon copied him, almost conspiratorially. "I'm sittin' 'ere listenin' to this lot talking about old Mrs. Teedle."

"Well, of course they're talking about her," Jonathon said quietly.

Paul huffed. "It's not so much that they're jabbering on. That's normal. It's more a case of what they're sayin'—or what they're *not* sayin', if you get my drift. Everyone's being nice as pie." He took a long drink of beer and wiped his lips.

"Is it just a case of not speaking ill of the dead?" Jonathon suggested.

Paul cackled. "Nah. If you ask me, it's more a case of not being caught sayin' something that might make you a murder suspect."

Mike nudged Jonathon. "Especially now." He inclined his head toward the door.

Jonathon glanced up as Graham Billings approached the bar, dressed in jeans, a thick sweater, and a heavy jacket. "Pint, please, Mike. I'm gasping." He sat on a barstool and gave Jonathon a friendly nod. "Good evening. You okay now?"

"I was okay then, but thanks for asking." Jonathon walked over to him. "Where are you up to?"

"Well, the body's gone. SOCO will be in the house first thing in the morning. And I've called her next of kin." Mike placed a pint glass in front of him, and Graham's face lit up. "You're a lifesaver. I've been dreaming of this all flipping day. So much for a peaceful Sunday on duty." He lifted the pint and drained a third of its contents.

"SOCO." Paul smacked his lips. "Sounds like something off the TV."

"Scene-of-crime officers to you," Graham said, nodding toward him.

"Who's minding the station?" Mike asked with a grin.

Graham let out a satisfied sigh. "I roped in Dan Fitch."

"The special constable?" Mike asked with a frown.

"That's him. About time he did a shift anyway. Not that he won't call me if things get hairy." Graham drank some more. "And Dave Frogatt will be back off holiday tomorrow."

"Who's Mrs. Teedle's next of kin?" Mike asked, pulling another pint for a customer.

"She's got a daughter in Australia. Married with three grown-up kids. She sounded awful. Not surprising, really. Said she's gonna book a flight over here as soon as she can, but it might take a while. Her husband's away at the moment."

Someone cleared their throat loudly, and Jonathon's attention was seized by a middle-aged man with a definite case of middle-aged spread, his round cheeks flushed.

"Don't you think we should all be raising a glass to the dear departed?" he said, addressing Mike. "To show our respect?"

Paul snorted. "If anyone but *you* had said that, I might have said yes." From behind him came murmurs of agreement.

Jonathon gazed at the pub's occupants in surprise.

The man's flush deepened. "I don't know what you mean, I'm sure."

Paul widened his eyes. "The dear departed? Respect? That *was* you, wasn't it, last week, mouthing off in 'ere about her? Something about charlatans, fake healers, con artists…. Didn't notice much respect in anything you had to say then." He narrowed his gaze. "And don't think for a second that we don't know who was behind that smear campaign. That had your mucky prints all over it." His eyes gleamed. "Yeah. Now *there's* a thought. Maybe Graham 'ere should be testing one of those flyers for fingerprints. If there are any left, of course. Mine ended up on the fire, where all rubbish belongs."

The man's eyes bulged. "I'm not going to stand here and be… maligned like this."

Paul gave him a sweet smile. "There's the door. Don't let it hit your arse on the way out." He raised his new pint. "Cheers, Mike."

The man glared at Paul before striding toward the door, pushing through customers.

Jonathon gaped from behind the bar. "Okay, who was that?"

"*That* was Nathan Driscoll, our chemist," Graham informed him. He glanced at Paul, his lips twitching into a wry smile. "And remind me never to get on your bad side."

Paul huffed. "Come on. He deserved it, the little shit. He's been bad-mouthing Naomi Teedle for as long as I can remember." He snorted. "'Dear departed,' my arse."

"What's this flyer you mentioned?" Jonathon was intrigued.

Before Paul could reply, Graham coughed. "You don't know he was behind it. He could do you for slander, if he was feeling vindictive."

Paul let out another derisive snort. "Yeah, right. Like *that's* gonna happen. It was Nathan, all right." He tilted his head. "*Could* you test for fingerprints, though?"

Graham sighed patiently. "Yes. But even if he did write it, that doesn't mean he murdered her."

"Will one of you tell me about this flyer?" Jonathon demanded. Both Graham and Paul stared at him, and he bit his lip. "Sorry, but I'm obviously missing something important here."

Graham took another long drink from his pint before responding. "A while back, before you came to the village, we all received a flyer through the post. It was about homeopathic remedies and what a load of rubbish they are. How you should only trust tried-and-tested medications from reputable sources... like your local chemist."

"It didn't mention *which* chemist," Paul added, "but it was fairly obvious who'd put it together."

Graham coughed again. "Supposition."

Mike laughed. "You can cough as much as you like, Graham, but you won't change Paul's mind. Now, suppose we talk about more useful topics—like when we can get a look at Mrs. Teedle's house. From the inside."

Graham burst into laughter. "Oh God. Sherlock and Watson are back, aren't they?"

Mike gave him an innocent glance. "Well, technically speaking, Jonathon does have a right to look at his property... doesn't he?"

Graham stilled. "Oh. Yeah. I'd forgotten." He leveled a hard stare at Mike. "And I suppose you'd go along too, to take notes, right?"

Jonathon chuckled. "He knows you too well, Mike."

Graham cackled. "You're both as bad as each other. So I tell you what I'll do. When SOCO have concluded their investigations, I'll give you a call. Then you can go and search that creepy old place to your hearts' content. As long as that's *all* you do. No more sleuthing, okay? Leave it to the professionals this time."

Mike gave him a hurt look that didn't fool Jonathon for an instant. "Aw, but we helped last time, didn't we? I mean, we solved the case."

Graham studied him in silence, then sighed heavily. "I'm not gonna be able to stop you. I can see that. So all I'm gonna say is… if you turn up anything relevant, anything important… let me know? Don't go charging in and putting yourselves in danger." His eyes glinted. "This isn't like last time. Somewhere out there is a murderer."

That sent a shiver down Jonathon's spine, but the frisson of excitement that followed soon pushed it from his mind. *What if we could work out who the killer was? Graham wouldn't mind that, surely?*

He glanced across at Mike and found him grinning, as though he could read every thought in Jonathon's head.

Graham was right about one thing. He and Mike were as bad as each other.

Tuesday, November 7

JONATHON TOOK one last look at his editing suite. He'd just finished kitting it out and was pleased with the end result. A wide monitor sat on a long desk, and next to it was his PC. A shelf above the desk contained several cameras, and below that was a box filled with different lenses and filters. Two tripods stood against the wall, and next to them was a wide table where his large printer was located.

All ready to begin.

Jonathon's planned visit to Vietnam had been postponed due to Dominic's death and the subsequent events, and he'd assumed that once life had settled back into some form of routine, he'd reschedule the trip. Only, something had changed.

Jonathon had lived alone since he'd left home for college, before ending up in Manchester. He was used to traveling around the world, with nothing to tie him to one place. Except that was no longer the case. Living in the manor house wasn't exactly an encumbrance. He had no duties as such—those days were long gone.

No, what tied Jonathon to Merrychurch with silken bonds was Mike.

The thought of spending several months away from him made Jonathon's heart sink. It was bad enough when he didn't see Mike for a whole day, and although he said nothing, those nights when Mike slept above the pub were the worst. Not that Jonathon would ever let on how he felt. There was no call for Mike to know. Besides, it seemed too… demanding of him. Mike didn't need a man who clung to him. He had a business to run, his own life to lead.

And Jonathon wanted to be part of that life. For good.

From beyond the closed door, a phone warbled into life. Jonathon exited the room, switching off the lights, and walked over to the phone standing in its cradle.

"Why aren't you answering your mobile?" Mike demanded as soon as the call connected.

"Because it's charging in my bedroom, and I'm in the studio." Jonathon smiled to himself. "Were you worried?"

"'Course not. It's just... well, when you didn't answer, I wondered...."

A flustered Mike was absolutely adorable.

"What did you want?" Jonathon couldn't let him flounder like that.

"Graham called. SOCO left five minutes ago. So unless you're in the middle of something that can't wait...."

Jonathon glanced at his watch. The pub wouldn't open until six, so that gave them a couple of hours. Plus, he hadn't seen Mike since the previous evening. "Want to pick me up here and we'll go together?"

"Works for me. See you in ten." And then he was gone.

Jonathon chuckled. He loved Mike's abrupt manner, his decisiveness.

Let's be honest here. I love him. It didn't matter that they'd been together a relatively short time. Jonathon knew he'd fallen for Mike, hook, line, and sinker. Wasn't it love that was keeping him from making travel plans for exotic, far-off places?

I could always ask him to come along. Except Jonathon knew he couldn't do that. Mike couldn't just up and leave the pub for a few months at a time. And then there was the small but not insignificant detail that Jonathon had no idea how Mike felt about him. Sure, they acted like an old married couple at times, with the way they behaved around each other. And things certainly worked in the bedroom—not to mention the bathroom, the kitchen, the stable....

He hasn't said it, though, has he? The L word? Then Jonathon smiled. *Neither have I.*

The one thing Jonathon knew was that he didn't want to say something that might… change things.

There's no rush. We have time, right? It's still early days, remember.

And in the meantime, they had a mystery to solve.

Chapter Five

"I SEE they left her jam table where it was." Jonathon picked up a jar of mango-and-peach jam. "You never did buy me a jar when we were here last time."

"We'd just found a dead body," Mike remonstrated. "It was hardly the time to buy a jar of jam. And if you still want it, leave some money in the box." It didn't make sense to do such a thing, now Mrs. Teedle was dead, but to his mind, it felt… right. Respectful. He paused at the threshold. "Remember… they'll have fingerprinted in here, so you'll see that powder everywhere. They'll also have taken away anything they think relevant to the case."

Jonathon put down the jar. "This *is* my second crime scene, y'know."

Mike snickered. "Ooh, get you." He lifted the black-and-yellow police tape and pushed open the door. Jonathon followed him inside. "This is obviously the part of the house where she met customers. I'd guess that the rest of the house is through there." Mike pointed to a door in the corner. "Let's look around in here first." He walked over to the table where Mrs. Teedle had been found. "Looks like whatever she was cutting up has been removed too." Something about that had been niggling him ever since they'd left the house and awaited Graham. The gloves....

"What are you thinking?" Jonathon regarded him closely. "You've clearly got something on your mind."

"It was her gloves. Do you remember what they were like?"

Jonathon frowned, but then his brow smoothed out. "Black. Like hospital gloves, kind of matte-looking."

"Yeah, that's right. But *why* did she need black nitrile gloves?"

Jonathon absently rubbed the edge of his hand. "Maybe the stuff she was working with had prickles or something."

Mike reached across and grabbed Jonathon's wrist. "Let me see that. You've been doing that for the last two days." He peered at his hand. "Jonathon... what have you done? You've got what look like blisters here."

Jonathon pulled his hand back. "I know. They're itching too."

Mike didn't like this. "You brushed aside some of the plant she'd been chopping up, didn't you? It must be something fairly toxic to cause this reaction. Maybe you should see the doc."

Jonathon gave him a frank stare. "Then maybe we'd better find out whatever she was chopping. It'd help to know what I've come into contact with. That can wait. Let's look around here." He walked over to the wall of shelves lined with jars and bottles, peering at the labels. "I've never heard of some of these things.

Chaparral? Sounds like a western you see on those channels of old TV programs."

"Hey!" Mike gave him a mock glare. "*I* used to watch repeats of that, so less of the old, if you please." He joined Jonathon and perused the containers. "She does have a lot of ingredients." He pointed to one bottle. "I've heard of that one. St. John's wort. That's good for people who have depression, supposedly." His attention wandered to a section of wall without shelves, against which hung a photo frame, and beneath the glass was a cross-stitch of a country scene. A fox was leaping over a hedge, and below it lay a sleeping beagle. At the bottom he could just make out two lines of stitched words, not that he was close enough to read them.

"Ah, this is why she had ginger around the place."

When Mike turned to look behind him, Jonathon pointed to a neat row of jars at one end of the kitchen table. He picked one up and peered at the handwritten label. "Ginger jam, November 2017. She'd only made this batch recently, then." He shuddered. "I still say there was no need to stuff her mouth full of roots like that."

Mike cast a glance over the rest of the table, his gaze alighting on a large, heavy bound book, its cover still bearing the traces of forensic investigation.

He opened it carefully, scanning the pages of handwritten notes. "These are her remedies. Look at this. *Aconite—for the treatment of facial pain, neuralgia, vertigo*…. I thought aconite was poisonous." He turned a few pages and smiled. "Look at this one. *Gelsemium—for those who fear the dentist's chair.*"

"Seriously?" Jonathon joined him and regarded the pages with interest. "Wow. She's got cures for all sorts in here. Wonder if any of them worked." He stared at the chopping board, its surface clear. "Strange to think she'd need to protect her hands from whatever she was chopping, especially if it was going into a remedy of some sort." The knife they'd seen previously was gone, obviously removed by the officers.

Mike wasn't sure what else they could glean from the kitchen. "Let's take a look at the rest of the house." He approached the door in the corner, which was locked, and turned the brass key. Jonathon followed him into a room that was nothing like the kitchen. It was a small, cozy sitting room, with a fireplace set into a brick chimney breast. Thick red carpet covered the floor, and a comfortable-looking armchair sat beside the fire, with a high back and wings, perfect for falling asleep in on winter nights. Beside the chair was a table made of a warm wood, on which sat photos in silver frames.

"That must be Naomi's family in Australia." Mike peered closely at them. Naomi wasn't in any of them, but instead they featured a couple with three children of varying ages, all smiling for the camera.

"She wasn't kidding when she said she was partial to champagne," Jonathon remarked, pointing to the shelves set into the space next to the chimney breast. "Not to mention a drop of whiskey now and then." On one of the shelves sat two bottles of Johnnie Walker Black Label, and next to them were thick, green heavy bottles, all bearing labels that Mike knew to be champagne. "She had expensive tastes, our Mrs. Teedle."

Now that he mentioned it.... *That* was what had struck Mike since they'd entered the main part of the house. It was the air of... opulence. Heavy, rich fabrics hung at the windows. Not a speck of dust to be seen.

Good, well-made furniture, including a sideboard filled with delicate glassware.

"Did she come from money?" Jonathon asked. "Because looking at everything in here, it sure feels that way. We're talking nothing but the best."

Mike had to concede that Jonathon knew what he was talking about. Of course he would, coming from one of the oldest families in England. "I think we need to do some digging. We obviously don't know enough about her."

"Now that *is* weird." Jonathon pointed to a bookshelf. "She has some beautiful books here, and then you have those."

Mike peered closely, recognizing the slim volumes instantly. There were maybe fourteen or fifteen of them. "Those are the diaries Doris gives away free every New Year." He pulled one off the shelf, gazing at the faux black leather binding, the words *Merrychurch Village Grocers, EST 1899* embossed on the front, and below them was the phone number for the shop, and incongruously, its website address. In the top right corner was stamped in the same gold lettering: *2017 Week to View*.

Mike slipped it back into its prior position. He knew what Jonathon meant. Among books bound in leather with gold leaf on the spine, the cheap diaries seemed incongruous.

"I know. She gave me the 2018 version for the hamper." Jonathon pulled another from the shelf and opened it, frowning as he flicked through its pages. "There's hardly anything in here. Just some entries that don't make any sense."

"Let me see."

Jonathon handed him the small diary, and Mike gazed at the page. There were four entries for the end of October, on different dates, spread out over the week.

JWR 35/21

WRR 17/9

WRR 9/7

JWR 33/9

Next to each entry was a neat tick. Mike flicked back through the diary. The remaining pages for October were blank, but the same entries were found at the end of September, again with the same neat ticks beside them.

He glanced at Jonathon, who was already leafing through another. "Is that one the same?"

"Yeah." Jonathon closed the diary, replaced it on the shelf, and removed another. "This is weird."

Mike put the diary back on the shelf. "Let's have a look at the rest of the house." He walked through the sitting room to the door on the far side and found himself at the front door. "Wait a minute. This is obviously the main entrance to the house, but from the direction we approached, on the outside it looks like a side entrance."

"But with the table outside, and the signs, that was obviously the way people were encouraged to enter— by the back door." Jonathon peered at their surroundings. "You know what I think? Her customers only got to see that kitchen at the end. *Everyone* used the back entrance. Maybe no one ever saw how she really lived." He pushed opened another door and gave a triumphant smile. "*This* is her kitchen, not that dark room at the end. Sparkling clean and not a potion in sight." He whistled. "Top-of-the-line appliances too." Jonathon closed the door.

"Maybe she got a good divorce settlement or an insurance payout," Mike mused. "There's been no mention of a husband so far." He had to agree with Jonathon: the rest of the house reeked of money. Everywhere was parquet flooring, all gleaming varnished wood, covered in places by thick rugs that didn't look the least bit worn. Paintings hung on the walls, mostly oils or watercolors.

"Possibly." Jonathon absently rubbed his hand against his thigh.

Mike sighed. "Okay. We're going outside to see if we can find some more of that plant. *Then* I'm taking you to the doctor. You need to treat those blisters."

Jonathon frowned. "It's nothing, really."

"Sure. That's why you keep rubbing it." Mike glanced around them. "There's nothing more we can learn here anyway. Our next step is to see what we can find out about her."

"Strikes me your mate Keith might be good for that." Jonathon grinned. "He came up trumps last time, didn't he?"

Mike had already been thinking about his former colleague. "And all we'd be asking him to do is look up what info he can find. It's amazing what he can dig up with just a name, date, and place of birth."

"Graham will be doing the same thing," Jonathon added. "This way we're not asking to see police evidence."

Mike laughed. "I'm pretty sure that's not how Graham will see it." He knew what Jonathon was like. He'd want to know more. Then Mike was struck by the sudden silence. Jonathon was staring at a painting on the wall. "Is something wrong?"

With a start, Jonathon turned to face him. "Is it wrong that we've just… leaped right in and started…."

"Sleuthing?" Mike suggested with a smile.

Jonathon flushed. "She only died two days ago, and here we are, going through her things…. Feels awkward. I mean, it's not like I knew her."

"You have a right to be here. She was your tenant. And did it sound like Graham minded us taking a look?"

Jonathon bit his lip. "Not really."

Mike gave a satisfied nod. "So as long as we share anything we find out, I don't see a problem with it. Of course, if we discover who the murderer was, I'm not about to let you go off to confront them. Not that you'd do that anyway. You've got brains. Now, let's take a look outside, shall we, while there's still enough light?" The sun had just set.

Mike walked back into the far kitchen, and when Jonathon was through the door to the main house, Mike locked it before leading him outside into the garden. It wasn't a large space, with only a few neat borders, but it had obviously been well thought-out. Fruit trees, now bare, were trained against the fence, and there were raspberry canes to one side.

"Looks like she grew her own fruit for the jams." Mike pointed to a thick shrub. "That's a gooseberry bush." To the rear of the house were beds and pots containing what looked like herbs, but beyond them, plants sprang up all over the place, giving that part a wild look. He gazed at the thick growth, searching for the leaves he'd seen on Naomi's table. Then he spotted them, growing in the farthest corner of the garden.

Mike's heart sank. "Damn." He'd thought the plant had looked familiar.

"What's wrong?"

Mike sighed. "You're bloody lucky, do you know that?"

Jonathon blinked. "What do you mean?"

"You only came into contact with a little of that stuff." Mike pointed to the plant. "It's hogweed. Not sure if it's common or giant hogweed. It's certainly big enough."

"Nice name," Jonathon said with a smirk.

Mike gripped his shoulder. "Well, that nicely named plant nearly cost someone his leg this year. It was on the news. At least we can tell the doctor what you've come into contact with."

Jonathon widened his eyes. "Are you serious?"

"Put it this way. If you'd gotten that stuff on your fingers, then rubbed your eyes, right now we'd probably be talking with an eye surgeon, discussing how to save your sight." Cold crawled over Mike's skin. Something had niggled at him the first time he'd seen the plants lying on her table.

"Am I... going to be all right?" Jonathon was pale.

Mike downplayed his fears at the sight of Jonathon's reaction. "You've only got a couple of blisters. I'm sure they can be treated." He patted Jonathon's arm. "Don't worry."

Jonathon twisted his neck to stare back at the house. "What on earth was she thinking of? What remedy could require hogweed?"

Jonathon had hit the nail on the head. "That's just it. I can't think of any use for it. Hogweed has no medicinal uses, as far as I know. It's poisonous, full stop. And the giant variety is banned in this country. It's illegal to cultivate it." Mike followed Jonathon's gaze.

Then what was *she going to do with it?*

Jonathon squeezed his arm. "Come on. Let's get out of here. I need to see the doctor, remember? And you need to call Keith. We can always come back here if we need to."

Coming back was a given. There still remained the riddle of the strange notations in the diaries, because that was a mystery begging to be solved. Although he did have an inkling.

Before he could walk away from the house, however, Jonathon tugged on his arm. "Have you got any money on you?" He pointed to the table by the door. "What about this jam you promised me?"

Mike laughed. "Really?"

Jonathon speared him with a look. "It's not as if you won't benefit too. That *was* you Sunday morning, wasn't it? Eating my marmalade?"

He had a point. "Okay, let's see what she's got."

Jonathon chuckled. "Don't give me that. You've had your eye on that mango-and-peach jam since you first saw it." He peered at the jars before his attention wandered to the ground below. "Someone's had a dog here. Look at all these paw prints. Big dog too."

Mike glanced at the earth. Sure enough, there were several clear prints in the scuffed soil. "Well, it's not hers. There's no sign of a dog in the house."

Jonathon picked up a jar of mango-and-peach. "Definitely this one, then. There's also plum, marmalade, and raspberry." He glanced at the clipboard lying beside the jars. "Aw. There was also a cherry jam too. That must have sold out."

Mike liked that each jar was labeled with a bright picture of the fruit, and the lids were covered with red-and-white checked fabric, secured with an elastic band. "Well, have you made your choice?"

Jonathon picked up a jar of plum jam. "These two."

Mike shoved his hand into his pocket, counted out the correct money, and dropped it through the slit into the honesty box. "Right. Let's get you to the doctors and get that hand sorted out."

As they headed back to the car, Mike couldn't tear his mind away from that chopping board. *What were you up to, Naomi Teedle?* Because he had a bad feeling about it.

CHAPTER SIX

MIKE PULLED up in front of the main door to the manor house. "Will I see you this evening?" The lights that illuminated the front of the house were already in force, and the manor glowed a ghostly white.

Jonathon had to smile. "That depends which side of the bar I'd be on, and who you were expecting—your boyfriend or Tom Cruise. Because I don't think I have enough energy to be fabulous with a cocktail shaker."

Mike chuckled. "The lord of the manor will do just fine. You can sit on a barstool and look gorgeous." He narrowed his gaze. "And you'd better do what the doc says and apply that ointment as often as prescribed."

Jonathon rolled his eyes. "Yes, Mother." He gazed at the white paper bag in his lap, bearing the green cross and the name Driscoll's. "Was it me, or was that chemist nervous?" There had been none of Nathan Driscoll's bluster of Sunday night. Instead, he'd appeared flustered when they'd entered the shop, and the speed with which he'd served Jonathon made it look like he couldn't wait for them to be out of there.

"It was probably me," Mike remarked. "Some people get nervous around a copper—or even an ex-copper. Or maybe he was in a hurry. It was almost closing time, y'know." He grinned. "He probably wanted to get home to his dinner."

"Perhaps." Jonathon peered through the windscreen and caught sight of Ben Threadwell pushing a wheelbarrow. "Okay. You'd better get back to the pub. It'll soon be opening time. I'll see you later. Only, I won't be on pints tonight. I'll use the Jag."

Mike rolled his eyes. "Any excuse."

Jonathon affected an innocent expression. "What?"

"You love that car. You're forever having it cleaned and valeted. I swear one day you'll yell at me for… breathing on it."

There was a grain of truth in Mike's words. The sleek black 1969 Jaguar E-type had been Dominic's pride and joy, even though there were several cars in the garage that had belonged to him. The Jag was easily Jonathon's favorite. He had memories of going for a ride in it with Dominic when Jonathon was in his teens, and when he discovered Dominic had left it to him, he'd shed more than a few tears. But after a month of cleaning it and gazing at it, Jonathon had come to the conclusion that above all else, the car was meant to be driven.

Jonathon leaned over and kissed Mike's cheek. "Go open your pub. I'll see you later." He got out of the 4x4, closed the door, waved Mike off, then peered into the increasing gloom as he heard the squeak of Ben's barrow. "Shouldn't you have called it a day by now, Ben?" Jonathon called out. It was almost dark.

The elderly man walked over to him, unhurriedly pushing the even more elderly wheelbarrow. "Just sweepin' up the last of them damn leaves. I swear, it's a never-ending job." He lowered his gaze to the bag clutched in Jonathon's hand, and his eyebrows shot upward. "You okay? Nothin' wrong, is there?"

"Nothing that isn't my own stupid fault." Jonathon sighed, then told him about the hogweed. "Mike says I'm lucky, and that it could have been much worse."

Ben's eyes gleamed in approval. "Now there's a man what knows his plants. Good man. You should listen to 'im." He cocked his head to one side. "So... would you an' he be... courtin'?"

Jonathon thought it was a charming term. "I suppose we are."

Ben appeared to consider his reply for a moment before giving another single nod. "Fair enough. Not like it's something new, is it? Jus' nowadays, you 'ear more about it than when I were a lad. Back then, you didn't talk about such things. Well, not in public at any rate." He removed his cap and rubbed his bald head. "Well, I'd best be off now. I'll be back tomorrow."

"Is there much to do this time of year?"

Ben laughed. "More than you'd think. Now's the time for plantin' new trees an' shrubs, an' coverin' the winter and spring flowerin' shrubs with nettin'. Them bullfinches can eat their way through a mountain of flower buds if you let 'em. Then I got to check all the climbers, make sure they're secured. And then there's them roses you asked me about a while back. Now's the time for plantin' 'em. Plus I've got to see to the pond and—"

"I had no idea there was so much work to be done." Jonathon gave him an earnest glance. "Are you sure it isn't too much for you?" Ben wasn't exactly a spring chicken, and Jonathon hated the idea of him tiring himself out.

Ben burst into laughter. "Bless you, son. If I wasn't doin' this, I'd be bored to tears, potterin' around me cottage. On the days when I'm not 'ere, all I do is sit by my window an' watch the goings-on. Not that there's all *that* much a-goin' on normally, apart from the ramblers traipsin' along the lane, headin' for the forest." He pursed his lips. "'Course, that was why that young constable came a-callin'."

"Constable Billings?"

"That's the one. He wanted to know who I'd seen in the lane headin' to Mrs. Teedle's place that Sunday mornin'."

That got Jonathon's attention. "Had you seen many people?"

Ben gave a shrug. "There's always folks walkin', whatever time of year it is. But he was more concerned with anyone I recognized."

"And did you? Recognize anyone, I mean?"

Ben smirked. "Oh, *I* get it. You and that Mike, you're at it again, aren't ya? Tryin' your 'and at a bit of detective work? Well, I can't deny you came up with the goods this summer, right enough." He replaced his cap and started to count off on his fingers. "First off, there was that Rachel who runs the cafe or tea shop, whatever she calls it. She parked up early in the lay-by, an' when she came back, she was carryin' a big cardboard box. Looked heavy."

Jonathon thought it odd that Rachel hadn't mentioned seeing Mrs. Teedle that day.

"Then there was a few more villagers, but I'm bless-ed if I can remember what order they came by in. I just know I saw 'em, that's all. And they're only the ones I *recall* seein'. I wasn't by the window the whole mornin'. There must've been folks passin' by who I missed."

"So who else did you see?"

Ben continued on his fingers. "That chemist fella at some point. Always looks like he's in a hurry, that one. And there was some fella with 'is dog, great big German shepherd. Come to think of it, the mayor's wife was walkin' *her* dog too."

Jonathon frowned. "Any idea who the man was?"

Ben scratched his head through his cap. "Soft-spo-ken chap, came to Merrychurch about... five years ago? From somewhere up north, I think. Can't recall his name for the life of me. Never 'ad much to do with 'im. But I 'ad no trouble recognizin' that Brent fella." Ben huffed. "Seems every time I turn on my TV and they're reportin' from outside Big Ben, there he is."

"Brent?" Jonathon knew the name from somewhere.

Ben beamed triumphantly. "Joshua Brent. He's our MP. Gonna go far, that one. They're sayin' he's gon-na be prime minister one of these days." He chuckled. "Imagine that."

"Anyone else?"

Ben stroked his cheek and chin, deep in thought. "There were two walkers, but they 'ad their hoods up, so I didn't see their faces. An' they didn't exactly walk slowly. Not that them walkers ever do. You'd think they were in a race, some of 'em."

Jonathon made a mental note to write down all the names when he got indoors. "Sounds like you gave him a good list of possible suspects."

Ben scowled. "Except I can't remember who I saw last. I wasn't exactly paying all that much attention. How was I to know she was bein' murdered?"

Jonathon patted him on the shoulder. "You've been a big help. At least the police have somewhere to start."

Ben made a noncommittal noise. "I'll be off now." He picked up the arms of the wheelbarrow and trundled it off in the direction of the sheds where all the tools and garden stores were kept.

Jonathon entered the manor house and headed for the small drawing room where he usually relaxed, watched TV, and listened to music. There was a new squishy couch in there that was perfect for sprawling on, and it was just the right size for two. The room was a far cry from the large, impersonal rooms that took up most of the manor house. It seemed a pity to waste so much space, but as to what else could be done to best utilize the property, he had no clue. Well, nothing that wasn't outrageous.

Jonathon smiled to himself as he envisaged suggesting to his father that the manor house be turned into some kind of commune.

He'd have apoplexy.

Then he reasoned that telling his father about the new photography studio and his plans for his future might very well bring about the same result.

Janet appeared at the door to the drawing room. "Dinner will be ready at seven as usual. Will it be just you, sir?"

Jonathon nodded. "Although I'll be going to the pub later, so you can take the rest of the night off. I'll probably be back here in time for bed."

"Unless you decide to stay there," she suggested with the hint of a smile. "Shall I tell Ivy not to make solid plans for breakfast in the morning?"

"What an idea. As if I'd want to spend the night there," he joked, and Janet surprised him by giggling. "Actually, that's a great idea. Tell Ivy I won't expect her until lunchtime." *A night at Mike's? Why not?*

"Very good, sir." Janet inclined her head and withdrew.

Having a cook and a housekeeper *definitely* took some getting used to.

Jonathon pushed aside such thoughts and grabbed a block of Post-its and a pen from the table. He jotted down the five names Ben had given him, then sat back against the seat cushions, pondering the list.

Could one of them be the killer?

Such a question was a waste of time. There was too much he didn't know, and nothing to say that situation would change in the future. *Maybe this is best left to the professionals after all.*

What came to mind was Nathan Driscoll's nervous manner. Paw prints. The hogweed. The diaries. Mrs. Teedle's lifestyle. The inside of her house at odds with the almost derelict exterior.

Jonathon smiled. What harm could come from giving the professionals a helping hand?

CHAPTER SEVEN

Wednesday, November 8

"JONATHON."

No response.

Mike tried again, only this time he nudged the sleeping Jonathon's thigh with his own. "Jonathon!"

"Hmm?" Brown eyes gradually focused on him, blinking. When that familiar smile blossomed, Mike's stomach did a flip-flop. Jonathon first thing in the morning was always a gorgeous sight. Then Jonathon grinned as he slid a warm hand over Mike's fuzzy belly, moving lower….

Mike grabbed him firmly by the wrist. "Much as I love the way you're going—"

"Oh good, me too." Jonathon let out a sleepy chuckle.

"That was *not* why I woke you up." Mike gestured toward the bedside table on Jonathon's side. "Your phone was buzzing. You've missed a call."

"Good. Too bloody early to be calling me anyway." Jonathon shifted closer, until his lips were inches from Mike's nipple—then he froze. "Wait a minute. No one I know would be calling me at this hour." He raised his head and squinted at the window. "It's only just dawn."

Mike let out a patient sigh. "You're usually awake before dawn. Which is why I woke you up. I figured it had to be important."

With a huff, Jonathon rolled over, grabbed his phone, and peered at the screen. His face fell. "Oh God. Well, that's killed my mood."

"Who called?"

Jonathon sat up in bed and tapped the keys on his phone. "My father."

Mike could understand that reaction. One withering glance from Thomas de Mountford had been enough to shrivel Mike's nuts to the size of raisins.

He waited while Jonathon listened to a voicemail message, his facial expression not improving. If anything, it appeared to worsen. After a few minutes, Jonathon tossed his phone onto the bed and sank back against the pillows.

"He's coming to see me," Jonathon said in a subdued voice.

"When?"

"This weekend. And he's staying the night." A few minutes was all it had taken to change Jonathon's mood from playful to downright miserable.

"Any clues as to the reason for this sudden visit?"

"Maybe. He mentioned my birthday."

Mike smiled. "Oh? Is it soon?" He gave himself a swift mental kick up the backside. *Not knowing when your boyfriend's birthday is? Scandalous.*

"In a week's time. And I have a sneaking suspicion why he mentioned it. After all, I'm going to be twenty-nine. That's nearly thirty, y'know."

"Yeah, last time I looked," Mike said wryly.

Jonathon shook his head. "You don't get it. Nearly thirty, as in, time I settled down. Got married. Had kids." His face was glum. "And somehow I don't think a husband features in his plans."

Mike blinked. "Why—does one feature in yours?" His heartbeat sped up a little. Okay, so three months was way too early to be thinking about such things, but that didn't mean the thought hadn't crossed his mind.

Jonathon regarded him with obvious affection. "Well, at some point, yes. Not this week, though." His eyes sparkled with humor. "Though that would surely shut my father up."

"More like, give him a heart attack." Mike held his arm wide. "I'm sorry your dad spoiled your mood. Would a cuddle help?" Talking about it would only exacerbate Jonathon's mood.

Jonathon was snuggled up against him in a heartbeat, his face buried in Mike's neck. "It's a start." His breath tickled.

Mike held him, conscious of warm, soft skin against his torso. "You have something else in mind?"

Jonathon craned his neck and grinned. "Like you don't know."

Mike let out a happy sigh. "Just checking." His morning might have suffered a brief wobble, but it looked like things were back on track.

Until the weekend, at least.

He'd deal with whatever Thomas de Mountford had in mind when the time came. One thing was certain: Mike would have Jonathon's back.

MIKE POURED two more mugs of coffee, then placed them on the kitchen table. "Any plans for today?" His morning was remarkably clear for a change. His stocks were up-to-date, the grocery shopping was done, and everything was ready for opening. That was thanks to Jonathon, who'd insisted on helping clear up the previous night after closing time.

Jonathon bit his lip. "Actually...."

Mike knew that look. "Out with it."

After a sip of coffee, Jonathon put down the mug and looked him in the eye. "I think it's time we had a chat with Graham. He must have the coroner's report by now."

Mike laughed. "I know what I'm going to get you as a birthday present. A deerstalker hat and a long coat, like the one Sherlock wears on TV."

"Does that make you John Watson, then?" Jonathon flashed him a grin. "Because you *know* Graham will make a similar comment." He reached into the pocket of his jeans, removed a yellow piece of paper, and held it out. "And then we should do something about this list."

Mike unfolded the paper and read its contents. "What's this? And who is 'man with German shepherd'?"

"*This* is a list of people seen in the vicinity of Mrs. Teedle's cottage on the morning in question. It's the same list Graham has. I talked with Ben Threadwell last night, and he said these are the only ones he could recall. And the man with the dog? Ben didn't know his name."

"I do." Mike put down the paper. "He's George Tyrell. At least, he's the only person in the village with that kind of dog. Lives in a cottage opposite the church. Nice bloke, if a bit quiet. Not much of a drinker, though. I think he's only come into the pub once or twice for a pint. Not with the dog, obviously. Northerner."

Jonathon snickered. "And is that a bad thing? Being a Northerner?" He waggled a finger in Mike's face. "Be careful how you answer that. I lived in Manchester for a good while."

Mike laughed. "Ex-copper, remember? It's a distinguishing feature. You tend to mention things that stick in the memory, like unusual hair, accents, and such like." He leaned back in his chair and folded his arms. "And what do you propose doing with that list? You can't exactly go to each person and question them, y'know."

Jonathon's face lit up. "I've been thinking about that."

"Oh God." Mike let out a groan, and Jonathon whacked him on the arm. "Hey!"

"Serves you right. Now listen. What if I were to go to each house and say I was collecting feedback on the bonfire, with a view to doing it again next year?"

"And while you're there, you just *happen* to mention that they were seen near the house of a murdered woman, and did they have anything to do with it?" Mike couldn't hold back his smile.

Jonathon rolled his eyes. "Well, *obviously* I'd be a little subtler than that. Give me *some* credit." He grinned. "Besides, that's why I'm taking you with me. I figured you might come up with ways to… you know… slip it into the conversation. You know these people, and I don't."

Mike tried not to laugh. "So now you're planning my morning too?"

"Well, you've got nothing else to do, right?"

Mike feigned a gasp. "And there was I, thinking you were helping me clear up last night because you lo—" He broke into a bout of coughing, and Jonathon patted him on the back.

"Did a word get stuck in your throat?" Jonathon asked innocently.

Mike took a swig from his mug. "Finish your coffee, and then we'll go see Graham. He might be more inclined to share if I'm with you. *Then* we'll think about that list." He didn't know why he should be so flustered by the declaration that had almost escaped him. He only knew he was.

Jonathon emptied his mug, his Adam's apple bobbing. "I think we should start with Rachel. That way, we can mix business with pleasure."

Mike snickered as he got up from the table. "I swear, you have a one-track mind." When Jonathon gave him a lingering glance, he realized his mistake. "Scratch that—a two-track mind." He left the kitchen and headed up the stairs to the bathroom, aware of Jonathon's soft chuckles still audible below.

MIKE PUSHED open the door to the quaint police house and went inside, with Jonathon behind him. They made their way to the desk, where Graham was in conversation with the special constable, Dan Fitch. He nodded briefly in their direction before resuming his talk. When they were done, Dan disappeared through a door to the rear and Graham came over to where Mike and Jonathon stood.

"Well, well, well, if it isn't Sherlock and Watson. Finished looking for clues, have we? I suppose you're here to tell me you've solved the case."

There was a sarcastic edge to Graham's voice that caught Mike's attention. "What's wrong?" he asked softly. Graham was a mate, and it wasn't like him to be snarky.

Graham's shoulders sagged a little. "Sorry. I've had a call from Winchester CID. Seems they're not happy with the progress we've been making—or not, as they see it. They're sending a Detective Inspector Mablethorpe tomorrow to take over. Not that *that* should worry you two, because this has nothing to do with you—right?" He cocked his head to one side. "And why *are* you here?"

Mike shrugged. "We were just curious about the cause of death, that's all. And whether SOCO had turned up anything."

Graham's eyes gleamed triumphantly. "I knew it! Well, after this DI gets here, you won't get so much as a sniff of the evidence." He paused, then smiled. "So you'd better learn all you can now before he arrives. How does the saying go? 'What the eye doesn't see, the heart doesn't grieve over.'" Graham picked up a folder from the desk and opened it before glancing up at them. "Well, sit down and take notes if you're going to. I know full well you're gonna look into this, and it's not as if I could stop you, so why mess about wasting time?"

Mike grabbed a couple of chairs and moved them to the front of the desk before sitting. "Was the head wound the cause of death?"

Graham shook his head. "Strangulation. And those ginger roots were stuffed in postmortem, the coroner says. No fingerprints obtained from her throat."

"Is that even possible?" Jonathon asked, his eyes wide.

"It can be done. Sometimes iodine fuming works, but in this case, no. So we don't know if the killer wore gloves. And considering we found fingerprints around the place that weren't hers, it seems unlikely."

"There were prints?" Mike exclaimed.

Graham chuckled. "Yeah. Someone didn't read his or her Basic Killer's Handbook. You know, where it says wipe all your prints before you leave the scene? We've got one or two clear prints from the doorknob."

"And you have DNA too, right? From the knife?" Jonathon asked eagerly.

Graham chuckled. "Oh dear. Someone else who thinks real-life forensics is like what you see on TV. No, Mr. de Mountford, we don't have DNA results yet, because that can take weeks. But we *will* have them."

"I take it the fingerprints didn't match anyone on record."

"Nope. Though when DI Mablethorpe arrives, doubtless he'll have me taking the fingerprints of everyone seen in the vicinity." Graham eyed Jonathon. "I suppose you want to know who *they* were an' all."

"That won't be necessary, thank you," Jonathon said with a polite smile.

Graham blinked, then facepalmed. "You already know, don't ya? It's just come to me. Old Ben, he's your gardener, isn't he? Well, isn't that a coincidence?" His lips twitched, however. "Now, is there anything else I can help you with? Wanna see the SOCO photos, perhaps?" There was a hint of yet more sarcasm in his tone.

"There *is* one more thing." Mike leaned forward. "Do you have any idea why someone would want to kill her?"

Graham sank into his chair. "Not a one. All we know about her is what was on the last census, which is her name, and date and place of birth. For some reason she went by her middle name. She was born Jane Naomi Taylor, in Nottingham in 1943. We know she lived for a while in Australia, which must be where she got married and had a family, and came to live in Merrychurch in 1998. As for reasons why someone should do her in... I can't *really* see someone strangling her because some beauty cream brought them out in zits, can you?" Graham winked. "I hear the stories, same as you must do. But so far they don't add up to a motive for killing her." He clasped his hands in front of him on the desk. "Now, on the off chance that you two turn up something—and I'd be a fool to discount the possibility, especially after this summer's goings-on—you *will* make sure I get to see it, right? I mean, if *I* can solve this, rather than the DI, then it'd look good on my record, for one thing. And you never know, they might think about promoting me."

Mike got to his feet. "Of course. We'll let you know if we find out anything. Won't we?"

Jonathon nodded in agreement. "Of course." He got up too. "And thank you for sharing all this with us."

Graham laughed. "It's not as if I have all that much to share. Just remember, though—things will be different tomorrow. I don't know anything about this DI, which is worrying."

"What do you mean?"

"No one will tell me anything about him. And *that* doesn't bode well." He gave them a nod. "Good luck with the sleuthing, but remember—there's a murderer out there, and they might not take too kindly to amateur detectives sniffing around, so watch your backs."

Mike placed his hand around Jonathon's waist. "I'll watch his back, and he can watch mine."

Graham coughed. "Whatever. Just be careful."

Mike thanked him and led Jonathon out of the police station. As they approached the 4x4, Mike mulled over what Graham had told them. "We're not much better off, really."

Jonathon sighed. "You're right." Then his face brightened. "You know what we need?"

Mike didn't need to be Sherlock Holmes to know the answer to *that*. "A pot of coffee and some cake at Rachel's?"

Jonathon beamed. "Accompanied by a few questions."

Coffee, cake, and questions. All they *really* needed were some answers.

CHAPTER EIGHT

"So, HAVE you solved it yet?" Rachel said as she brought them a pot of coffee and two slices of coffee-and-walnut cake. Her eyes twinkled. "Go on, tell me whodunnit."

Jonathon couldn't resist. "Well, according to one witness, it could have been you," he joked, "seeing as you were there that morning." Not that he believed for one nanosecond that Rachel Meadow was capable of murder. She was a sweet lady, usually with a warm, friendly expression, and streaks of gray in her hair that were quite stylish.

Rachel stilled. "Oh my God, how exciting! Of course. I went to pick up my supply of jams."

"How did she seem to you?" Mike asked as he poured the coffee.

"That presumes I saw her." Rachel glanced around the shop before pulling out a chair and sitting at their table. "It was the same as always—there was a box waiting for me by her back door, all taped up. We didn't normally see each other. I'd already paid her when I placed the order last week. I prefer doing it that way." She grinned. "Wow. I've never been a murder suspect before."

"It sounds like you were her first visitor that day." Jonathon took a bite of cake and let out an appreciative sound. "This is delicious."

Mike chuckled. "When you've finished getting sidetracked…." He addressed Rachel. "So there was nothing unusual at the house?"

"I don't think so." Rachel frowned. "Her table was there, like it always was, and the box and clipboard. I think there were about eight or nine jars left, maybe three or four varieties."

Jonathon made a mental note. He'd counted five jars on Sunday morning. "Did you take one?"

She rolled her eyes. "Didn't I just say I picked up a whole box of them? Why would I need another?" Her mouth went down at the corners. "I gather that means you don't have a clue who did it, then. Does Graham know you're 'helping'?" She air-quoted.

"First rule of amateur detectives—always keep the professionals in the loop," Mike said gravely. Then he smiled. "Well, *one* of us is an amateur. Jonathon needs me around to make sure he doesn't get into trouble."

Jonathon poked him in the ribs with his elbow. "I seem to recall it was *me* insisting we give Graham those bits of plastic from Melinda's greenhouse. I also recall a certain 'detective' being reluctant to enter said greenhouse for fear of—now, what was the reason? Oh yes—spiders." He beamed at Mike, who glared back.

Rachel burst into a peal of laughter. "You two are priceless. You already sound like an old married couple. It's adorable."

Jonathon smiled to himself. It wasn't the first time he'd heard such a statement.

Rachel got up from the table. "I'll leave you two to enjoy your coffee and cake. Thanks for brightening my day." She gave them a sweet smile, then went over to greet a couple who'd just entered the shop.

"Well, it wasn't as if either of us thought she was involved," Mike said under his breath. "And it backs up what Ben said about her carrying a box. So tell me, Sherlock, who do you want to see next?"

Jonathon pulled the Post-it from his pocket. "I think I've run out of aspirins," he announced emphatically.

Mike laughed. "Driscoll's it is, then. But that will be it for me for this morning. I have a pub to run, after all."

Jonathon didn't reply. He was too busy enjoying the coffee-and-walnut cake.

Some things should *never* be rushed.

JONATHON'S IMPRESSIONS as he took in his surroundings hadn't changed since his first visit to the chemist's shop. Nathan Driscoll couldn't be a very good businessman. The interior of Driscoll's cried out for a revamp. The shelves were full, but there was room in the middle of the floor for standing displays. It was a chemist's shop heavily rooted in the seventies, although above their heads were oak beams that added a little character to the otherwise drab decor.

"Christmas is coming," Jonathon whispered to Mike, his gaze trained on Nathan, who was dealing with a prescription, "but you wouldn't know it in here. If I owned this place? There'd be stuff out that people might consider buying as gifts. You know, perfume, talc, soap, bath stuff... not to mention accessories like back scrubs and body mitts. Those things always go down well as Christmas presents." He glanced around the shop. "Not exactly inviting, is it?"

"Word is, he's not doing so well," Mike said quietly.

"And now that I've seen the place a couple of times, I'm not surprised. He needs marketing advice." That had to be the understatement of the week.

The gentleman in front of them paid for his prescription and exited the shop, leaving it empty but for Jonathon and Mike.

Nathan looked up from the till, and for a second, Jonathon was sure he appeared a little flustered. Then he straightened and pasted on a smile. "Good morning, gents. What can I do for you?"

Jonathon gave a nod toward the shelves behind the counter. "A box of aspirins, please."

Nathan reached behind him and picked up a small box. "Anything else?"

Mike cleared his throat. "I can't see condoms anywhere. Do you stock them?"

Jonathon did his best to stifle the chuckle that bubbled up inside him, thinking of the almost-full box in his bedside cabinet. *As if Mike would let us run out of those.*

Nathan's cheeks flushed. "Yes, but we only have a limited range. Not much call for them in Merrychurch, I have to say from experience. I keep them under the counter."

"You might sell more of them if people could actually see them," Jonathon suggested innocently. "And you also might find out that there's a bigger market for them than you suspect." His impish sense of humor rose to the fore. "I mean, there are other related products that could prove very popular. Some gels and lubricants, for instance, to make life more... interesting." He grinned. "After all, they're being advertised on TV nowadays, so there's obviously a call for them." He shrugged. "Just a suggestion."

Nathan's flush hadn't receded. "I'll... er... bear that in mind. So, did you want a packet of... condoms? I just have... ordinary ones, I'm afraid."

Jonathon nudged Mike. "Wait until I go to the supermarket. They've got those ribbed ones that you like."

The strangled noise that escaped Nathan told him they'd better quit before Nathan had a heart attack.

"I think that's everything," Jonathon added quickly.

Nathan bundled the box into a small paper bag and told them the price.

As Jonathon counted out his change for the payment, he asked nonchalantly, "Did you enjoy the bonfire party?"

Nathan appeared relieved at the change of topic. He tugged at his tie, loosening it a little. "Yes, it was splendid. I hope you'll be doing it again next year."

"If feedback shows it was well received, then possibly," Jonathon admitted. "However, the event *was* somewhat marred by the following morning's news. I only got to meet Mrs. Teedle for the first time that evening."

"A remarkable woman," Nathan intoned solemnly. "Gifted, I always thought."

Jonathon caught Mike's less than subtle cough but surged ahead. "Did you know her well?" It was as if Nathan had completely forgotten the episode in the pub. *That* was *Nathan the regulars were calling out for lying his arse off? Does he have amnesia?*

"Not exactly," Nathan said hesitantly. "I wouldn't have called us friends."

Jonathon frowned. "That's funny. I'd kind of gotten the idea that you knew her better than that. Now, where could I have got that from?"

Mike took up the hint. "Ah, *I* know. It was because you paid her a visit Sunday morning. That must be it."

There was no mistaking Nathan's reaction. He paled. "Me?" he squeaked.

Mike nodded. "You were seen walking toward her house."

Nathan stared at him in silence for a moment, swallowing hard once or twice. Then he gave a weak smile. "Ah yes. I was walking the dog. I often go past her cottage on my way into the forest."

"Past… then you didn't go in?" Jonathon asked.

Nathan blinked several times. "I had no reason to call on her. I did stop and buy a jar of jam, however. She makes—*made*—lovely jam."

"I bought some myself," Mike said with a bright smile. "Which flavor?"

For a moment Nathan stilled, his chest rising and falling rapidly. "Just a sec." Then he darted out of sight.

Mike turned to face Jonathon. "That man is very nervous. I'd like to know why."

Before Jonathon could reply, Nathan appeared behind the counter again, holding aloft a jar. "Plum," he declared with a relieved smile.

"Ooh, I must have missed this variety," Jonathon lied. "Can I see?" When Nathan handed over the jar, Jonathon peered closely at it. The label bore the same date as those on the table, and the red-and-white checked cloth was still in place. "I won't open it and take a sniff, because it's still sealed, but I bet it's delicious." He handed it back to Nathan, who placed it under the counter. "And she wasn't around when you bought the jam?"

Nathan shook his head. "I just put my money in the box and the jar in my pocket. Then I carried on with my walk. Frisky loves the forest."

"Frisky?" Mike inquired, his lips twitching.

Nathan narrowed his gaze. "My cockapoo."

"And is he? Frisky, I mean?" Jonathon asked playfully.

Nathan's manner thawed a little. "Not since he had the snip," he said with a half smile. Behind them, a bell rang as the door opened to admit more customers.

"We'd best be off." Jonathon gave Nathan a polite nod before pulling on Mike's arm to lead him out of the shop. When they were outside, he looked back toward the shop. "Yeah. Very nervous. More of you than me, I think."

"Told you. It's the ex-copper bit. And I didn't buy his compliments for a second."

"Well, of course you didn't. Who would after his past performance? But it doesn't tell us why he could possibly want to kill her. Unless we're thinking his flyers about fake healers are a motive." The visit hadn't been a complete waste of time. Nathan Driscoll was definitely going on the list of suspects. All they had to do was figure out why he would have wanted Naomi dead. Killing off the competition, however much they might like it as a motive, wasn't all that likely.

"Time I went back to the day job and opened the pub." Mike unlocked the car. "After dropping you home first."

"Thanks." Jonathon wanted to make sure there'd be a room ready for his father's arrival. "Will I see you tonight?"

Mike smiled. "As soon as I've closed those doors. You can warm the bed for me."

"I'll keep you warm, have no fear of that."

Mike stepped closer to him and kissed him languidly, sending heat spreading through him. "Good to know." He walked around the car and got behind the wheel.

As Jonathon got into the passenger seat, an idea occurred to him. "You do know I'm expecting you to be around this weekend, right?"

Mike squeezed Jonathon's thigh. "Don't worry. I'll be there, as much as I can, at least. I've got your back." He switched on the engine.

Jonathon breathed a little easier. He could cope with a small dose of his father if he had Mike in his corner.

CHAPTER NINE

JONATHON WAVED Mike off, then headed for the house. He'd taken some photos of a magnificent sunset the previous week, and now that the editing suite was finished, he was itching to work on them. Getting a room ready for his father could wait.

As he drew closer, he spotted a figure sitting on the top front step. Jason Barton was on his phone, lost to the world as he scrolled, his earbuds in place. When Jonathon's shadow crossed over him, he gave a start, his head jerking up.

"Hey." Jason pulled the buds from his ears and scrambled to his feet.

"To what do I owe the pleasure?" Jonathon frowned. "How long have you been sitting out here? You must be chilled to the bone."

"Your housekeeper said that I could wait inside if I wanted and that you'd be here for lunch. I preferred to stay out here." Jason tilted his head. "Is it okay for me to visit? I wanted to talk to you on Saturday night, but there was no time at the bonfire party. Since then, I've had college."

"Shouldn't you be there now?"

Jason smiled. "Wednesday afternoons are for clubs and sports. No classes."

Jonathon opened the door. "Come on in. And seeing as you're here now, you might as well stay for lunch. I'm sure Ivy can rustle something up for you."

"Oh, I don't want to be a bother," Jason protested, but then his stomach grumbled and his face flushed.

Jonathon laughed. "That settles it. You're staying for lunch." He held the door open for Jason, then stepped inside. "Was there a reason for this visit? Or is it just a social call?"

"I wanted to talk to you about… photography," Jason said shyly. "It's something that really interests me. Is that okay?"

"Of course. You can be the first person to see my newly completed studio." Jonathon let out a wry chuckle. "Which makes it sound a lot grander than it is, I assure you." He led Jason through the house, and Janet met them at the dining room door.

"I've already spoken with Ivy, and I've set another place for lunch," she said with a smile. "It will be ready in half an hour."

"Thanks, Janet." Jonathon tugged on Jason's arm. "That gives us time to look at the studio. Take off your jacket, and I'll give you the guided tour."

Jason shrugged off his jacket, and Janet took it. Then Jonathon led the way, guiding him through the rooms.

"This place is huge," Jason exclaimed. "Do you ever get lost?"

"When I was little, I used to play hide-and-seek with my uncle. Not often, but now and again. Since I've come to live here, however, I've taken over one wing. The rest of the house is shut up."

"I can understand that," Jason said quietly as Jonathon opened the door to the studio. "It can't be easy, knowing this is the place where he… you know…."

A fragment of a conversation came to mind, and Jonathon gazed thoughtfully at him. "I meant to ask. Are *you* okay? I forgot, you knew Mrs. Teedle." For all Jonathon knew, this was Jason's first brush with death.

Jason stepped into the large room and stared at the walls, where Jonathon had hung some of his favorite photos. "Oh wow. These are amazing."

Jonathon recognized evasion when he heard it but let Jason take his fill of the prints. He'd chosen a mixture of views, from crumbling ancient ruins in India to the breathtaking color of Ayers Rock against a brilliant blue sky. There were portraits, too, faces that had spoken to him as he'd traveled, capturing the mood of a place. Seeing them all before him made Jonathon long for the time when he could leave England behind again and head for Vietnam as planned.

An easy enough plan but for that silken rope around his heart, keeping him in Merrychurch….

After a few moments of silent contemplation, Jason turned to face Jonathon. "You asked me if I was okay. The truth is… I'm not sure. Kind of. I didn't really know her all that well, but I've been hearing that story of how she delivered me since I was a little boy."

"Your mother must have been glad she was around that day," Jonathon commented.

To his surprise Jason's brows knitted. "That's the weird thing. I'd have thought so too, but every time

I asked her—well, more like begged her—to tell the story, she didn't seem all that keen. Other people did. My dad. Their friends. The ladies in the WI who pinch my cheek every time they see me and tell me what a beautiful baby I was."

Jonathon laughed. "I think Women's Institute ladies are the same all over the country."

His laughter didn't ease Jason's frown, however. "You know, I got the impression Mum didn't like Mrs. Teedle. Not that she ever said as much. It was more like… a feeling. And then the day after Mrs. Teedle was murdered…." He shivered.

Jonathon went over to him and laid a hand on his arm. "Hey, what's wrong? Did something happen?" He guided Jason to the red leather couch against the wall. "Here, sit down."

Jason complied but didn't relax, perching on the edge of the cushion instead. "It wasn't much. Just… a bit of a phone conversation that I overheard. I thought at the time that Mum was talking to Dad. I was coming out of my room and heading downstairs when I heard her. She said, 'It's a horrible thing to say, but it's a huge weight off our shoulders.' Then she gave this laugh, only it was kind of… weird, almost nervous. 'Ding, dong, the witch is dead,' she said. Then she paused, said something about she'd have to see, then bye for now. It was the way she said goodbye that made me think she was talking to Dad. You know how parents talk to each other sometimes and you try not to think about… stuff?"

Jonathon snickered. "Trust me when I say I know what you mean, but *my* parents? Sentiment was in short supply. I could never imagine how they ever got around to producing me."

Jason laughed at that. Then he sighed. "Except… it couldn't have been Dad. A couple of minutes after that, his car pulled into the driveway. And the first thing he did when he got in the house was apologize for not calling her as usual to say he was on his way, only his battery was dead."

Jonathon knew when evening came, he'd be relating all of this to Mike. It could prove important. But one look at Jason's strained expression told him a change of topic was in order. "You said you were interested in photography. Do you have any photos you could show me?"

"Now? Really?" Jason's face lit up.

"Yes, now. I'd love to see them."

Jason pulled his phone from his jeans pocket and scrolled through. "I've got a ton of photos on here. And now you've suggested it, it's difficult to decide which ones to show you."

"What do you take photos of?"

Jason's eyes were bright. "Everything. The village, my friends, sunsets, sunrises—you name it." He held out his phone. "Here's one I took the night of the bonfire."

Jonathon gazed at the image. It was of him and Mike, standing by the fire, holding hands, their faces glowing in the light, the two of them caught in a moment where no one else existed. "That's beautiful," he said at last.

"Seriously?" Jason gazed at him earnestly. "Coming from you, that… that means a lot."

The hairs on the back of Jonathon's neck stood on end. There was something in the air, an electric current that teased his skin, in anticipation of… what? Jonathon had no idea but knew with all of him that there was more to come.

His phone buzzed. Jonathon peered at the screen and laughed. "There you go. In the past when a meal was ready in this house, there was a gong. Now? I get a text." He held up Janet's message: *Lunch is ready when you are.*

Jason laughed. "I like it." He pocketed his phone and followed Jonathon back to the dining room.

Jonathon was content to wait until after they'd eaten to see if anything else was forthcoming. He had a feeling Jason's motivation for this visit was more than just an interest in photography.

"WILL THERE be anything else, sir?" Janet asked as she cleared away the plates. "Apart from coffee, of course."

Jonathon smiled. "I don't think so. Tell Ivy that pie was delicious."

"God, it was mega," Jason added. "Steak-and-kidney is my favorite."

Janet beamed at him. "Glad you enjoyed it. Would you like a coffee too? Or there's orange juice, apple juice, mineral water...."

"Apple juice would be great." As Janet left the room, softly closing the door behind her, Jason sagged into his chair. "Your cook is amazing."

"Ivy? She's a treasure." Jonathon leaned back, content. "And it was nice to have company."

"Mr. Tattersall must visit you a bit." Jason's cheeks pinked a little. "I mean, what with you and he...."

Jonathon sighed. "It's difficult. He has the pub to run, after all. We try to grab all the moments we can." He took in Jason's keen gaze, his still-flushed cheeks, and the way he worried his lower lip with his teeth. Jason was a gorgeous young man, with dark brown hair, short at the sides but longer on top where it curled a little. His most striking feature had to be those green eyes.

He's going to break a lot of hearts.

In that instant Jonathon had a burst of clarity, and his heart went out to Jason. *Oh. I think I know what it is you want to talk about.*

Janet entered with a pot of coffee, a cup and saucer, a milk jug, and a tall glass of juice. After placing them on the table, she withdrew.

Jonathon poured himself a cup and handed the glass to Jason. "You know we mentioned parents briefly? Well, when I was your age, I lived in a large house. Not as large as this one, but definitely on the grand side."

"I can understand that. Your family goes way back, doesn't it?" Jason sipped his juice.

"You could say that," Jonathon said with a wry smile. "I didn't ever think I'd end up living here. I love the house, the village… but in some ways, it means my life isn't my own. Other people… expect things of me." He wasn't sure if he'd chosen the right tack, but he wanted to see where it led.

"Like what?" Jason asked with a faint frown.

"Take my father for instance. He expects me to carry on the family line. Now I'm getting on in years—and before you ask, I'll be twenty-nine soon, which to you is pretty ancient, I'm sure—but—"

Jason spluttered apple juice over the tablecloth. "Sorry," he said, wiping his chin with his napkin.

Jonathon chuckled. "I still remember what it was like to be seventeen. But back to my father. He wants me to get married and produce the next little de Mountford. Which is where we hit a snag."

Jason's eyes widened. "Does... does he know you're gay?"

Jonathon nodded calmly, his eyes focused on Jason.

"And... how does he feel about that?"

"I think you can guess," Jonathon said dryly.

"Can I ask you something?" Jason paused and took a long drink of juice. "How did he react when you first told him you were gay?"

Jonathon sighed. "Like I'd just said something in a foreign language that he didn't understand." He looked closely at Jason. "Not all parents are like my father, thankfully. Mike's, apparently, have no problem with him being gay. I haven't met them yet," he added, "but I'm not worried. I do get why so many kids are scared to tell their family. It's a scary thing to do, right? But I also believe you do get a sense of how things will work out, especially if you have a good relationship with your parents." He fell silent and drank his coffee. It was up to Jason now.

Jason stared into his glass. "Yeah. You can tell if they're going to be assholes about it." He jerked his head up, his eyes large. "Oh. Sorry."

"I've heard worse," Jonathon told him with a wave of his hand.

Jason took another drink, then straightened in his chair. "I suppose it's easier to... come out if you have someone to talk to who understands how you feel."

"You tell me." Jonathon locked gazes with him. "*Does* it feel easier?" His heartbeat sped up a little.

Jason blinked, and then a smile gradually blossomed. "Yeah, it does," he said softly. He tilted his head. "How did you know?"

Jonathon chuckled. "Sometimes you get a sense for these things. Some call it gaydar. It can be very useful, especially when there's someone you're interested in and you have no idea whether making a move will earn you a kiss—or a smack in the mouth. And yes, there *will* be occasions when you'll get it wrong." He smiled. "*Is* there someone?"

Jason's cheeks appeared flushed. "Not yet. I've had a crush on one or two guys, but nothing serious. Enough to realize girls don't do it for me."

"Okay. Now for the important bit." Jonathon leaned forward. "You don't have to come out. That's your decision, all right? It's no one's business but yours. *But…* if you ever want to talk about stuff, my door is always open. Anytime."

Jason heaved a relieved sigh. "Thank you. That means a lot."

An idea occurred to him. "I was going to spend some time in the studio this afternoon, working on some new photos. Would you like to stay? I could show you some of my equipment." He grinned. "Okay, that sounds really creepy, and not the way I meant it at all. Let's try that again. You could play around with my filters."

Jason laughed. "That would be cool." He finished his juice, pushed back his chair, and stood.

On impulse, Jonathon rose to his feet, walked over to him, and gave him a brief hug. "It'll be fine," he said reassuringly, hoping the mayor of Merrychurch would react favorably to his son's news—whenever he chose to deliver it.

"I'M GLAD Jason came to talk to you," Mike said as he undressed.

It was past midnight, but Jonathon was wide-awake, lying in his bed, awaiting Mike's arrival. Mike carefully removed his prosthetic foot and placed it on the floor beside the bed. It was a practice that seemed commonplace after these last months. Mike pulled back the sheets, climbed in, and shifted across the mattress to where Jonathon lay, his arms wide.

"Me too. I wish I'd had someone like me around when I came out—if that makes any sense." Jonathon wrapped his arms around Mike and held him close. "And that means he can talk to you too. We come as a package deal."

Mike smiled against his chest, gently rasping the skin with his beard. "Does that mean we come together?"

Jonathon let out a soft chuckle at Mike's play on words. "I think if we put our minds to it, we could achieve anything. It might take a few tries." He spread his legs slightly, knowing Mike would recognize the motion as an invitation. Jonathon couldn't think of a more perfect way to end the day.

"Practice makes perfect, they say, so let's start right now." Mike reached up and switched off the lamp, plunging the room into darkness. "I think I'll start… *here*."

Jonathon gave a low moan as Mike's tongue found its target. "No arguments from me."

CHAPTER TEN

Thursday, November 9

"Do you want that last piece of toast?" Jonathon asked in a nonchalant manner.

Apparently there was no fooling Mike. "D'you mean that piece you're already dying to smother in *my* mango-and-peach jam?"

Damn it. "If you want it, have it," Jonathon said resignedly. He didn't recall there being anything about love that meant giving up the last bit of toast, but then again, how would he know? This was his first time dipping his toes into that particular pool, and so far, the water was lovely.

Apart from the whole giving-up-the-last-piece-of-toast part.

Mike picked up the toast rack and passed it to him. "Here. I've had plenty." Then he poured another cup of coffee. "What are your plans for today?"

Jonathon had been thinking about that since he'd woken up. Jason's words from the previous day lingered in his mind. "I think I'd like to pay a visit to the mayor's wife."

"Is this you checking out why she was near the cottage that day, or because of what young Jason said?"

"Well, you have to admit, that was a bit strange. And it does bring a couple of ideas to mind." Until Jason's visit, Jonathon had never really entertained the idea that the mayor's wife was a likely suspect, but now? It was a possibility.

"Like, she's having an affair and they could have had something to do with the murder? Because that was what came to *my* mind."

Jonathon smiled. "Good to know we're on the same page."

"Yeah—and it's headed 'suspicious,'" Mike added with a grin. "Make sure you don't go ruffling the mayor's feathers, okay? And I take it you won't be mentioning the rest of Jason's conversation?"

"God, no." Jonathon was still honored that Jason had confided in him.

Whatever else he'd been about to say fled from his mind when there was a light tapping at the french doors. Jonathon glanced across and smiled. "Ben must want something." He got up, went over to the windows, and unbolted the door. "Good morning. Would you like to join us for coffee?"

Ben touched his cap. "Thanks for the offer, but I already got a flask of coffee with me. I'm only here to tell you I need to do some work on the pond. There's a problem with the filter."

"Can you fix it or do I need to call someone in?"

Ben smiled. "'Course I can fix it. An' if it needs a new filter, I'll let you know."

"Ben?" Mike called out. "You got a minute?" Seconds later he was at Jonathon's side. "You know those people you saw on Sunday morning? Can I ask if any of them regularly walk that way?"

Ben grinned. "Funny. That's what that constable wanted to know too. Well, I'll tell you what I told 'im. Rachel Meadow came by regularly enough, but I think that was 'cause she 'ad business there. The German shepherd is a regular—and 'is master, of course. We get a lot of dog-walkers going that way. Take Mrs. Barton, for instance. She comes by now and again, same as does that Brent fella."

"And Nathan Driscoll? With Frisky?" Mike asked.

Ben frowned. "Yeah, that was odd. I seen 'im with Frisky that day an' wondered if something was up with Mrs. Hardcastle."

"What do you mean?"

"Well, Frisky's her dog, ain't he?"

Jonathon blinked. "Are we talking the same dog?"

Ben's brow was still furrowed. "Cockapoo. Pale cream and brown. Curly coat."

Jonathon recalled Nathan's words. "But... he said he often takes Frisky for walks in the forest because the dog loves it."

Ben chuckled. "Oh, Frisky loves his walks, sure enough, but not with Nathan Driscoll. Come to think of it, I reckon that's the first time I've seen 'im go past. I see 'im in the village all the time, always scurrying from one place to another." He cocked his head to one side. "Was that all you wanted to know?"

"Yes, thanks. You've been a big help." Mike extended a hand, and Ben shook it.

"Glad to assist. I'll be gettin' back to work now an' leave you to your... detectin'." Ben winked. "You'd better get a move on if you're gonna solve the murder, though. I do 'ear tell there's an inspector comin' to take over the case."

Mike laughed. "Who needs informants when you live in a small English village? Everyone knows everything."

Ben touched his cap again. "As it should be. Good day, gents." And with that, he walked off toward the rear gardens.

Jonathon closed and bolted the french doors. "Interesting. Nathan Driscoll 'borrowed' a dog and took a walk. A coincidence? Was he doing Mrs. Hardcastle a favor? Or did he borrow Frisky as a cover?"

"We could always ask Mrs. Hardcastle," Mike suggested. "She helps out in the village shop."

Jonathon smiled broadly. "I feel the urge to do a little shopping this morning. Want to come along?"

Mike sighed. "Can I finish my coffee first? And there's still that last piece of toast."

Jonathon grimaced. "It'll have gone cold by now. Still, it was worth it. We learned something." He smacked Mike's backside. "Now, drink your coffee. I've got the mayor's wife to see too, remember? You've only got your pub to run." Then he scooted out of the room before Mike could return the smack.

He laughed as Mike yelled, "*Only* got a pub to run?"

Teasing Mike was such fun.

DORIS BEAMED at Jonathon from behind the counter as he entered the shop. "I was gonna call you later. Your, er... order has come in." Her wrinkled cheeks pinked.

It took him a moment to realize what she meant. Then the penny dropped. "Oh, great." His amusement died when she reached under the counter and withdrew a brown paper bag that she placed beside the till. Jonathon took out his wallet and removed a five-pound note.

Doris leaned over the counter and lowered her voice. "My granddaughter says you can order these online."

"Really?" Jonathon paid her and took the bag.

"I was only thinking, it might be easier if you did, that's all." She gave a half smile. "Save you the trip to the shop."

Jonathon thanked her and looked around for Mike, who was perusing the magazine rack. He glanced up as Jonathon approached, then dropped his gaze to the bag. "What's in there?"

"A failed experiment," Jonathon said with a sigh. When Mike gave him a quizzical look, he explained. "Actually, it's a copy of *Attitude*. I ordered it last week."

Mike arched his eyebrows. "Why the long face?"

"Because I didn't expect to be handed it as if it was pornography. It's just a gay magazine. There isn't even a seminaked bloke on the cover this month."

Mike gave him a compassionate glance. "Nice idea, but take a look." He swung his arm to encompass the shelves before them. "*Horse & Hound. Country Life. Harper's Bazaar. Woman's Weekly. House Beautiful.* Puzzle books and crosswords. Knitting patterns. Children's coloring books. Can you really see *Attitude*, *DNA*, and *GT* on the same shelves?" He tilted his head. "Or was that the plan, to bring Merrychurch into the twenty-first century?"

"Kind of." Except, deep down, Jonathon had known how it was going to work out.

Mike put his hand on Jonathon's shoulder. "I know," he said quietly. "And you're right. Having a gay magazine on a shelf in here would've been a great first step. But how about you let the village get used to a gay lord of the manor first? You don't have to rub their noses in it, though… maybe walk through the lanes holding hands with me, for one thing. Or give me the odd peck on the lips when you're in the pub. Stuff like that." He smiled. "There you were, talking about having a husband. Well, that's the goal, to get to the point where you announce you're getting married—to a guy—and have the whole village ready to celebrate it with you." He leaned in and kissed Jonathon's cheek. "Baby steps, love."

Jonathon caught his breath at the unexpected term of endearment, and Mike chuckled. "See? I managed to get it out that time." He cocked his head to one side. "Too much? Too soon?"

A warm glow filled Jonathon. "Just right." Then he caught sight of the magazine rack again, and scowled, his newly acquired glow dissipating. "When I think about the eloquent, fascinating articles you find in gay magazines and then compare them to all these celebrity mags…."

"And while you're on that track, take another look at the top shelf. No magazines for men, if you get my drift. If the shop won't even stock the latest equivalent of *Loaded*, they're not gonna stock gay magazines. And here's a thought for you. Are they being homophobic—or merely reacting to the adult nature of the magazines?"

Mike had a point. Before Jonathon could respond, however, Mike tugged his arm.

"Now, how about we go over to the deli section, where Mrs. Hardcastle is slicing bacon as we speak, and ask her about her dog? That *is* why we came here, right?"

"Yes, it is," Jonathon admitted. He followed Mike to the rear of the shop, where the long fridge was filled with cooked meats, cheeses, pork pies, and pates. Sure enough, Mrs. Hardcastle was carefully easing a joint of meat through the bacon slicer while keeping up a verbal battle with a teenage girl who was filling a stainless-steel tray with the rashers.

"I still can't believe you'd do such a thing," Mrs. Hardcastle muttered. "Don't you have any brains? As if that would work in the first place."

"She said it would," the girl retorted.

"Of *course* she'd say that. You were giving her money, you—"

The girl glared and dropped the tray onto the counter with a clatter. "Sod this. I'm out of 'ere." She pulled off her clear plastic gloves, slung them to one side, strode toward the door at the rear, and banged it shut behind her.

Mrs. Hardcastle stared after her for a few seconds, then resumed her task, muttering under her breath.

"It's difficult when they reach that awkward age, isn't it?" Mike offered.

Mrs. Hardcastle jerked her head up and stared at him. "Mark my words, Laura has been at that awkward age ever since she learned how to say *no*." She sighed. "And all of this over a *love potion*, if there *is* such a thing." When neither Mike nor Jonathon responded, she let out another heavy sigh. "Laura's my niece. She's staying with me while her parents are away on business. I found this bottle of… stuff in her room, and when I asked her what it was, she said it was this love potion she'd asked old Mrs. Teedle to put together for her." She rolled her eyes. "A *love* potion, I ask you. But still, taking money off a kid...."

"I take it the potion didn't work," Jonathon said, biting back his smirk.

Mrs. Hardcastle leaned closer. "Poor lass. She's got her eye on young Jason Barton. Well, he's a bit out of her league, to be honest. And then she gets all riled up when he doesn't pay her a blind bit of notice." She shook her head. "I'd go round there and give that woman a piece of my mind—if it weren't for the fact that she's dead." She put down the bacon joint and removed her plastic gloves. "Now, what can I do for you?"

"I was just checking you were okay," Jonathon said smoothly. "I happened to see the chemist walking your dog the other day, and I had the idea you might be ill."

She gazed at him with wide eyes. "Aw, bless you. No, I'm right as rain. Nathan—he's my next-door neighbor—called around on Sunday and said as how he was thinking of getting a dog, and how he'd always liked cockapoos, and could he take Frisky for a walk to kind of try him out?" She smiled. "Like I'd say no to someone taking him for a walk. I said yes, and off they went."

"And what did he decide?" Jonathon asked.

"Why, he—" Mrs. Hardcastle frowned. "Well, that's strange. He never did say. In fact, he took off sharpish right after he brought Frisky back. I'll have to ask him this evening when I see him." She gestured to the fridge. "Now, are you sure I can't tempt you to a nice bit of bacon?"

Five minutes later, they left the shop, Jonathon clutching his brown paper bag and a white plastic one secured with a red tie, a label stuck on it. When they reached their cars, Jonathon came to a halt. "I am *not* going to see the mayor's wife armed with a bag containing half a kilo of bacon." He thrust it at Mike. "Here. Take it back to your place. We can have it for breakfast the next time I stay over."

Mike grinned as he took it. "What makes you think there'll be any left?"

"Because I'll stay every night for a week until it's all gone," Jonathon flung back at him. "And that includes tonight."

Mike chuckled. "Aha. Now I know the secret. If I want you in my bed, I need bacon in the fridge. Gotcha."

"It isn't true, you know—'the way to a man's heart is through his stomach.'" Jonathon kissed him lightly on the lips.

Mike pulled him close. "Then how do I get to your heart?" His voice was low.

Jonathon smiled. "Maybe you're already there." And without waiting for Mike to reply, he pulled free of Mike's embrace, got behind the wheel of the Jag, put it into reverse, and steered out of the little car park behind the shop, waving at Mike as he passed him.

It was the closest he'd come to saying those three little words, but he figured they wouldn't be far behind.

CHAPTER ELEVEN

THE MAYOR'S house wasn't what Jonathon expected. It was a detached cottage with a dark gray slate roof, standing among three or four similar houses in a narrow lane not far from the water mill. The front garden was beautifully maintained with neatly shaped shrubs and flower beds behind a low stone wall. A couple of windows were set under a kind of eyebrow where the roof curved over them, something seen in a few houses in the village.

Jonathon locked the Jag and strolled up the path that led to the wooden front door. He rang the bell and waited. A minute later Mrs. Barton answered, her eyes widening in obvious surprise.

"It's… Mr. de Mountford, isn't it?"

Jonathon gave a polite nod. "I hope it's not an inconvenient time to call."

"Not at all. You're just in time to join me for a cup of tea, or coffee if you'd prefer."

Jonathon beamed. "I never say no to a cup of coffee."

She stepped aside, and he entered a low-ceilinged hallway, the floor covered with stone flags and thick rugs. "Go straight ahead, through the kitchen and into the conservatory. I'll make us some coffee."

He followed the direction through the sunny kitchen that opened out into an even sunnier space with glass all around. The comfortable-looking rattan furniture was inviting, and Jonathon took a seat on the couch, gazing out at the garden beyond. The rear was as perfectly maintained as the front.

"Your gardens are delightful," he called out toward the kitchen.

Mrs. Barton stepped into the conservatory. "Nothing like the ones up at the manor house," she said with a smile. "Your uncle used to show me around when John—my husband—would go up to see him. Your uncle was so proud of the gardens."

It always warmed Jonathon when people spoke well of Dominic. "It's nice to meet someone who knew him."

From behind her came a beep. "Kettle's boiled." She disappeared from view, but it wasn't long before she returned with a large tray that she set down carefully on the low coffee table. "Help yourself to cream and sugar. I've brought out some of my homemade biscuits too. I didn't know if you have a sweet tooth." She sat beside him on the couch and poured out two cups. "You were lucky to catch me in. Thursday is usually my day for working with John, but he had a few meetings. I wasn't about to say no to a morning of leisure."

Jonathon had to admit, for someone spending a morning doing nothing, she was immaculately dressed in dark gray slacks, a cream blouse, and a lace cardigan. Her glossy brown hair fell to her shoulders, where it curled under at the ends, and she wore only the lightest touch of makeup. It was easy to see where Jason got his good looks.

"I'm glad to find you in, then." Jonathon helped himself to a biscuit.

"What brings you here today?"

He relaxed against the seat cushions. "I'm conducting research, actually, by way of feedback. I'm asking people if they'd like a similar bonfire party next year, and if they can think of any way to improve it. This was my first such event, and I'd like to do it again."

Mrs. Barton's face lit up. "It was a wonderful night. And as for improving things, I think you got it just right. Those fireworks were magnificent."

At that moment, a golden retriever walked sedately into the conservatory, heading for them.

Mrs. Barton smiled. "Ah, I wondered when *you'd* appear. You think you're missing out on something, don't you?"

The dog laid its chin on Jonathon's knee and gazed up at him with liquid brown eyes. When Jonathon stroked the sleek gold head, the dog closed its eyes, but when he stopped, the dog brought up its leg and placed a heavy paw on Jonathon's arm, opening its eyes to stare at him.

He laughed. "Oh, I'm sorry. Was I not allowed to stop?" Jonathon resumed his stroking, and the dog lowered its paw.

"This is Goldie, who knows better than to beg for cuddles, not that you'd know it." Mrs. Barton gazed fondly at Goldie. "He's getting on, poor old thing. His hips aren't what they used to be. We've had to cut his walks down. He used to drag me all over the place three times a day when he was a puppy, but not anymore." Her eyes held a look of sadness. "We've had him ever since Jason was one, possibly two years old, so there's not much time left, I'm afraid. The lifespan of a golden retriever…." She swallowed.

The love in her voice tightened Jonathon's throat. He bent over and looked into the dog's eyes in an effort to hide the tears that pricked his own. "You're gorgeous and you know it," he told Goldie, who chuffed and pushed his head into Jonathon's hand.

"Do you have a dog?" Mrs. Barton asked as she dropped a cube of brown sugar into her cup, then stirred it.

Jonathon looked up and shook his head. "I've spent too much time traveling to think about getting a dog. It seems cruel to have a pet that I then have to kennel when I go away on a trip."

"I understand. And I've seen the results of your trips. Jason was showing me some of your photos of India and Australia. I think you have a fan there." She smiled, the sunlight catching in her pale blue eyes. "Actually, there's no 'think' about it. Jason has a mild case of hero worship."

"You don't appear concerned." Jonathon left off his stroking to drink his coffee, but fortunately Goldie seemed to understand and sat at his feet—well, *on* his feet.

Mrs. Barton chuckled. "It's definitely bringing out his creative side, and there's nothing wrong with that."

Jonathon sipped his coffee, his gaze focused on Goldie. "Now that I think about it, I knew you had a dog. My gardener mentioned it."

"Oh?"

Jonathon raised his chin to look at her. "He lives on the edge of the forest, and he was commenting about the number of people who walk their dogs there. He likes people-watching." He paused, awaiting her reaction.

Mrs. Barton stilled. "Really? And he mentioned me? I can't think why."

He didn't break eye contact. "He was watching out of his window on Sunday morning, and I think he counted four villagers all walking their dogs along that path." He chuckled. "I bet you probably ran into all of them when you took Goldie for a walk."

For the briefest moment, Mrs. Barton's face tightened and her eyes widened, but then she smiled. "Funny. I don't think I saw a soul that morning. Not even Mrs. Teedle, when I stopped to buy a jar of marmalade."

"Ooh, I haven't tried that one. Mike loves the mango-and-peach jam. In fact, the way he's going, he'll have eaten through the entire jar before I get so much as a spoonful." Jonathon kept his tone light, but that moment had been enough to assure him they were right to keep her on the list.

It was not the reaction of an innocent woman.

Jonathon did his best to put her at her ease. "I'm very fond of marmalade. Is it a chunky version or more like a jelly?"

"Do you know, I haven't opened it yet. Let's see." She got up from the couch and went into the kitchen.

Jonathon gazed thoughtfully at Goldie, who brought his head up at the movement before settling back to sleep. "You're doing a great job of keeping my feet warm," Jonathon told him quietly.

Mrs. Barton came back, carrying the now-recognizable jar. "I can see chunks in here, if that helps you decide if you'd like to buy some." She placed it on the table.

"Not that I suppose it matters now. She won't be making any more," Jonathon added in a low voice.

She gave a slight shudder. "A horrible business. Jason was quite upset."

"Is it true that Mrs. Teedle delivered him?" Jonathon helped himself to more coffee from the pot. "Someone told me a story about that."

Mrs. Barton laughed and settled back against the cushions, apparently more at ease. "Perfectly true. To be honest, I shouldn't have gone to the fete in the first place. I *was* overdue, after all. But it was such a lovely day, and I was fed up being stuck at home. John was away that day on business—not that he wanted to go, it being so close to the birth. So there I was, strolling through all the stalls, when I suddenly realized my waters had broken."

"You must have been scared."

"I didn't expect it to happen so quickly. Everyone had said the first labor usually lasts forever. Not mine. But Mrs. Teedle was wonderful." Mrs. Barton smiled. "I remember lying on a first-aid cot, covered in this coarse green blanket, with Jason wrapped up in a clean tea towel, and thanking her. She laughed and said it wasn't as if that was the first baby she'd ever delivered."

"Then you were fortunate to have her around," Jonathon commented.

"That's what I'm always telling her." Mr. Barton came into the conservatory, smiling. "I *thought* I heard voices out here." He walked over to his wife and kissed her cheek. "Meetings all done for the day." Then he came over to Jonathon, his hand outstretched.

Jonathon attempted to rise to his feet but was prevented by the very solid Goldie.

Mr. Barton laughed. "Stay where you are. It looks like the old boy is comfortable, though how he could possibly be so on someone's feet is beyond me." His gaze settled on the coffee table, and his eyes lit up. "Ooh, coffee, good." He promptly took the empty space next to Jonathon.

Mrs. Barton got up. "I'll fetch another cup."

Mr. Barton gave him a jovial smile. "To what do we owe this honor?"

Jonathon explained quickly about the feedback on the bonfire party, and he beamed.

"Fantastic evening. I think making it an annual event would be wonderful." He leaned back, his arm resting along the edge of the couch. "I hear you had a visitor yesterday." His bright blue eyes twinkled.

"Ah. Jason told you he came up to the manor house?"

Mr. Barton nodded. "This was the first time I'd heard of his ideas for a career. I must admit, it came as a surprise."

"What career?" Mrs. Barton asked as she placed a cup in front of him.

"Our son wants to be a photographer," Mr. Barton said as he poured himself a cup.

Mrs. Barton stared at him.

"That's right," he told her. "We talked about it Wednesday night. I got the impression he was going to talk to you about it tonight. Not that we didn't already know he was interested in photography—that's been obvious for the last six months—but as for a career in it?"

Jonathon's stomach churned. "My father certainly doesn't see it as a career. He'd be happier if I went into law, like the rest of the family."

To his surprise, Mr. Barton scowled. "Reminds me of *my* father. He wanted me to go into medicine, to follow in his footsteps. I did try. I went to medical school, but it became clear to me—*and* him—that it wasn't the path for me. I told him that I wanted to go into business and that it was my life, after all. I dropped out of medical school and got a job with a large retail company in Reading. Worked my way up." His scowl deepened. "Caused a rift between us that has never healed. Well, I'm not going to let the same thing happen with Jason. If this is what he wants to do, then he should do it, with our blessing. We can be there for him, advise him, support him, but ultimately he has to lead his own life, make his own mistakes—not that I'm saying this would be a mistake, you understand," he added quickly.

"Having seen some of his photos, I think he has a real gift," Jonathon said, his tension bleeding away.

"Then I'm glad he came to see you," Mr. Barton said warmly. He lapsed into silence as he drank his coffee. Goldie shifted to place his chin on Mr. Barton's knee, and he stroked the soft, silky coat.

Mrs. Barton drank as she stared out over the garden.

Jonathon drank too, conscious of being torn. On the one hand, he had a really good feeling about Jason's father. Every sense in Jonathon told him that coming out to him would not be as scary as Jason feared. Although nothing specific had been said, Jonathon thought it would be strange if someone who was so supportive of his son's career choice turned out to be an asshole about his sexual orientation. In his—somewhat limited—experience, the trait of being an asshole tended to permeate through all aspects of a life.

But that left Mrs. Barton.

Jason had said how she'd been reluctant to talk about his birth, but Jonathon had gotten no sense of that. In fact, she'd appeared relaxed as she retold the story. And the only thing that had changed was that Mrs. Teedle was now dead.

Then there was her reaction to being seen near the cottage. There had been no mistaking that initial spasm of fear or her first attempt at denial. She wasn't going to admit to being there.

Why, Mrs. Barton? Why don't you want to be linked to Mrs. Teedle?

What exasperated Jonathon was the lack of motive.

We don't know enough yet. Especially about Mrs. Teedle.

It was time to call Mike's friend Keith. They needed more information.

CHAPTER TWELVE

JONATHON PARKED the car behind the Hare and Hounds, and strolled around to the front entrance. From inside the pub came music and chatter, inviting sounds for a cold night. But as he reached the door, Jonathon heard another noise.

"Will you flippin' well do your business so I can get back inside?"

He peered into the dark toward the village green. A man stood there, illuminated by the streetlamp, watching a large dog sniffing at the ground. The man hugged himself, dressed in only jeans and a shirt and a pair of plaid slippers. In his hand he held a chunky metal dog leash.

"Come on, Max, for Christ's sake. Just find a shrub to piss up," he hissed.

Jonathon chuckled, and the man jerked his head in Jonathon's direction. At that moment the large dog noticed him too, and ran over to him, tail wagging ten to the dozen.

"Max, no jumping!" the man called out, but Max apparently wasn't listening. A few seconds later, two large, heavy paws were at Jonathon's shoulders, and a gorgeous German shepherd was attempting to lick his face by way of introduction. The man hurried over and grabbed his collar, pulling him off Jonathon. "I'm so sorry. He really is a friendly dog. That's why I let him off the leash. Absolutely useless as a guard dog, however. He'd lick the burglars to death." He was a tall man, maybe in his early fifties, with receding hair, his eyes appearing dark in the poor light.

Jonathon laughed and bent over to pet the dog. "He's great."

The man scowled. "Not when he whines to be let out to have a pee, then spends ten minutes investigating every interesting scent he can find. Meanwhile, I'm freezing my nu—I'm getting cold."

Right on cue, Max ran over to the lamppost and cocked his leg.

"Thank God." The man waited until he'd finished, then whistled. "Come on, boy. Back inside."

Max raced across the green, through the front gate of a nearby cottage, up the path, and stopped at the front door, whining.

The man raised his eyes heavenward. "*Now* he's cold." He started to walk toward the house, then stopped and turned back to Jonathon. "Sorry. That was rude of me. And not quite how I wanted to introduce myself to the lord of the manor." He extended a hand. "The name's George Tyrell. I was going to say hello at the bonfire party, but you were always surrounded by people. And when I thought I'd got my chance, the mayor got in first." George laughed. "Well, he *is* the mayor."

Jonathon gestured toward the pub. "I'm going for a drink. Would you care to join me? Then we can talk properly." He couldn't believe his luck. He'd been racking his brains for how to arrange an "accidental" meeting with George, and fate lent a hand.

George sighed. "Thanks, but I tend not to drink outside of the house." When Jonathon blinked, he snickered. "That sounded awful. Truth is, I'm a narcoleptic. I don't socialize much. I do have a drinks cabinet that's well-stocked, however, so if you'd care to join me for a drink one evening, that would be wonderful. The only thing you need to know is if I fall asleep, it's not a comment on your conversational skills." He tilted his head to one side. "And a little bird tells me you're a dab hand with a cocktail shaker. I have this book—*Two Hundred Cocktails*—and I've never made a single one."

That settled it. "How about tomorrow evening?" Mike would be working anyway, and Jonathon could combine cocktail shaking with a little sleuthing. "If you're sure."

George smiled. "I'd love the company. Shall we say eight o'clock?"

"Sounds good."

"In that case, I'll get in the warm." George gave a cheerful nod in Jonathon's direction. "Good to meet you at last—even if it *was* while my dog was, er… relieving himself. Eventually." He pushed open the door, and Max nipped inside. George gave one last wave and closed the door behind him.

Jonathon hurried into the pub, pleased with the way things had worked out. Based on first impressions, he liked George. Then he had to remind himself that nice or not, George could be a suspect. And those large paw prints around the base of the table outside Naomi's cottage *could* have been made by a German shepherd.

Or a golden retriever. Don't forget Goldie.

At least Frisky was off the hook. Nathan Driscoll, however, certainly was *not*.

MIKE TOOK one last look around the pub, checked that all the doors were locked, then switched off the lights and climbed the narrow wooden staircase located behind the door marked Private. At the top, the only light came from the lamppost outside, whose glow filtered through the gap in the curtains, and from under the door to Mike's bedroom.

Smiling to himself, he pushed open the door and found Jonathon sitting up in bed, his chest bare, his attention locked firmly on a notepad in which he was writing carefully.

"Not what I *thought* I'd find," Mike commented with a chuckle.

Jonathon raised his head and gave Mike a bright smile. "I've been making notes." His brow creased slightly. "What did that mean?"

Mike gave him an innocent glance. "Nothing. It's only… when you said you were going up and you'd be waiting for me, it all sounded a lot… sexier."

Jonathon snickered. "That's because you, too, have a one-track mind. And are you implying my chest isn't sexy?"

"Not in the least. I just want to know what's waiting for me under the sheets."

Jonathon's eyes gleamed. "Later. Now, do you want to hear what I've written?"

"Sure." Mike sat on the edge of the bed and began unbuttoning his shirt.

"I've been writing down what we've learned so far, and I have to say, it's not a lot." He cocked his head. "Can you call your friend Keith? We need to know whatever he can find out about Naomi Teedle's life. There's too much we don't know. There has to be *something* in her past that would lead someone to kill her."

Mike removed his shirt. "So you don't think the chemist murdered her to get rid of the competition?"

Nathan Driscoll was certainly acting in a suspicious manner, but as motives went, it was pretty thin.

Jonathon worried his bottom lip with his teeth. "I think he did send those leaflets to everyone, but having seen his shop, I also think his lack of business success is down to his high prices and lack of vision, rather than her stealing all his customers."

"*Nathan* might not see it that way," Mike argued. "For all you know, he might think that his shop is absolutely perfect and that she *was* stealing his customers."

Jonathon gave a shrug. "I could be wrong. He *was* seen near the cottage, after all—*and* he borrowed a dog under dubious circumstances."

"So we're not crossing him off the list?" Mike stood, removed his boots and sock, then casually unzipped his fly.

Jonathon's focus shifted momentarily, and he narrowed his gaze. "You're doing that on purpose."

Mike grinned. "No—going commando was me doing things on purpose." He lowered the zip just enough that Jonathon's pupils darkened. Mike stifled a chuckle. "Now, where were we?" He sat on the edge of the bed again and shucked off his jeans, his back to Jonathon, who cleared his throat.

"I've been thinking. We have a thirty-year gap when she lived in Australia. I might be able to help with that. Remember I told you I stayed with a guy and he taught me to mix cocktails? Well, his dad is a cop. He could run a background check on her, find out about her life over there. I'm pretty sure Wayne would ask him for me. We parted on good terms, after all, and it *was* an amazing three weeks."

Mike wasn't sure he liked hearing about an amazing ex, but he had to admit, it was a great idea. "Fine. Get him on it, and we'll see what he turns up. Meanwhile, I'll call Keith in the morning and get him to run a check too." He unfastened his prosthetic and placed it out of harm's way. From beneath his pillow, he pulled a neatly folded pair of pajama bottoms and put them on, not missing Jonathon's slight noise of disapproval. "What did you learn at the Bartons'?" When no reply came, Mike twisted around to look at Jonathon, who was staring at his notepad. "Sweetheart?"

Jonathon smiled. "I like the sound of that." Then he tapped his notes with his index finger. "It's hard to picture her strangling Mrs. Teedle, I have to admit. But something tells me she's involved somehow. It's not much, just a feeling, but…."

Mike knew all about such feelings. "Sometimes we have to go with our instincts." Like the one that had been niggling him ever since he'd seen those village shop diaries. "I've been thinking. Why would Naomi write in code?"

Jonathon stared at him. "I've been thinking about that too. We need to look at those diaries again. She obviously didn't want anyone to know what she was writing, but she also needed to keep track of something.

My first thought was…." He hesitated, letting out a nervous laugh.

Mike gave a nod of encouragement. "Say it."

"Do you think she was… blackmailing people?"

Mike grinned. "Very likely."

Jonathon's eyes widened. "But… she was a little old lady."

"With a beautifully decorated home and a taste for expensive champagne," Mike added.

"So how do we prove it?"

Mike had already considered that question. "First off, we have to get evidence. Show monies going to her on a regular basis."

Jonathon huffed. "I don't see how we can do that. For all we know, her victims paid her cash and she stuffed the money under her mattress. No trail to follow." He stilled. "Maybe we should check there."

Mike let out a gruff chuckle. "If she was blackmailing people in the village, they would *not* want to be seen regularly going to her cottage. No, it would be easier for them to pay cash into her bank account."

Jonathon groaned. "The police will have asked for her financial details. I can't see them willingly letting us have a look. Especially now there's a new DI in charge."

"There's no reason for them to look into her finances—not yet, at least. But I'd be willing to bet she has paper copies at the cottage."

"Who does that these days? Everyone's gone paperless, with online banking."

Mike smiled. "You said it yourself. She was a little old lady. Can you see her with her banking details on her phone? No. She's old-fashioned enough to stick with paper, which means somewhere in that cottage are all her bank statements. We simply have to see if anything matches. Then there's the small but important task of cracking the code."

"Oh, why didn't you say so?" Jonathon rolled his eyes. "I'm an expert. I crack codes instead of doing crossword puzzles."

Mike leveled a stern gaze at him. "Sarcasm is not helpful." He got into bed. "Who's left to see from the list Ben gave the police?"

Jonathon consulted the notepad. "I'm having a drink tomorrow night with George Tyrell. That leaves our MP, Mr. Joshua Brent."

Mike chuckled. "Good luck trying to run into him by accident. Now *there's* a very busy man." He removed his glasses before prizing the notepad from Jonathon's hands and placing it on the bedside cabinet. "No more sleuthing tonight."

Jonathon gave him a lazy, sexy smile that sent heat pulsing through him. "Oh, really? And I thought you wanted to discover what was hiding under the sheets...."

Mike glanced down at the tented sheet and grinned. "I hate to tell you this, but your secret has just been blown."

Jonathon switched off the lamp. "Not yet, it hasn't," he whispered.

CHAPTER THIRTEEN

Friday, November 10

"IS EVERYTHING as you'd want it, sir?" Janet asked, adjusting the vase of flowers on the dressing table.

Jonathon glanced around the sunny bedroom that had been prepared for his father. Fresh towels and fresh bed linens, in what had been Dominic's former bedroom.

And on the other side of the house to where I sleep. Jonathon didn't want to even entertain the possibility of having his father anywhere near, especially as he could see Mike wanting to stay the night. Not to rub his father's nose in it by any means, but Mike wouldn't change his plans for fear of upsetting him.

What am I thinking? That would be Mike's way of cutting through the bullshit and forcing my father to face up to this.

God, he loved that man.

"Everything is perfect," Jonathon assured her. "My father should be arriving at some point tomorrow morning, and he'll be leaving Sunday afternoon."

"A short visit this time," she said with a smile.

Not short enough, in Jonathon's book.

"Ivy wants to know numbers for meals. What shall I tell her?"

At that moment Jonathon had no idea. "Let me check with Mike first. Tell Ivy I'll let her know ASAP."

Janet nodded and left the room. Jonathon got out his phone and dialed Mike.

"You only left here an hour ago," Mike said with a chuckle as he answered the call. "Can't keep away, can you?"

"Nope. You're irresistible. Now, will you be here for lunch or dinner on Saturday? Ivy needs to know."

"Hey." Mike's voice softened. "I said I'd be there, didn't I? Abi is opening the pub at lunchtime and Saturday evening, and she assures me she can cope. It's not like she hasn't done it before. So tell Ivy she'll be preparing lunch and dinner for three."

A wave of relief crashed over Jonathon, so acute that it left him shaking. He sat at the foot of the bed. It wasn't until that moment that he realized how much he'd been dreading this visit.

"You still there?"

Jonathon drew in a deep breath. "Yeah, still here. And thank you."

"No problem. And I had an idea after you'd left. How about we go to the cottage and see if we can find her bank statements?"

Jonathon had been thinking too. "Do you think we should tell Graham our suspicions?"

"Not yet. Let's wait until we have something definite to tell him. Do you want me to pick you up first?"

"Sure. Now let me go tell Ivy the good news."

Mike laughed. "Tell her I'll be expecting something delicious as always." He disconnected.

Jonathon got up and smoothed the bedspread flat. Then he left the bedroom and headed down to the belowstairs kitchen, a roomy space painted in a pale green that made it feel peaceful. Ivy was busy making pastry on the huge wooden table, and she looked up with a smile as he came into the room.

"Lunch and dinner for three, I see." Before he could ask how she'd known, Ivy added, "When you walked in smiling, I knew." She inclined her head toward the pale lump of dough she was busy manipulating. "I'm keeping things simple. Steak pie, mashed potatoes, plenty of veg, and lots of gravy. And for dessert, fruit tart with cream. None of that fancy cooking I expect he gets in London in all those posh restaurants."

Impulsively, Jonathon came over to where she stood and kissed her cheek. "I'd rather have *your* food any day."

"Get away with ya," she said, her face flushed, her eyes bright, and her smile wider than ever. "Now out of this kitchen so I can finish this pastry."

He left her to it and went upstairs to the main hall to await Mike.

His father's visit was looking less like something to be endured.

JONATHON STARED at the chair where they'd found Mrs. Teedle and tried not to think about how she'd looked. Instead, he peered behind her chair, gazing intently at the fireplace, with its blocks of rough-hewn stone and thick hearth.

"What are you looking at?" Mike joined him and peered too.

"I was thinking about that head injury. Did they hit her head with something, or did she bang it?" Jonathon scanned the stone for signs of blood or hair.

"I'm pretty sure SOCO would have gone over this, so don't expect to find anything, but it's a thought. Bashing your head against this would make one hell of a dent—not in the stone, of course."

"Did they hit her first to knock her out, *then* strangle her? And what about that knife? Whose blood was on the blade—hers or the attacker's?" Still so many questions unanswered.

Mike straightened. "Let's remember why we're here. I don't think her bank statements would be in this part of the house. I can't see anywhere she'd keep them. So let's look in the main part of the house." He unlocked the door, and they walked through into the living room. Jonathon headed for the bookshelves to search for a folder of some kind, while Mike pulled open the drawers beneath them.

"While I'm here, I want to take a photo of some of the diary pages." Jonathon pulled out the latest diary and opened it to the previous month. Mike held it open while he took a shot. Then Jonathon skimmed through, looking for any months that had different entries. "Something's different in the early part of the year. The code changed for one of the entries. Not the figures." He took another photo before placing the diary back on the shelf. Then he pulled more diaries out and leafed through them. "There were more entries prior to this year. What do you think? She was blackmailing more people but decided to be *nice* to some of them and let them off the hook?"

"We don't know for sure that she was blackmailing anyone yet," Mike remonstrated. "It's merely a theory until we find those statements." He crouched down and pulled out the wide bottom drawer. "Aha." Inside was an A4 folder with a white label on the cover, which said Bank Statements. He removed it and found a thick sheaf of sheets with holes punched through them. Mike went to September 2017, then looked up at Jonathon, pointing to the diaries. "Find me this month."

Jonathon opened the diary to the last full week of September. "You're looking for deposits on or near the twenty-fifth, twenty-seventh, twenty-eighth, and thirtieth."

Mike beamed. "Yup. There are corresponding entries. Hang on a minute." He flipped back to August. "Yeah. Again, the same entries."

"How much are we talking?" Jonathon wanted to know.

Mike chuckled. "Wow. Some of her victims were lucky, others not so much. There are deposits of £150 and £500."

"Go back to January."

Mike flipped through the sheets again. "Yes. Ah. You were right. The amounts changed. There's only one deposit of £500. Another is for £250."

Jonathon whistled. "She started demanding more from one poor wretch, then."

Mike stared at him over the rim of his glasses. "Before you start feeling *too* sorry for the poor unknown wretch, they had to be doing *something* wrong or illegal for her to be blackmailing them in the first place."

"You don't know that for sure. Maybe she had something on them that they didn't want to come out into the open."

Mike sat back on his haunches, the folder in his hands. "You do realize we could be looking at two entirely different lists of suspects now. Those who were seen near here that day, and those she was blackmailing."

Jonathon gave a slow nod. "What *I'd* like to see is where the two lists intersect. Because if we have someone on *both* lists—" He froze at the sound of a door creaking. "Someone is here," he whispered. As silently as he could, Jonathon replaced the diary on the shelf, and Mike slipped the folder back into its drawer. They crept toward the door—which opened as they reached it, bringing them face-to-face with a middle-aged man in a pale gray suit, who glared at them.

"Who are you, and what are you doing here?" His voice was loud, with a rough edge to it. Equally pale gray eyes regarded them with suspicion.

From behind the man came more noise, and Graham appeared in the doorway, in full uniform. His mouth fell open when he saw them, but he recovered quickly. "Ah. Sir, these are the gentlemen you asked me about yesterday." He cleared his throat. "Mike, this is Detective Inspector Mablethorpe, Winchester CID."

Before Mike could respond, the DI gave him a hard stare. "So, *you're* the ex-copper I was warned about. And who gave you permission to enter a crime scene?"

"I did." Jonathon straightened, lifting his head high. "This is my property. And I was given to understand that SOCO had completed their investigations here."

DI Mablethorpe's eyebrows shot up. "Indeed. In which case, that would make *you* Jonathon de Mountford. Well, for your information, *gentlemen*, the investigations will only be completed when we have someone in custody for the crime. And as we are not at that point yet, I must ask you both to leave. Should you wish to enter this property again, for whatever reason, you must first inform a police officer at Merrychurch police station. You will then be accompanied here by an officer, who will supervise your visit at all times." His eyes glinted. "Is that understood?"

Mike laid a hand gently on Jonathon's arm before addressing the DI. "Perfectly." He gave Jonathon a flash of a smile. "It's time we were out of here anyway."

The DI didn't move. "You are not, I trust, removing anything from the property?"

"Of course not." Mike's smile was a lot cooler. "Please, feel free to search us."

"That won't be necessary." The DI stood to one side to let them pass, and they walked through the old kitchen and out of the door.

Graham followed them. "I'll just escort them to their vehicle, sir," he called back to the house. With a sigh, he gestured toward the lane.

Mike led the way, with Jonathon behind him.

Graham cast an uneasy glance toward the cottage. "Sorry, guys," he muttered as they approached Mike's 4x4. "The DI is a strictly by-the-book copper and a real stickler for protocol. I knew he'd be trouble when he asked about you yesterday. By name too."

"How could he know about us?" As soon as he'd asked the question, Jonathon realized there could only be one answer. "Gorland. He knows DI Gorland, doesn't he?"

Mike groaned. "Oh, please, let's hope he's a better detective than Gorland."

Graham came to a halt at the car. "Yeah, he knows Gorland, all right. They're golfing buddies, I found out this morning." He sighed heavily. "Well, I hope you learned something from your visit, 'cause heaven knows when he'll let you back in there again." He rubbed his hand through his hair. "God, is it six o'clock yet? That's when I'm done for the day."

"I think *you* could do with a pint this evening," Mike said, his eyes twinkling.

"*Now* you're talking." Graham grinned. "Save me a stool at the bar. I'll be there before closing." He looked closely at Jonathon. "*Have* you found anything out?"

Jonathon opened his mouth to respond, but Mike got in there first. "Maybe. Nothing concrete. When we have more than a theory, we'll let you know."

Graham nodded. "Fine. Good luck to you. I'd best be heading back. He wanted to see the crime scene for himself." And with that, Graham hurried toward the cottage.

Jonathon watched him go. "You know what I think? That DI is going to be a real pain in the arse."

Mike burst into laughter. "And to think, when I first met you at the station, you were this polite, eloquent guy who wouldn't say boo to a goose. And here you are, referring to a senior member of the Hampshire Constabulary as a pain in the arse." He puffed out his chest. "I feel like a proud father."

Jonathon chuckled. "I hate to burst your bubble, but you're only now seeing what I'm really like. I haven't changed—well, perhaps in one way I have. I feel comfortable enough around you to be myself." In fact, he couldn't remember ever feeling so comfortable with another man.

Maybe the fact that I'm in love with him has something to do with that.

Mike gave him a warm smile. "That makes me feel good. Now, how about I take you home so I can go and open the pub? I'll be seeing you later, right?"

"Of course. After I've been for a drink at George Tyrell's. I'll tell you all about it tonight after closing."

Mike unlocked the car and they got in. As they drove toward the manor house, Jonathon realized he was taking it as written that they'd be spending the night together. Then he realized he wasn't the only one.

It really *was* good to be on the same page.

CHAPTER FOURTEEN

JONATHON EXAMINED the bottles in George's drinks cabinet. "You've got a great variety here. Except... most of them haven't been opened yet." A shiny stainless steel cocktail shaker stood beside the bottles, along with four cocktail glasses. Then there was a small jar of cherries, a container of cocktail sticks, and a saucer filled with lemon and lime slices. "This is all very impressive, you know."

George laughed. "Yeah, well, I had no idea what you'd want to make, so I needed to think of everything. And as for all those bottles... I started with scotch and vodka. Then it seemed every time I went to the supermarket, I'd see another that looked interesting, so I'd buy that. I drew the line at a melon liqueur, though." He shuddered. "Melon. Who'd even come up with such a thing?"

Jonathon was enjoying the conversation. It was easy to talk to George, who seemed relaxed and friendly. "That doesn't explain why you haven't opened them."

George sighed. "I'm not a big drinker. And alcohol just sends me to sleep." He snorted. "I don't need something else to make me do that. I can manage *that* part all on my own."

Jonathon gazed at him in sympathy. "It must make work difficult."

"Bless you, lad, I don't work anymore. Had to take early retirement. That's how I ended up living here."

"How about I mix us a cocktail, and then you can tell me about it," Jonathon suggested. He'd had a few ideas of basic cocktails to show George, based on the contents of the cabinet.

George beamed. "That sounds great. There's ice in the ice bucket. I thought I'd be prepared."

Jonathon spied the small book on the coffee table. He picked it up, thrust it into George's hands, and told him to choose one. George leafed through the pages and finally pointed to a vodka martini.

Jonathon laughed. "Very James Bond."

George sat in the chair, watching as Jonathon measured, poured, and shook. "You look like you could do that for a living."

"I did once. For all of three weeks. I think photography pays better, though. The tips were atrocious." Jonathon took a sliver of lemon and pressed it onto the rim of the glass before handing it to George. "Try that. I used equal quantities of sweet and dry vermouth. There's also a dirty version that uses olives and olive juice."

George sipped the cocktail tentatively, then grinned. "This is delicious." He relaxed against the cushions, clearly content.

Jonathon took his own glass and sat on the couch. From his place on the rug in front of the fire, Max raised his head, his nose trembling.

Jonathon laughed. "Definitely not for dogs."

Max lowered his head onto his front paws and huffed.

Jonathon turned his attention to George. "You were going to tell me how you came to live in the village?"

George nodded amiably. "I used to live in Nottingham, where I worked in the town council offices. Not the most exciting job—I worked in accounts. That's bound to send anyone to sleep, right? Well, after I was diagnosed with narcolepsy, I tried to keep on working, but it soon became obvious that it just wasn't possible. You can't have an employee falling asleep at his desk at the drop of a hat."

"So they arranged for you to take early retirement?"

"Yup. They were very generous—gave me a decent payout, seeing as I'd worked for them since I was eighteen. But I didn't want to stay in the North."

"I lived in Manchester for a while," Jonathon told him. "It's a great city, with so much going on, but the light…." It was hard to explain.

"It's a bit… grayer up there, isn't it?" George smiled. "Down here there seems to be more sunshine, more blue skies. That might not be the case, but it feels like it."

"Exactly!" George had nailed it. "Carry on with your story."

"Anyway, one day I was watching one of those daytime TV programs where a couple tries to relocate to a house in the country. They get shown three properties, then have to choose. Well, one of the properties was in Merrychurch."

Jonathon had to smile. "It *is* a pretty village, isn't it? All those thatched roofs, twisting country lanes, the bridge, the river, that picturesque village green…."

George chuckled. "Like something off a box of chocolates or an old-fashioned jigsaw puzzle. I came down here on a visit to check the place out."

"And obviously liked what you saw."

"Yeah. That was five years ago. When I made inquiries about properties to buy or rent, I got put in touch with the vicar. Seems the church owns this house and the two next to it. The rent was reasonable, and I fell in love with the village. That was that." He lowered his gaze to Max and gave him a fond look. "I found Max at a local animal shelter. He loves it here too, I think. Lots of places for our three daily walks—by the river, through the forest, past the water mill…. Doggy heaven."

Max clearly knew he was the topic of discussion. He got up, walked over to George, and rested his chin on George's lap.

George stroked him softly. "Yeah, we love it here, don't we, boy? You'd have hated Nottingham. All that traffic, no rabbits to chase…."

"Do you still have family up there?"

He sighed. "My grandparents passed away a few years ago, after I moved here. My mum… well, she was in a home until last year. She died."

"I'm so sorry."

George gave a sad smile. "It's okay. These last few years, she had no idea who I was anyway."

"Are you an only child, like me?"

For a moment George's face tightened. "Yeah. There's just me now." He drank the contents of his glass in one long gulp, grimacing slightly. Then he relaxed. "I think I'd like another cocktail. Something more... exotic."

Jonathon got up and scanned the bottles on the back row. "George, you have three different kinds of rum here."

"Is that important?" George asked with a frown.

Jonathon grinned. "It is if you want to make a rum runner—well, *my* version of it at any rate. But we'd need juice too."

George's frown faded. "I've got orange, pineapple, tropical—"

"Stop right there." Jonathon pointed to the kitchen. "I'll need all of them."

George got up and went to the kitchen, chuckling. "Well, I did ask for exotic."

As Jonathon selected the bottles he needed, he thought about George's story. There was something about him that invited trust, and yet.... *What's puzzling me?* He strove to recollect George's exact words. *There's just me now.* It seemed an odd response. Then Jonathon realized that he still didn't know if George had anything to do with Mrs. Teedle. *That* was *the purpose of this visit, right?*

Jonathon had been sidetracked by cocktails and pleasant conversation.

George returned, carrying three juice cartons. "That's all of them." He placed them on the drop-down flap of the drinks cabinet, then sat down. "So, are you settling into life in the village?"

Jonathon emptied the contents of the cocktail shaker into a pint glass, then added more ice. "Slowly but surely. Seems like every day I'm meeting someone new. And I thought this was a small village."

George laughed. "You're telling *me*. Five years I've been here, and I still don't know everyone."

"Did you know the old lady who died?" It was the perfect moment to ask.

George studied Jonathon's hand movements as he measured juice into the shaker. "No. Well, I'd heard *of* her, of course. Some people get talked about, and there were certainly lots of tales going around about her."

"I only met her for the first time at the bonfire party." Jonathon moved on to measuring the rum. "It's funny you mentioned me talking to the mayor. It was just *after* that when she introduced herself." He snuck a glance at George, but George wasn't meeting his gaze. "And you talked about walks in the forest too. The path goes right by her cottage, did you know? Not that you could miss that table full of jams."

George gave a half smile. "You're right. Her cottage always struck me as a spooky old place. Not that I ever saw the inside, you understand. But the jams? That's another matter. I always bought a jar if I'd run out. She made really good jam."

"I bought two jars myself." Jonathon regarded him closely. "Were there many jars left when you went past on Sunday morning?"

George stilled, his bright blue eyes wide. "How did you know I went past there?"

"You mentioned taking three walks a day, and the forest being one of your favorite routes." Jonathon frowned. "But you're right. What made me assume you'd been there that particular morning?" He rubbed his chin, then nodded triumphantly. "My gardener mentioned seeing a German shepherd who's a regular. I figured he had to mean you."

George's breathing grew a little labored. "Oh, I see. Now that you mention it… yes, I did go by there. In fact, I bought a jar of jam from the table."

"Oh? Which flavor? I was sad to have missed the cherry variety. I love cherries."

George frowned. "I don't think it was cherry." He got up and went into the kitchen. "Tell you what. If it *is* cherry, you can have it."

"Aw, you don't have to do that," Jonathon protested. What made his heart beat a little faster was George's change in mood. *Someone else who gets nervous talking about that morning.* He realized it could all be entirely innocent, the reactions of people who didn't want to be considered suspects. That would make anyone nervous.

George returned to the small living room, clutching a jar. "Sorry. It's ginger." He held up the jar with its white label, on which had been scribbled Ginger Jam, Nov 2017.

Jonathon arched his eyebrows. "Oh wow. That's different. You'll have to let me know what you think of it." He went back to his task, placing the cap on firmly before vigorously agitating the shaker. "I hope you like this."

"I'm sure I shall. But I think this will have to be the last one. I'm starting to feel tired." George went back into the kitchen with the jar. By the time he was in his chair again, Jonathon had strained the brightly colored concoction into a clean glass, then added a cherry on a stick.

He handed George the glass. "Then this will make a great nightcap." He picked up his own. "Cheers."

George echoed the toast before sipping the cocktail. He let out a groan. "Oh my. This tastes amazing."

Jonathon chuckled. "Folks, we have a winner." He took a drink from his own, the sweetness of the cocktail making him wince. "Wow."

From next to George's chair, Max licked his chops.

Jonathon laughed. "And *you* can forget it, and all. I am *not* pouring some of this into a bowl for you." When Max let out a soft whine, Jonathon gave him a stern look. "Dogs do *not* drink cocktails, no matter how hard they beg."

Max dropped his head back down, looking for all the world like he was pouting.

"Thanks for coming round here this evening." George raised his glass. "To an excellent cocktail master. Long may you shake and pour."

Jonathon raised his own. The earlier relaxed atmosphere appeared to have been restored, but Jonathon wasn't about to forget those moments when George had appeared genuinely nervous. When he'd not volunteered the information that he'd been past Naomi's house. When he couldn't look Jonathon in the eye.

Of course, it could *be me. I might make all these people nervous.*

Then Jonathon dismissed that idea. Compared with his father, Jonathon was as intimidating as a soft cushion.

CHAPTER FIFTEEN

Saturday, November 11

"HE'S HERE." Jonathon glanced across at Mike, who wore black jeans, black boots, and an open white-collared shirt visible above the neckline of his navy sweater. "Nice look, by the way. Casual."

"Too casual?" Mike touched his collar. "I *had* thought about—"

"Relax. It's only my father, not royalty."

Mike snickered. "Funny. The way he acted when he first met me, I'd have sworn they were the same thing."

Jonathon glared at him. "Do *not* make me laugh. And don't go out of your way to rile him. He doesn't need any help in that department. He could win medals for England." He took another look through the window at the driveway beyond, where his father was locking the Bentley, and sighed. "Come on. Let's get this over with."

As he opened the door that led to the main entrance hall, Mike caught hold of his hand and squeezed it. "Say the word and I won't let go," he whispered.

Jonathon laughed softly. "Nice idea, but do you recall what I said less than a minute ago? That would class as riling him. Big-time."

Mike raised Jonathon's hand to his lips and kissed it, just as the heavy front door opened. He relinquished his hold, and Jonathon strode over to where his father stood, removing his dark brown trilby before pulling off his driving gloves and depositing them in the up-turned hat. He looked up and gave a brief smile that faded when Mike stepped into view.

"Good morning, Father." Jonathon did as was expected, extending his hand. His father shook it, then gave a single nod in Mike's direction.

"Mr. Tattersall. I didn't expect to see you. I felt sure you would be running your *pub* today."

Jonathon marveled at how much disdain his father could squeeze into a word of one syllable. He flashed Mike a glance, but Mike smiled politely.

"I felt it would be rude to miss your visit, Mr. de Mountford, so I made alternative arrangements. Besides, we didn't get much of a chance to talk during your last visit, and I wanted to rectify that."

"Indeed," Father murmured. He focused his attention on Jonathon. "Some coffee would be most welcome. I didn't stop on the journey here."

Janet appeared in the doorway. "Good morning, sir. Let me take your coat and hat."

His father blinked. "I see some changes have been made around here. And for the better." He unbuttoned his long black coat.

"This is Janet, my housekeeper." Jonathon could have placed bets on his father's reaction to him having taken on staff. "Janet, could you bring us some coffee to the drawing room?"

"Certainly, sir." She took Father's coat and hat, then waited for them to leave the hall.

"How long have you had a housekeeper?" Father inquired as they passed through the long hallway that led to the drawing room.

"About a month. There's Ivy too. She's the cook. And Ben works in the gardens." Jonathon glanced over his shoulder at him. "And that is as much staff as I can cope with. Although Mike feels I need an estate manager too."

Father's eyes widened slightly. "Then we are in agreement. Such an appointment would mean you could dedicate more time to other... pursuits."

Jonathon had a sneaking suspicion his father was *not* referring to photography. He was also pretty certain his father had never expected to agree with *anything* Mike had to say.

They reached the sitting room, and Jonathon stood aside to let his father enter, with Mike following.

Father glanced around the cozy, comfortable room, his expression impassive. "Is this where you entertain your guests?"

"I don't have all that many visitors," Jonathon explained before he realized his father's question had implied disapproval and his reply was almost an apology. Jonathon breathed deeply and sat on the couch next to Mike, facing his father. Having spent most of his life feeling as though he was a disappointment, he was determined not to allow that state of affairs to continue. "This room is perfect for my—*our*—needs."

"I see."

Exactly *what* his father saw remained a mystery, since Janet entered at that moment, carrying the coffee tray, which she placed on the table, then withdrew. Jonathon wasted no time pouring the coffee and handing cups around.

Father sipped the aromatic brew. "I only realized yesterday that one of my acquaintances is your neighbor."

Jonathon frowned. "Really? Who?" He didn't think he knew anyone in Merrychurch who would move in his father's circles.

"A chap I met at a dinner in London a few months ago. A politician. One never knows when it will prove useful to have such an acquaintance, of course. By all accounts, this chap will go far. The meteoric way he's risen through the ranks in the party attests to that."

Jonathon didn't have to ask which party. Furthermore, his father could only be referring to Joshua Brent.

"Would that be our MP?" Jonathon asked after swallowing a mouthful of coffee. "I'm afraid we haven't met yet, although that *was* something I was hoping to rectify—very shortly, as a matter of fact." Not that his father needed to know *why*. Jonathon caught the catch in Mike's breathing, the way his shoulders shook, and did his best to avoid meeting his gaze.

"That's the fella. Brent. And in my opinion, that's a very good idea. It pays to have friends in high places, and an MP who could one day be prime minister would be an extremely valuable friend." Father cleared his throat. "I don't believe in wasting time, beating about the bush, and as I came here for a specific purpose, I think it best to... get it out into the open, so to speak."

Jonathon seemed to have developed a severe case of snakes in his belly, because *something* was unfolding and writhing in there, leaving him uneasy. He remained silent.

His father took another drink from his cup. "I'd like to begin by sharing a piece of family history of which I am certain you are unaware. In the early 1800s, the manor house's incumbent at that time was William de Mountford. There were fears that the line would die with him, as he was the sole male and his wife, Ann, seemed unable to bear a child. This situation continued for several years. Then suddenly Ann produced a son, John, and followed him with yet more children, much to the family's relief."

Jonathon met Mike's gaze. Mike's knitted brows, occasional blink, and grimace spoke of his confusion. Jonathon gave a shrug, equally lost.

"Doubtless, you cannot see how this could possibly relate to you."

Jonathon bit his lip. "You took the words right out of my mouth."

That earned him a slight scowl. "Then I will continue. Years later, several diaries were discovered, which cast new light on this situation. It seems William's father had an illegitimate son, also named John, who had 'stepped in' to provide what his half brother could not. There was no chance that this John would ever inherit. And in fact, there *is* evidence that Ann and John had been involved in a relationship long before her marriage, and that this relationship continued for a great many years after." Father pursed his lips. "Imagine the scandal if that had all come out at the time."

"William knew about the affair?" It sounded like the plot of a racy historical romance.

"Strange as this might seem, he appears to have been perfectly content with the situation. The family line remained unbroken, and his half brother took over what must have been an onerous task." Father wrinkled his nose. "You, more than any other de Mountford, are in the position of truly understanding just *how* onerous." He fell silent, his gaze focused intently on Jonathon.

Jonathon stared back at him, nonplussed.

Beside him, Mike let out a snort. "Don't tell me you haven't guessed. Seems like you're not the only gay in the de Mountford closet. Well, apart from Dominic."

Father coughed. "Yes. Quite."

Jonathon sagged against the cushions. "Okay, so he was gay, and his brother from another mother did the deed for him so there'd be lots more little de Mountfords. I still don't see what this has to do with—"

"You have *got* to be kidding." Mike sat upright, gaping at Jonathon's father. "You can't possibly think Jonathon would agree to that—and if you do, it only goes to prove how little you know of your son."

Jonathon frowned. "Did I go out at some point and miss several pages of dialogue? Because I'm lost."

Father gave Mike a wry smile. "I seem to have misjudged you, Mike—if I may call you Mike. You possess a remarkably quick mind. Please, tell me what you *think* you understand the present situation to be."

Mike took a long, steadying breath before twisting in his seat to face Jonathon. "What we have here isn't *exactly* like what happened back then, but… I think your father has finally realized that this is *not* a phase, you *are* gay, and *I'm* not going away." Jonathon opened his mouth to speak, but Mike held up his hand. "Let me finish. Because this is where it gets fantastical. Right now, the family is in the same situation. End of the line, and all that. I think he's proposing that you marry—a *woman*, mind you—and then close your eyes and think of England. More than once, if you can manage it. While in the background would be me. I'd be there to keep you happy. So to the eyes of the world, there'd be Jonathon de Mountford, plus wifey and whatever children you can produce, and I'd be your secret."

Jonathon could only stare in stunned silence as he went over Mike's words. Finally he gaped at his father. "Well? How far off the mark is he?"

Father sighed. "Yes. I have definitely misjudged you, Mike." He met Jonathon's wide-eyed stare. "What can I say? To use the vernacular of your generation, he nailed it."

Jonathon drained his cup and leaned forward. "Then here's another scenario for you. I marry Mike, we find a surrogate, and bingo—more de Mountfords. Family line goes on."

His father frowned. "You don't understand. You can't just marry *anyone*. It's like a… a king marrying a commoner. You need to find a… partner, to use the more modern term, who is at least your equal socially. Someone with good breeding who'll produce strong, healthy, intelligent children. *You* would not be blessed with the intelligence and talents you have, were it not for good breeding."

"I don't think I'm going to ask a prospective surrogate to undergo a MENSA test, and then look her up in *Who's Who* to see if she has an entry." This was worse than Jonathon had expected.

"You already have someone in mind, don't you? Someone for him to marry?" Mike's eyes gleamed. "Well, don't stop now. You've got this far."

Father arched his eyebrows, then addressed Jonathon. "It's not as if I'm proposing you should marry a complete stranger. You've known Ruth Ainsworth since you were a child. She's about your age, a little younger perhaps, but the biological clock is ticking."

Jonathon stilled. "Ruth? Are you telling me Ruth is okay with this idea?"

"Never mind that," Mike interjected. "It's 2017, and he's trying to arrange your marriage like we're still in the Dark Ages." He lurched to his feet, his hands clenched at his sides. "Does Jonathon even get a say in this? Or is it a fait accompli?"

For a moment Father stared at Mike in silence. Then his shoulders sagged. "Of course he gets—" He turned his attention to Jonathon. "*You* get a say in this. You're an adult. It's your life. I'm simply trying to preserve what has existed for so many years. And you're right. I had entirely dismissed surrogacy as an alternative, which is stupid of me, considering how often one sees it in the news."

Jonathon gave him a rueful smile. "Just checking you weren't about to establish some draconian measures to make sure you got your way."

Mike's eyes were almost bulging. "You... you can smile? After everything he's said?"

Jonathon could understand Mike's anger and frustration. He'd also been on the point of exploding—until his father pricked the bubble that was his rage without even knowing he'd done it. "He's merely made a proposal. I can consider it, can't I? If my father can admit surrogacy is an alternative, then I can look at his proposal with a clear head." What he really needed at that moment was to breathe some fresh air—and to prevent Mike from going ballistic.

He got up from the couch and pulled on the faded green velvet rope beside the fireplace. A couple of minutes later, Janet appeared.

"Janet, would you please show my father to his room? I'm sure he'd like to freshen up before lunch."

"Certainly, sir. Ivy says she'll serve at twelve thirty, as arranged."

His father rose to his feet. "That's an excellent idea. And you two need some time to… digest my suggestions." He followed Janet from the room.

Mike watched him go, his gaze narrowed. "Yeah," he said as the door closed quietly behind them. "Because let's face it, those suggestions are gonna take some chewing to make sure they don't stick in my throat."

Jonathon inclined his head toward the door. "Let's go for a walk."

He needed to clear his head, and Mike needed to cool down. The brisk November wind would accomplish both.

CHAPTER SIXTEEN

"I DON'T know which I dislike more," Mike said as they exited the house via the dining room's french doors and walked toward the Italian garden. "The fact that your father came up with that... harebrained notion, or the fact that for a short while back there, he was starting to like me." He gave an exaggerated shudder. "And you wanna know what I found most interesting about that little historic tale he told? The stuff he *didn't* say."

"Such as what?"

Thank God. Jonathon hadn't said a word since they'd left the drawing room, and Mike was starting to panic. He'd expected a rant or at least *some* kind of backlash the whole while Thomas had been talking. Okay, so it wouldn't be in Jonathon's nature to smart-mouth his dad, but was it wrong for him to hope that Jonathon would have told Thomas in no uncertain terms to fuck off?

And how many times have you heard that *word pass his lips?*

Mike had to face reality. Jonathon was definitely a lover, not a fighter.

"Mike?"

With a start Mike realized he'd dropped off into his own little world. "Huh?"

"What stuff didn't my father say?"

"Well, he talked about the family being happy and relieved that Ann was finally producing kids. He said William was happy he didn't have to… you know… do the deed, as you put it, with his wife. What about John?"

"What about him?"

"Well, how did *he* feel in all this? Ann obviously loved him—they had a good relationship. But there he was, kept hidden. A dirty secret. It was down to him that the line continued, but no one knows that. And then there's William. Was *he* allowed to have someone in his life? Ann got *her* man, that's for sure. She got *her* itch scratched. But what about William? Because I'm damn sure no one would have turned a blind eye to *William* having a fella on the side."

Jonathon sighed. "We don't know. I hope he had someone. Perhaps he did. Look at Dominic. If you didn't know any better, you'd have thought he lived all those years alone. But now we know. He loved Trevor. They had ten years together. It doesn't matter that Trevor was a secret all that time."

"Hmm, I don't know about that," Mike murmured. "You have no idea. Maybe it really tore up Dominic and Trevor to have to keep their love a secret."

"The point is, Trevor isn't a secret now. Maybe one day we'll dig up something that proves William de

Mountford had a male lover, or even a string of lovers. By that time, you know what the reaction will be to that news?" Jonathon smiled. "People will just nod, like it's nothing." He stopped at the top of the stone staircase, decorated with urns standing on posts, that led to the ornamental pond. At the far end, statues of two Grecian men faced each other, arms outstretched, poised to spring, as though about to fight. Jonathon pointed to them. "Is it wrong that when I was in my teens, I believed that when no one was looking, they reached each other and made love on the path?"

Mike snickered. "Actually? Yeah, I can believe that about you." He gazed out at the structured garden, with its long, thin reflecting pools, the ornate fountain that was dry, and the neatly sculpted lawns. "I had no idea this existed."

"There are several different gardens to the rear of the house," Jonathon told him. "Apparently one of the past owners wanted it to be like a series of rooms, separated by walls and hedges, so you never knew what you were going to find around the corner." He pointed to the high hedge beyond the fountain. "For instance, anyone going behind there might have a surprise, especially if it's summertime."

"Why? What's behind there?"

Another smile, only this one was accompanied by a glint in his eyes. "My naturist garden. It's a regular little sun-trap. I found it at the end of the summer."

"And you're only telling me now?"

Jonathon laughed. "I'd known you how long? Besides, you're still in your probationary period."

Mike came to a halt. "Oh really?" Then he caught that glint again. It was no good. They had to discuss the elephant in the room. *Or should that be, the garden?*

"Tell me about Ruth Ainsworth."

Jonathon raised his eyebrows. "It seems I'm not the only one with a retentive memory."

"Ex-copper. It went with the job. Now quit stalling and tell me who she is—and more importantly, why you're not freaking out about her."

Jonathon sat on a nearby low wall, tugging his jacket around him. "My father is correct. I've known Ruth most of my life. When you have as many social gatherings as our family, you get to see the same faces again and again, especially those who are of a similar age. I can remember Christmas parties when I was maybe nine or ten, and Ruth was this little thing with a ponytail tied up in a bright blue ribbon. Her favorite color, I think. Her parents knew mine from way back—university, maybe—and they stayed friends. Same social networks, same clubs… you get the picture."

"Another old family?" Mike guessed, joining him on the wall.

"Pretty much. What surprises me is my father saying she'd be up for all this. I recall an engagement a while back, but it got broken off. One or both of them changed their minds, apparently. Now, maybe I got the wrong end of the stick, but the Ruth I knew wasn't into the idea of marriage much."

"When did you last see her?"

"We lost touch when I moved to Manchester and spent less time around my family. But that wasn't all that long ago. A year, at most."

"Jonathon, if I ask you a blunt, personal question, would you answer it?" Mike couldn't let this drop.

"It depends *how* personal, Mr. Probationary Boyfriend." Jonathon's eyes twinkled.

Mike took hold of his courage. "It's just… part of me wonders why you don't stand up to him and tell him to—"

Jonathon flashed that wry smile. "Tell him to go do something involving sex and travel?"

Mike snorted. "Another way of putting it, but yeah."

Jonathon leaned forward, his elbows on his knees, his hands clasped between them. "I'm trying to keep the peace. And believe it or not, I'm trying *not* to rub his nose in my sexual orientation, so to speak. It's my hope that he'll come around, one day. When I get married, I want him there, wishing me all the best for the future. That's not going to happen if I alienate him. And besides, you heard him. I don't think he'd *force* me to marry Ruth, or whoever. But he's not at the stage yet where he can truly accept that I'm gay, for all the things he says. So until then, I have to bide my time… *and* buy a little time too."

"What does that mean?"

Jonathon shivered. "It means it's time to get the hell inside, because my arse is just about frozen to this wall." He got up and held out a hand to Mike. "And as for the rest, you'll have to trust me."

Mike grasped his hand firmly, allowing himself to be hoisted to his feet. "Never mind frozen. My arse is numb." He walked at Jonathon's side as they made their way back to the house, his mind going over that last statement.

You'll have to trust me.

Mike pushed down that niggle of unease. *Why, Jonathon? What are you going to do?*

"I did have one wicked thought," Jonathon said as they walked briskly.

"What was that?"

"I'd love the murderer to be Joshua Brent, just to see the look on my father's face."

The laughter that rumbled out of him echoed against the walls of the house. "You've got an evil mind."

"Don't tell me you weren't thinking the same thing," Jonathon retorted.

Yeah. No comment.

BY THE time dinner arrived, Mike was climbing the walls. He'd been on his best behavior, the sarcasm had been nonexistent, and he'd even tried to engage Thomas in conversation. It had been about as successful as trying to braid fog. And he couldn't wait for Thomas to leave. Unfortunately, there was still breakfast—and possibly lunch—to endure.

Thomas wiped his lips with his napkin before placing it beside his dessert plate. "That was delicious. You've found yourself a good cook."

Jonathon smiled. "I'll be sure to pass on the compliment. Do you still smoke a cigar after dinner, or has your doctor finally convinced you to quit?"

Thomas coughed harshly. "No, I don't, and that is down to your mother. And before you ask, no, I will *not* tell you how she got me to quit. Now, what's this I hear about another murder in the village?"

"News travels fast," Mike murmured.

Thomas glanced at him. "Not really. I had drinks with Brent in London this past week. He told me all about it."

Jonathon widened his eyes. "Drinks? At your club, perchance? You really are keeping in with him, aren't you?"

"You never know when you'll need friends in high places. At least this murder is nothing to do with us."

Jonathon's gaze met his, and Mike couldn't miss that evil glint. *No. Don't do it. We're almost there. Don't get Thomas all worked up.*

"Well, strictly speaking, she was *my* tenant."

Thomas stilled. "You are *not* to get involved, do you hear me? I will *not* have the lord of the manor running around chasing clues like some little old lady amateur detective."

Jonathon bit his lip. "I always did like Miss Marple."

Mike did his best not to snort.

"Leave it to the professionals, Jonathon." Thomas stared at Mike. "And *you* should be convincing him to stay out of this."

Mike let out a loud chuckle. "I might not have known your son for long, but even *I* know how futile it is to tell Jonathon not to do something. Red rag to a bull."

To his surprise Thomas echoed his chuckle. "Yes. You're quite right—I should have known better. How does the saying go? 'A man convinced against his will is of the same opinion still.' You cannot convince Jonathon to change his mind once he's decided upon a course of action. And as that is a family trait which I recognize, in this case the fault lies solely in his genes."

Jonathon cleared his throat. "Then maybe I need to break away from past patterns of behavior."

Both Mike and Thomas gazed at him in confusion.

"Meaning what, precisely?"

Mike had been about to ask the same thing.

Jonathon lifted his chin and locked gazes with his father. "I'll meet with Ruth."

Silence.

Mike blinked, but his tongue refused to work.

"To what end?" Thomas asked quietly.

Jonathon narrowed his gaze. "That would count as pushing your luck tonight, Father. We both know you want this, so be content with knowing I *will* meet with her. Not that I am promising anything, do you understand?"

Thomas nodded, appearing as if he were in a dream.

Mike was in a dream, all right.

It was beginning to feel like a nightmare.

WHEN THOMAS declared himself tired and bade them good night, Mike was still no clearer about what the hell had happened—or how he wanted to deal with its implications. He kept his mouth shut, but when they reached Jonathon's bedroom, he couldn't remain silent a second longer.

"Look, I might go home tonight." Mike's pulse was rapid, his hands clammy.

Jonathon came to a dead stop, his eyes full of confusion. "What?"

Mike scrubbed his hand through his hair. "You… you dropped a pretty huge bombshell tonight, and I'm not sure how I feel about that."

Jonathon sighed. "Come in here for a second." He pushed open the door, led Mike to the bed, and waited until he'd sat on the foot of it. Jonathon switched on the bedside lamp, then came to stand in front of him. "First of all, I know how all that must have sounded."

Mike snorted. "It sounded like you were agreeing to meet the woman you're gonna marry."

Jonathon blinked. "I did no such thing. Your brain heard one thing and made a connection. Understandable. But all *I* did was agree to meet her."

Mike did his best to recall Jonathon's exact words. "You're right. I jumped to a conclusion. But why meet her at all? Unless you really *are* considering marrying her. That part about breaking away from past patterns of behavior…. My brain didn't conjure up *that* part, did it? And what was that, if not another way of saying…." Mike didn't know what to think anymore.

Jonathon knelt at his feet. "Which brings me to my second point. Do you trust me?"

Mike's throat seized. "I thought I did," he croaked.

Jonathon's gaze locked on his. "Then you need to go on trusting me." He took Mike's hands in his. "I have a plan. I'd love to tell you about it, but I have to… discuss it with Ruth first. There are a couple of things I'm not sure of, and I don't want to talk about this, only to find I've got it completely wrong." He brought Mike's hand to his lips and kissed it. "All *you* need to know is that *nothing* is going to change between us. I wouldn't let anything or anyone—and that includes my father—come between us."

Mike stared at Jonathon's earnest expression. "This plan of yours… is your father going to like it?"

Jonathon's lips twitched. "Oh, I sincerely doubt it."

Mike gave a single nod. "Then I'll wait until you're ready to share." He smiled. "I'll trust you."

Jonathon beamed. "*That's* what matters to me right now—that the man I love trusts me." Beautiful brown eyes focused on him.

Oh, holy hell.

Mike searched for the right response, the right words that could even begin to communicate how deeply Jonathon had just touched him.

There was only one way to go.

"I love you too." His heart pounded, flooding him with an exhilaration that left him dizzy.

Jonathon's face lit up. "Good to know. Now… do you still want to go back to the pub tonight?" Lamplight sparkled in his eyes.

Mike unbuttoned Jonathon's collar in a leisurely manner and worked his way lower.

Jonathon grinned. "And there's my answer."

CHAPTER SEVENTEEN

THE WINDOWS to the dining room were closed, but that didn't stop the sound of the church bells from filtering through. Jonathon smiled as he helped himself to their traditional Sunday cooked breakfast. Ivy had sourced some local sausages, and they were plump and succulent-looking. The bacon came from Paul Drake's farm, and seeing the thick pink rashers always gave Jonathon a crisis of conscience.

"Stop it," Mike muttered beside him, lifting a couple of rashers onto his plate. "We've talked about this."

"But… this might have been Maisie." Jonathon had gotten into the habit of walking to Paul's farm, where he chatted with the pig farmer while they leaned over the sty and laughed at the antics of the piglets. Maisie had been a sweet-tempered sow who loved it when Paul scratched her back with a stick.

Mike sighed. "And if you thought that way about all your food, you'd never eat. If you want to become a vegan, now's the time to tell me. You know, so I can get out before I get in too deep." He bit his lip. "Oops. We're already past that. I guess I'm stuck with you, vegan or carnivore."

"Before you get in too deep? Is that a euphemism for being in love with me?" Warmth filled him.

Mike gazed at him over his glasses. "You just wanna hear me say it again, don't you?"

"Yes," Jonathon replied promptly. "I also want another kiss before my father walks in here. I don't think he'd approve of public displays of affection."

Mike put down his plate, cupped Jonathon's cheek in his large, gentle hand, and kissed him unhurriedly on the lips. Jonathon closed his eyes and lost himself in the tender kiss. Mike broke away but brought his forehead to Jonathon's.

"I love you." His words were soft.

The sound of the door opening had them separating, and Mike resumed his task of filling his plate. Jonathon turned to greet his father. "Good morning. If you'd like cereal or porridge, please ring for Janet. Otherwise, there's a cooked breakfast here."

Father strode across the dining room, smiling at the old-fashioned sideboard covered with trays. "This reminds me of breakfasts here when your grandfather was alive. It set you up for the day."

"Which is probably where I got the idea from." Jonathon pointed to the scrambled eggs, bacon, and sausages. "These are local. The black puddings are sent from Bury. I got a taste for them when I lived in Manchester. And Ivy makes the bread herself from flour produced at the water mill."

Father nodded in approval. "Excellent. Well, I shall have a good breakfast, and then I shall head back to London, seeing as I accomplished what I set out to do."

Jonathon wasn't going to let him get away with *that*.

"You're fond of sayings, aren't you, Father? Ever heard the one about putting the cart before the horse? All I said last night is that I would meet with Ruth. Please, do *not* read more into that statement. And don't go making plans that include me."

Father gazed at him in silence for a moment before glancing at Mike with a sigh. "Do you have more luck persuading him to follow certain courses of action?"

Mike smiled politely. "That depends on what means I use to persuade him."

Jonathon was *so* thankful not to be drinking his coffee at that moment. A flush rose up his father's neck, staining his cheeks.

"Yes, well, breakfast."

Jonathon had to admit, Mike had found the perfect way to ensure a quiet meal.

AS SOON as his father's Bentley was out of sight, Jonathon heaved a sigh of relief. "Hopefully we won't see him for a while." He turned to Mike. "Now, can we get back to the important stuff?"

Mike laughed. "And would that be solving a murder by any chance?" He tut-tutted. "If your dad knew…."

"Well, he's not going to know." Jonathon was still amazed that he'd found out in the first place. "Especially as the only person left to see from Ben's list is his new pal, Joshua Brent. I still haven't worked out how I'm going to do that."

"Then isn't it a good thing I have?" Mike gave a smug smile. "What would you do without me?"

"Have more sausages and toast for breakfast, for one thing." Jonathon took no notice of Mike's mouth falling open. "Now quit looking so self-satisfied and tell me how we get to see him."

Mike pulled out his phone. "According to his website and Facebook page—and yes, he has them—every second Monday in the month, Brent meets with his constituents in Merrychurch village hall. He's there for a couple of hours before lunch, and anyone can come along and ask him questions, voice concerns, whatever." Mike grinned. "And tomorrow happens to be the second Monday in November."

Jonathon sighed happily. "Guess where *we'll* be tomorrow morning? I'm still not sure how I'm going to bring up the whole topic of 'Hey, that *was* you walking your dog past a cottage where someone was murdered last week, wasn't it?' That might require some forward thinking."

"Or some on-the-spot inspiration," Mike added. "And that still leaves us with the rest of today. Any ideas about what you'd like to do?"

Jonathon couldn't hold back his grin. "I might have a couple."

Mike gave him a hard stare. "Ones that *don't* involve going back to bed?" He rolled his eyes when Jonathon huffed. "Honestly, you really do have a one-track mind. I was thinking more along the lines of trying to crack Naomi's codes." He shivered. "In front of the fire, with hot chocolate."

"*Now* you're talking." Jonathon headed toward the main door, more aware of the cold morning wind.

"Lying on the rug on piles of cushions, in front of a roaring fire, applying our minds to the task…."

Mike sighed as they stepped inside the house. "I notice you said *task*. A nice, nonspecific word. Don't think I don't know what you're contemplating."

Busted.

Monday, November 13

MIKE HAD only been inside the village hall once, the first Christmas he'd spent in Merrychurch. It was a quaint stone building with a thatched roof, and at one end, a stage had been set up, complete with deep red velvet curtains. At the other end was a tiny kitchen, and in between was a wooden floor, heavily varnished. Windows lined both sides, lace curtains frothed against the leaded glass, and a small vase with tiny flowers sat on each deep sill, an indication of the thickness of the walls.

"They have a carol concert here every year," he told Jonathon as they stepped into the warm interior. Wall heaters glowed orange above the windows. There were only a handful of people in the hall. A few ladies were arranging flowers on the stage, and Mike spotted Melinda Talbot, deep in conversation with one of the women.

Along one wall was a wide table, and behind it sat a very handsome man, dressed in a dark gray suit, reading a newspaper. The two lines of chairs in front of him were empty, as were the two chairs facing him.

"Perfect timing," Mike whispered. "It looks like he hasn't got any villagers beating down the door to ask him questions."

Just then, Joshua Brent glanced up and saw them. He smiled widely. "Good morning." He closed his newspaper and put it to one side.

Jonathon hadn't budged from Mike's side, so Mike nudged him. "Come on. Let's go and talk to him."

"Hmm. Oh. Sure." Jonathon went over to the two empty chairs and sat down. Mike joined him, waiting for Jonathon to introduce himself.

Nothing.

Mike peered at Jonathon, who was staring intently at Mr. Brent. Mike nudged Jonathon again, this time with his thigh.

"Can I help you, gentlemen?" Mr. Brent appeared amused by Jonathon's intense observation.

If you want something doing....

Mike stretched out his hand. "Good morning. We haven't met before, but I'm Mike Tattersall. I own the Hare and Hounds. And this is Jonathon de Mountford."

Mr. Brent shook his hand. "Delighted to meet you." He winced as Mike let go.

"I didn't think my grip was that strong." Then Mike winced too when Mr. Brent turned over his hand, revealing cracked skin that appeared very sore. "Ouch."

Mr. Brent sighed. "The weather's turned colder. It always sets off my eczema." He regarded his hand sadly. "I've spent my life avoiding irritants and wearing gloves, but when you're meeting the general public, that doesn't go down too well." He smiled. "Shades of Howard Hughes." He clasped his hands in front of him. "I've been intending to meet you for some time. I wanted to talk about the pub's opening hours. I've had several people—" He broke off and stared at Jonathon. "De Mountford?" His smile widened. "I know your father. In fact, I was only having drinks with him last week." He extended a hand to Jonathon. "I'm pleased to meet you at last."

Jonathon said nothing but shook his hand, blinking.

Mike had never seen Jonathon so tongue-tied.

"Thomas was talking about you this weekend, when he came to visit." Mike took a closer look at Mr. Brent. He had to be in his forties, with thick brown hair, green eyes, and what his sister Sue described as a Gillette jaw, clean and well defined. His first impression of a handsome man quickly gave way to the admission that Mr. Brent was drop-dead gorgeous. Not *his* type, of course—Brent's shoulders were way too wide, his chest too broad, and there was this sneaking suspicion that the man spent a lot of time taking care of that body—but he could see how Brent might break hearts.

Then it hit him. Apparently Brent was Jonathon's type, judging by his starstruck, glazed look.

Mike wasn't sure if he was amused or jealous.

"Was he? I'm sorry I missed him."

Jonathon cleared his throat. "He spoke very highly of you. In fact, he was the one to bring you up in conversation."

Mike heaved a silent sigh of relief. *Finally*.

"Really? I'm flattered." Brent's smile revealed gleaming white, perfect teeth.

"Yes. He said you told him about our recent murder." Jonathon sighed. "Terrible business, of course."

"Yes, terrible." Brent's facial expression grew more solemn. "An elderly lady, I believe."

"But… you knew her, didn't you?" Jonathon frowned. "I'm sure that's what I heard."

Brent arched his eyebrows. "I can't think where you heard that. I'd never spoken with her."

"Ah, that's it." Jonathon's eyes gleamed triumphantly. "*I* know what it is. I got my wires crossed. You were one of the last people seen in the vicinity of her cottage the day she died. That was it. You were walking your dog." He spoke with conviction, although Mike wasn't convinced Ben had mentioned a dog in connection with Brent.

"Was I? When was that?" Brent stroked his jaw.

"Last Sunday. The day after the bonfire party." Jonathon gazed at him steadily.

"Ah, yes. I was sorry to miss that. Apparently it was very successful. Now, let me see. I do recall walking my dog that morning. I often do when I'm down here for the weekend. Where did she live?"

"Close to the edge of the forest. The lane through it runs right past her house," Mike volunteered.

"The forest… that rings a bell." Brent straightened in his chair. "Ah. The cottage with the jam table. *Now* I remember. I thought it was such a charming thing to do. I even bought a jar myself."

"It seems a lot of people were very fond of her jam," Mike admitted. "I like the—"

"Which flavor did you buy?" Jonathon interjected. "I'm trying to find someone who tried the cherry. It's a favorite of mine. Not that I could buy a jar now."

Brent tapped his finger against his lips. "Hmm. I think it was raspberry jam. Although the mango-and-peach was very tempting."

"And you didn't see Mrs. Teedle?"

Brent appeared to consider the question. "I didn't see anyone, come to think of it. I dropped my money into her box and continued on my way." He tilted his head to one side. "Why did you come here this morning? Surely not to ask me about walking my dog."

Jonathon chuckled. "Of course not. I felt it only proper to meet you, after my father had spoken about you. He seemed surprised that we hadn't met yet." He gave a shrug. "I felt it was time to rectify that."

Mike was impressed. Jonathon's laid-back response came out as natural and genuine.

"I'm delighted that you did. I shall definitely mention this visit the next time I see him."

The scrape of a chair behind them told Mike their time was at an end. He rose to his feet, holding out his hand once more. "I'd be happy to see you in the pub, although I do understand if you feel you couldn't do that. I'm sure a person in the public eye as much as you are must have people wanting to talk to you all the time. I don't imagine you get much peace."

Brent smiled. "You hit the nail on the head. But I will stop by one of these days so we can talk about the licensing hours." He shook Mike's hand once more before doing the same with Jonathon. "And at least now I can say I've met the lord of the manor."

Jonathon laughed. "Compared to you, I'm no one. You're the one who's always on TV."

Brent groaned. "Don't remind me. The press…. You have *no* idea what they can be like." He glanced between them. "And now I must speak with these good people."

Mike and Jonathon thanked him, then vacated the chairs. From the stage, Melinda beckoned them, and Mike headed toward her. She greeted them with a hug.

"So pleased to see you. I was *only* thinking about you this morning. I told Lloyd it was high time we had you both for afternoon tea."

"But we'd taste awful on sandwiches," Mike joked.

Melinda rolled her eyes. "Really. Just for that, I'll expect to see you both at four. No buts."

"Yes, Melinda," Jonathon said with a sigh of resignation.

They left her to her flower arranging and headed for the door. When they reached it, Jonathon paused.

"Something wrong?" Mike asked.

"Damn it. There was one question I should have asked." Before Mike could inquire what that was, Jonathon turned and looked back into the hall. The elderly couple who'd arrived after them had concluded their conversation with Mr. Brent and were getting up to leave.

"Mr. Brent?" Jonathon's voice rang out clearly.

The MP gave him a polite smile. "Mr. de Mountford."

"I forgot to ask—what kind of dog do you have?"

Mr. Brent blinked. "A Yorkshire terrier." He grinned. "Are you conducting some sort of a survey into the village's dogs?"

Jonathon laughed. "No, merely curious." He gave a nod, then exited the hall.

Once outside, Mike tugged on Jonathon's arm. "Okay, want to explain what that was all about?"

Jonathon gazed at him innocently. "What? I wanted to know what his dog was. The paw prints by the jam table, remember?"

"Don't you give me that. I'm talking about *before* that, when you went all bashful on me."

"I asked him the questions, didn't I?"

"Sure—when you finally remembered where you kept your tongue. *And* when you'd got a good enough look at him." Mike smirked. "Oh, wait a minute. That was your tongue I kept tripping over, wasn't it?"

Jonathon's cheeks were flushed. "Oh, come *on*. Who wouldn't want to get an eyeful? He's gorgeous."

Mike stared at him. "Jonathon de Mountford. You've got a crush on our MP."

Jonathon's eyes widened. "So what if I have? I can look, can't I?" His lips twitched into a smile. "It's not *him* I'm in love with, is it?"

Mike huffed. "Just you remember that." He groaned. "And now we're seeing Melinda at four. You know what *that* means."

Jonathon grinned. "Tea and gossip. I think we're about due for a chat with the vicar's wife, wouldn't you say? Only, be careful what you say in front of Melinda., all right? Last time was bad enough."

"What was bad about last—?" Mike snickered. "Oh yeah. You said I had a nice arse."

"Exactly. She doesn't need any more ammunition."

"What—like knowing you think our MP is dishy?"

Jonathon's growl as he made his way to the car was adorable.

CHAPTER EIGHTEEN

"I THINK you should get one of these, Mike," Jonathon murmured, stroking Jinx between his ears. The black-and-white cat purred, lifting its chin, and Jonathon scritched him under there. "I can just picture a cat strolling around the pub, getting cuddles from all the regulars." There was something about stroking a cat that always made him feel at ease—not drowsy, but in that pleasant state of not giving a damn about anything.

"Jinx has this unerring knack of finding the right lap," Melinda commented. "But I'm afraid if you want some cake, he'll have to find another place to snooze."

In seconds, Jonathon grasped the cat around its middle, lifted it into the air, and deposited it on the rug. "Bye, kitty."

Melinda, Lloyd, and Mike all laughed.

Melinda cut a slice of carrot cake, which Mike passed to him. "Here," he said, thrusting the plate at Jonathon. "Start eating this and Jinx will be back in a heartbeat. And why *me* have a cat? You could have a cat at the manor."

It was on the tip of Jonathon's tongue to say it wasn't fair to have a cat when he didn't plan on being there for a few months at a time. But something stopped him. For one thing, he hadn't mentioned anything to Mike, and for another, he wasn't about to do it in front of the vicar and his wife.

"Can we leave the subject of cats alone for a moment and get to my reason for inviting you to tea?" Melinda poured Jonathon a cup of coffee.

Jonathon blinked. "We're not here because we're scintillating good company?"

Mike snickered.

Lloyd peered at his wife over his rimless glasses. "My dear? What are you up to?"

Melinda patted his knee. "Nothing you need worry about. I just wanted the opportunity to talk to Jonathon about the parish council."

"I see." Lloyd met Jonathon's gaze. "Run, dear boy. Run while you still can." He smiled, however.

"Should I be worried?" Jonathon asked before swallowing a mouthful of carrot cake.

Melinda gave her usual musical laugh. "Not at all. I simply felt that you might like to become a member of the council. Your uncle was for a great many years."

"That's a good idea," Mike commented.

"Who's on it?" Jonathon had no aversion to following in Dominic's footsteps, and he liked the idea of becoming more involved in village life.

Melinda counted off on her fingers. "There's myself; the mayor, John Barton; Grant Spencer, the planning officer; Doris Pullman, who runs the village shop; Esther Thompson, who runs the WI; and our MP,

Joshua Brent." Her cheeks pinked. "You remember, the gentleman who so captivated you this morning."

Jonathon should have realized that nothing escaped Melinda.

"That man will never become prime minister, you mark my words." Lloyd's voice quavered.

Melinda regarded him with mild surprise. "And why is that?"

Lloyd huffed. "He's far too good-looking. Let us be brutally honest here. When has there ever been an attractive prime minister in this country?"

"Oh, I don't know." Mike's eyes gleamed. "I dare say there are some who might like a good-looking PM. Eh, Jonathon?"

Jonathon gave him a hard stare, and Melinda aimed an intense gaze at Mike. "I sense someone is being teased. Pay no attention to him, Jonathon. Joshua Brent might be prettier than him, but we all know Mike has *your* heart, don't we?"

Jonathon's stare softened, and he smiled.

Mike, however, almost choked on his mouthful of coffee-and-walnut cake. "Prettier than me? Says who?"

Melinda ignored him and addressed Jonathon. "Besides, I'm the only one allowed to tease in this house." Her eyes twinkled. "Now, what do you think about the council? Is it something that might interest you?"

Jonathon grinned. "I think so."

Mike was still spluttering.

Melinda beamed. "Excellent. Our next meeting is tomorrow evening in the village hall. I'll tell everyone to expect you."

Jonathon almost choked on his coffee. "Talk about short notice. You don't waste time, do you?"

"Why do you think I got you here today?" Melinda leaned forward conspiratorially. "Now, boys, how are you doing? Are you close to solving the case yet?"

Mike burst out laughing. "What makes you think we're doing anything?"

Melinda arched her thin eyebrows. "That wasn't a serious question, was it? I remember how you were this summer. As soon as I heard you'd been to her cottage, I knew you were doing a little sleuthing." She poured herself another cup of tea and dropped a slice of lemon into it. "So, what progress have you made?"

"I should think you have a great many suspects," Lloyd commented. "One has only to listen to village gossip to glean *that* much."

"Surely *you* don't listen to such things," Mike said innocently.

Melinda hurriedly put down her cup. "Mike, you really shouldn't say things like that when I'm drinking. That might have been disastrous." She eyed her husband. "And the less said about Lloyd's propensity for gossip, the better."

"It's not gossip," Lloyd remonstrated. "*Everyone* knows that little upstart sent those flyers. Sheer jealousy. It wasn't Mrs. Teedle's fault his business is doing so appallingly. The man should look to his own house first."

"I take it we're talking about Nathan Driscoll, the chemist?"

"Indeed. Although, I must admit that killing the competition is perhaps a little too strong an action to take."

Melinda chuckled. "Agreed, dear."

Jonathon concluded that there was little point hiding anything from the elderly couple. "We started with a list of people seen near the cottage that morning. Nathan was on that list, by the way. And as of today, we've spoken with all of them."

"Hmm. Fat lot of use *that* was." Mike scowled. "None of 'em went into the cottage, none of 'em spoke with her, and they all just bought a jar of jam."

"How frustrating for you," Melinda murmured. "Especially when one of them must be lying."

"Yeah, but then it gets more complicated." Jonathon shot a glance at Mike, who nodded. "We found some diaries, and they point to Mrs. Teedle being a… blackmailer."

Melinda's mouth fell open.

Lloyd removed his glasses and cleaned them on his napkin, shaking his head. "You think you know people, and then…."

"Are you certain?" Melinda's brow furrowed. "Do you have any idea who her victims were?" She shivered. "Blackmail. Such a nasty crime."

"Right now, it's a theory, but her bank statements seem to back it up. There's a snag, however. All the diary entries are written in code."

Melinda bit her lip. "Code? That hardly points to an innocent activity, does it?"

"We've worked out some of the amounts just by matching them to the deposits made, but as for who was making them, we have no clue," Jonathon said glumly. "We spent virtually all of Sunday trying to crack it." Mike coughed, and Jonathon gave him another hard stare.

"So, unless you happen to know anyone who can crack codes, that avenue of inquiry is closed off to us." Mike forked off another piece of cake.

"Plus, the investigation is now headed by a Detective Inspector from Winchester. We had the pleasure of meeting him the other day." Jonathon grimaced. "Delightful man."

"Can't be worse than that Gorland fella," Lloyd commented. "Officious little—"

"Thank you, Lloyd." Melinda gave him what could only be described as A Look. She gazed thoughtfully at them. "And what if I did?" she asked quietly, before sipping her tea.

"Did what?" Jonathon was momentarily lost.

"Know someone who can crack codes," she replied simply.

Jonathon stared at her. "Seriously?"

She put down her cup. "One of my duties as the vicar's wife is to go visiting, and that includes going to the Cedars."

"What's that?" Jonathon asked.

"A retirement home on the road to Lower Pinton, just inside the village boundaries," Mike supplied. "Nice place. It's a big house set back from the road. Lovely gardens."

"That's the place. One of the residents is a sweet elderly lady by the name of Lily." Melinda sighed. "She's in her nineties, bless her, and getting about is sadly a chore for her, but her mind is still rapier-sharp."

"And what makes you think she'd be any good at cracking codes?"

Melinda arched her eyebrows again. "Well, there's the fact that during the war, she was a young cypher clerk at Bletchley Park," she said dryly.

It took Jonathon a second or two to register her words. "Bletchley Park... isn't that where Alan Turing worked on cracking Enigma?"

Melinda sighed. "A lot more went on there than what you *might* have seen in a film. The point is, she has experience that might prove useful. So, do I arrange a meeting, or do you want to stumble around a little more? Because it strikes me that if you want to dissect something, you need a scalpel, not the garden spade that you two are currently using."

Mike snickered. "Seems to me we'd be stupid not to."

Melinda beamed. "Perfect. I'll set up a time to introduce you. Now, who wants that last piece of carrot cake?"

Mike gazed at Jonathon with narrowed eyes. "I'll arm wrestle you for it."

"Fine. And while you're rolling up your sleeve…." Jonathon reached over and grabbed the plate on which the cake sat. "I'll eat the piece." He held the plate to his chest.

Jinx appeared at his feet, pawing at his leg.

Mike appeared to take it in his stride. "That's okay. You have it. Just remember one thing. I know where you live. I know where you *sleep*."

"If you didn't know that by now, I'd be very surprised," Melinda said matter-of-factly. When Jonathon, Mike, and Lloyd stared at her, she regarded them with mild surprise. "Didn't you know? Vicars' wives are unshockable. It comes with the job."

Jonathon gazed at her with affection. "I think vicars' wives are wonderful." This new turn was an exciting one. He wanted to see who Naomi had been blackmailing.

Then all they had to do was work out why.

CHAPTER NINETEEN

Tuesday, November 14

JONATHON SLID a hand across the mattress, then opened his eyes when his fingers didn't encounter Mike's warm flesh. A glance at his phone revealed it to be seven thirty. He sat up and scraped his hand through his hair. Mike's clothes were still on the chair where he'd deposited them, but the robe he usually wore when he stayed over was not. Jonathon peered over the edge of the bed—the prosthetic wasn't there either. He pushed back the covers, got out of bed, reached for his warm robe, and tied it securely around his waist.

As he approached the drawing room, he heard Mike's voice, and he pushed open the door. Mike was on the couch, slippered feet propped up, his phone on the arm and earbuds in place while he scribbled notes.

"Yeah, I've got all that." He glanced up as Jonathon came into the room, smiling at him. "Thanks again, Keith. … No, it's fine. I was gonna get up early anyway." Mike laughed. "Bastard. Life of leisure indeed. … I owe you one." He disconnected, then beamed at Jonathon as he pulled the buds from his ears. "Good morning, sleepyhead. Some of us have been up for a while."

Jonathon sniffed before he spied the mug. "Where's mine?" he demanded.

Mike rolled his eyes. "You were asleep. And besides, I didn't make it. Janet brought it for me. She was a little surprised to find me awake and on the phone." He put down his pen and picked up his mug, inhaling the aroma. "God, I need this."

Before Jonathon could inquire about what he'd learned, Janet entered, carrying a tray.

"I thought I heard you. Good morning, sir. And as you're both awake, you'll need more than a mug. Shall I have Ivy serve breakfast earlier or at the usual time?" She set the tray down on the coffee table.

Jonathon chuckled. "I want to stay on Ivy's good side. Breakfast at eight thirty as usual, please."

"Very good, sir." Janet left the room.

He joined Mike on the couch and poured himself a cup before leaning over to kiss Mike's cheek. "Good morning. Now tell me what Keith discovered. Hopefully something useful."

Mike flipped back through his notepad. "He's been a busy boy. Our Naomi didn't exactly have an incident-free life before she went off to Australia. She trained as a nurse before becoming a midwife when she was about twenty-three. The interesting bit? She got herself pregnant, and her family basically disowned her. They were pretty well-to-do, and yes, it might have been the late sixties, with more liberal attitudes everywhere, but not in *their* house, thank you very much. So she left home and set up in a place of her own. She was working at a little cottage hospital in Nottingham, where apparently she delivered a great many babies."

"Aha. *Now* that remark she made when she delivered Jason Barton makes sense. No wonder she did it so efficiently. What about her own baby?" Jonathon sipped his coffee.

Mike sighed. "A boy. Gabriel. But... he died when he was two months old, from what sounds like what they later came to call cot death. A couple of months after he died, she went back to work, although it seems there were concerns that it was too early. Maybe it was," he mused, "because not long after that, she immigrated to Australia on their Ten Pound Poms scheme."

"What was that?"

"The Australian government had this Assisted Passage Migration Scheme, which started after the Second World War. They promised employment opportunities, affordable housing, and a new way of life, and it only cost ten pounds for the fare to get there. I think it ended in the early eighties, and over a million people made the journey there."

"How old was she? Twenty-fiveish? And she'd just lost a baby. Yet she decided to move to the other side of the world. Brave lady."

Mike's phone pinged, and he scrolled through. "Keith's sent me something. It's a photo of her birth certificate, her baby's, *and* the subsequent death certificate. Not sure why, but there you go."

Jonathon sighed. "Not exactly what I'd hoped for." His phone vibrated in the pocket of his robe. He peered at the screen and let out a whoop. "Wayne, you little beauty."

"Wayne?" Mike frowned. "Your ex in Oz?"

Jonathon nodded. "He's heard back from his dad." He grinned. "Talk about good timing." He scrolled through the email, trying to take in the gist of the information. "Okay. Jane, as she was then, met and married Wayne Teedle, a builder. One daughter, Gabriela." His heart went out to Naomi. "She must have named the baby after the little boy she lost, to remember him. No more children, however. Seems there were complications arising from the birth." He scanned the rest of the email.

"Anything juicy to report?"

Jonathon shook his head. "Her husband died in an accident—work-related, by the look of it—and left her provided for. Insurance. Daughter got married, has three kids. And when Naomi was fifty-five, she made the move back to the UK, but going under her middle name. Wayne says there's nothing untoward about her life in Australia. No scandals. No dramas. Just an ordinary life. She studied homeopathy there." He lowered his phone to his lap. "So we're no nearer to finding a motive."

"Maybe not. We know she wasn't blowing smoke, if she'd studied homeopathy. And maybe things will become clearer when we find out who she was blackmailing. Because the more I think about it, the more convinced I am that the answer lies there." Mike gave an emphatic nod. "You wait and see. Her murderer will turn out to be one of her victims." He leaned forward and poured another coffee.

Jonathon had to agree. Of the five people seen near her cottage, they'd already discounted Rachel, and the others appeared to have no motives for killing Naomi. Well, except for Nathan, but Jonathon really couldn't

picture the dumpy little man strangling Naomi to eliminate the competition.

He put down his cup and rubbed his hand, trying
desperately not to scratch it. The blisters hadn't healed
yet, and the doctor had told him he'd been very lucky
not to have broken the skin.

*But what if that stuff got into the bloodstream? By
means of a cut, for example?*

"It's been nearly a week since we asked Graham
about the forensic results," Jonathon mused. "Do you
think he might have more in by now?"

Mike snorted. "Oh sure, and that DI is going to
be more than happy to hand over the report so you can
take a look at it."

"What if we asked him just to let us see a copy?
Would he do that?" Graham had done it before, after
all. Jonathon stroked Mike's thigh. "He'd do it if you
asked him."

Mike appeared mesmerized by the movement of
Jonathon's hand, especially when he pulled aside the
soft fabric and stroked bare flesh instead, shifting a little higher with each caress.

"I... could ask him, I suppose." His breathing
caught as Jonathon casually undid the tie around Mike's
waist. "Can I point something out here?" There was an
urgent quality to Mike's voice that was a definite turn-
on. "Janet might come in at any minute."

Jonathon shifted off the couch and onto his knees
in front of Mike, pulling open the robe. "Then I'd better
make it quick, hadn't I?" He grinned. "Is the adrenaline
flowing? Heart racing? Blood pumping?" He glanced
down. "Stupid question."

"God, yeah," Mike whispered, before Jonathon lowered his head, still grinning. "Okay, enough talk," he said breathlessly.

Jonathon locked gazes with him. "My father always taught me it was rude to talk with your mouth full."

"BLOODY HELL. We're open in fifteen minutes," Mike exclaimed with a groan when someone knocked on the pub door. "Surely they can wait that long."

"I'll get it," Jonathon told him. Mike had connected a new barrel and was checking it before the lunchtime opening. Jonathon unlocked the door and smiled when Graham stuck his head inside. "Good afternoon—well, almost."

Graham came into the pub, scowling. "You two are gonna get me shot, you know that?" In his hands he carried a plain brown envelope.

"Hey, wait a minute." Jonathon shut the door after him. "Like Mike said on the phone, only if it was no trouble *and* it wouldn't get you into hot water." He peered anxiously at Graham. "You're not, are you?"

Graham hoisted himself onto a barstool. "No," he said with a sigh. "And I shouldn't have come in like that. It's just... he's pissing me off. He's got me doing paperwork. I flippin' *hate* paperwork." He placed the envelope on the bar and tapped it with his index finger. "Anyhow, that's the latest forensics report. Wanna tell me what you're hoping to find?"

Jonathon decided to come clean. He held up his hand. "See this? That's what I got for brushing aside some of the leaves Naomi Teedle was chopping when she died. Horrible stuff brought me out in blisters. Hogweed, Mike says."

"Yeah. We came up with that too." Graham pulled a face. "Nasty stuff."

"Well, I started thinking about the blood on the knife. Whether it was Naomi's or not. Because if not, then whoever's blood it is, they've possibly come into contact with this stuff too, and we've already seen what a mess it makes."

Graham opened the envelope and removed the sheet of paper. "It wasn't hers. We've got DNA, but of course it's no one on file. At least when we catch them, we can nail them for sure. But we do have something else to go on." He pointed to a paragraph. "There was a residue on her neck, a trace of something that the killer had on their hands or gloves." He smiled. "Although, having analyzed it, I'd go with gloves."

Mike joined Jonathon and peered over his shoulder at the report. "A leather treatment?"

Graham nodded. "Stuff you use to keep leather looking good. You can apply it to handbags, gloves, saddles, furniture—just about anything. Only this particular compound? The forensic guys even narrowed it down to the actual brand. It's a leather treatment used in valeting cars."

"Really?"

Graham chuckled. "That's given you something to work on, hasn't it? Now, quid pro quo. You got anything for me?"

Jonathon gave Mike an inquiring glance.

Mike cleared his throat. "You might want to look into her finances. We know she was provided for by her husband's insurance policy, but… she had expensive tastes, mate."

Graham's eyes widened. "Blackmail? We've got statements from her bank, but there's nothing to point to blackmail. No large deposits."

"Ah, because they'd show up as regular payments. The only way we knew they weren't was because of the coded diary entries. There's a set of diaries at the house—you know the ones, you've probably got one free from Doris, same as me—and they contain the codes and payments. And before you ask, no, we haven't cracked the code yet."

Graham grinned. "You two are amazing. I'll get onto that ASAP."

"Feeling better?" Like Jonathon had to ask.

"Miles better. Sod him and his bloody paperwork—I'm gonna pay another visit to that cottage and get those diaries." He extended a hand to Jonathon. "Thanks, mate."

Jonathon shook it. "You're welcome. Just remember this next time we ask a favor, okay?"

Graham stared at him with wide eyes. "Yeah, right. This was quid pro quo, remember? *Now* we're even." He got off his stool and headed for the door. "Don't go showing that report around, all right? Otherwise he'll have my guts for garters." He patted Jonathon's shoulder. "Play nice with the parish council tonight. I know it's only your first meeting, but don't go suggesting they have a Pride parade or something like that. You'll scare the pants off them."

Jonathon gaped. "How did you know about tonight?"

"I *am* a policeman, right?" Graham gave a nonchalant shrug. "We have our sources." Then he winked. "I ran into Melinda Talbot as I was coming here, and she told me all about it."

"Now *that* makes sense." Jonathon followed him to the door, let him out, and bolted it behind him. Then he reconsidered and unbolted it again. It was opening time. When he got back to the bar, Mike was grinning.

"Let's see if *they* have more luck cracking the code."

"I notice you didn't mention Lily," Jonathon remarked.

"'Course not. She's our secret weapon. And I've been thinking. There are a few garages we might visit to see if they use that brand of leather treatment. Plus we'll see if Doris stocks it."

"I can see our suspect list growing even more." Not that Jonathon minded all that much. After Ben's list hadn't rendered them any obvious clues, it was clear they needed to widen the scope of their investigation.

Investigation sounded *so* much better than snooping.

CHAPTER TWENTY

DORIS PULLMAN beamed at Jonathon. "I was *so* pleased when Melinda said you'd be joining us."

"It was nice to be asked," Jonathon admitted. Not everyone had arrived yet in the village hall, and Doris had made tea for those who had. A table stood near the stage, with seven chairs around it, a pot of tea and a milk jug in the center, and two plates of biscuits, one at either end. Melinda, it appeared, was the council's secretary, and it was she who took the minutes. The mayor, John Barton, had greeted Jonathon warmly, and they'd talked for a few minutes about Jason's plans, which now included studying photography. John was plainly supportive, and Jonathon was delighted things were working out well.

Esther Thompson was slightly cooler with him, and Jonathon responded to her questions with politeness. It was their first meeting, and he could almost hear Mike's advice in his head, given before he'd set out for the meeting: "You can't make everyone like you. You're not chocolate."

"Grant Spencer called a moment ago," Melinda announced. "He's on his way back from Salisbury. And Joshua—"

Whatever else she'd been about to say was lost in the *click click click* of nails on wood as a very enthusiastic Yorkshire terrier scurried across the floor, heading straight for Jonathon.

Melinda laughed. "Toby spies a new friend," she said as the dog jumped up, his paws on Jonathon's knees, his head narrowly missing the table.

"Well, hello. Aren't you friendly?" Jonathon patted the dog's head and was rewarded as Toby bounced a little higher and landed a lick on Jonathon's chin.

"Toby!"

At Mr. Brent's voice, Toby was back on the floor, running toward him, then circling him, barking the whole time.

Mr. Brent sat in the chair next to Jonathon, and Toby eventually sat at his feet under the table. "Twice in two days, Mr. de Mountford," Mr. Brent commented. "When we spoke yesterday, I had no idea you'd be joining us this evening."

"At that point, neither did I," Jonathon confessed. "Someone had other ideas, though."

"Guilty as charged." Melinda held up her hand. "I felt the timing was right."

Brent held out his hand. "Glad to have you aboard." They shook, and Brent cast a glance in the direction of the kitchen before whispering, "Be careful with Esther. She has been known to turn the odd man into ice with a single stare."

Jonathon quickly stifled his chuckle. "Thanks for the warning. And it's Jonathon, by the way." He half wished Brent had taken the empty seat facing him. That way Jonathon could have gazed at him all evening without it appearing obvious.

"Then I'm Josh. Seeing as we're going to be on the same council." There was that smile again, the one that had made Jonathon go weak at the knees the previous day. *Why does he have to be so gorgeous?*

The door to the street opened once more, and a man entered, bundled up in a thick coat. "Sorry I'm late," he said as he approached the table. "Traffic was murder this evening." He glanced at Jonathon and blinked. "Oh. Hello."

Jonathon rose to his feet and held out a hand. "Jonathon de Mountford. Here because Melinda twisted my arm," he teased.

The man shook before heading for the empty chair across the table. "Grant Spencer." He glanced around the table, then toward the kitchen. "Oh my. Mrs. Thompson won't like that. Four men, three women? Such inequality will never do." His eyes sparkled.

Jonathon liked the look of Grant. He was possibly in his thirties, with a kind face, brown eyes, and short black hair.

At that moment Esther Thompson left the kitchen and made her way sedately across the floor to them. She frowned when she saw Grant. "Late *again*, Mr. Spencer."

"It really wasn't my fault," he protested. Then he laughed good-naturedly. "Who am I kidding? My wife says I'll be late for my own funeral."

"Then let's not waste any more time," Melinda said in a patient tone.

When Esther had taken her seat, John Barton stood.

"I'd like to formally welcome Jonathon de Mountford. He fills the space left by his uncle, and it's a pleasure to have another de Mountford on the council."

"Agreed," Josh added warmly, amid murmurs of assent from the others.

"Although I'd like to go on record as saying if we are approached by any new future members, I think we should consider them very carefully," John said gravely.

Melinda blinked. "But… I proposed Jonathon."

The mayor held up both hands. "And *now* look where we are. We have a John, a Josh, and a Jonathon. Awfully confusing." His eyes twinkled with good humor. "No more Js, please, everyone?" Then he grinned. "My son will be pleased he's off the hook."

And with that—and a few chuckles and snickers— the meeting finally started.

Jonathon had anticipated a rather plodding pace, with lots of red tape and boring items of which he was blissfully unaware, and was not disappointed. There were few points of contention, and everyone seemed to get along—until the final item on the agenda.

Grant Spencer led off. "As you will know, Brian Calder has applied for planning permission to develop the plot of land at the end of Mill Lane, having submitted outlines to this council—"

"He can submit as many outlines as he likes," Doris interjected. "Fat lot of good it may do him, after the last time. No one in their right mind would give him permission to build more houses, especially if they're anything like the last lot."

Grant coughed, his face flushing. "Actually… planning permission has been approved."

It was as if someone had flicked a lit match into a pool of petrol.

"Surely you're not serious." Melinda stared at him openmouthed.

"What the hell?" Josh gaped.

"How can this be?" Esther demanded.

"Wait a moment—*you're* the planning officer, damn it." John Barton's face reddened. "That means *you* gave permission. Just like you okayed it last time."

"There was nothing wrong with his proposal," Grant protested. "And the houses weren't an eyesore, were they? They look fine."

"And I'm sure they'd look equally fine in some suburb of Winchester, or some council housing estate in Reading, but *not* in Merrychurch village," the mayor remonstrated.

"An appeal was launched against the original decision, if you recall." Grant's voice shook slightly. "That decision was upheld at county level."

"Then someone from the county offices needs to come down here and take a good, long, hard look at this village. Because to build a development of houses like the ones Calder built in Turnbull Lane is an abomination." Josh's face darkened. "And now he wants to do it again—at the end of Mill Lane? For God's sake, man, why didn't you turn him down flat?"

"Because, in case you missed the news reports, there is a housing shortage in this country, *Mr.* Brent." Grant glared at him. "You of all people should be aware of that issue, seeing as you brought it up in Parliament on more than one occasion."

"Agreed, but there is a great deal of difference between developing a piece of common land and building good, low-cost houses for those trying to get onto the property ladder—and privately—secretly—buying a piece of land and proposing to build twenty or so houses on it that have *nothing* in common with the appearance of this village. They were *not* designed sympathetically. He made *no* attempt to—"

"I think we should call an end to this meeting." Melinda's voice rose above the clamor. "There is clearly no way we are going to reach a consensus on this matter, and indeed, I feel there should have been some public forum on this. If I may make a suggestion? We should timetable another meeting to discuss this issue at a later date, but I would ask that Brian Calder be invited to take part, along with any interested members of the village. And that in the interim, Mr. Calder does *not* begin work on this development."

"I can certainly convey that to him." Grant Spencer stood and put on his coat. "I trust I'll be informed of the date of this meeting?"

"Of course," Melinda said gravely.

Grant gave a curt nod to those around the table, then walked out of the hall.

Melinda sagged into her chair. "Well. I didn't see *that* coming. I thought it was a simple item."

John Barton still appeared stunned, as did Esther and Doris.

"As you're relatively new to Merrychurch, you probably have no idea what all that fuss was about," Josh said with a wry chuckle.

"I'm afraid not." Only one reference had made any sense to Jonathon. He'd visited Mill Lane that summer. It was a narrow road full of old-world charm, containing listed buildings and an ancient water mill that was still in working order. A more picturesque part of Merrychurch he'd yet to find.

"Talk about a baptism by fire." John sighed unhappily. He got up from the table and went to pick up his coat where he'd left it over a chair. One by one, the council members took their leave, until only Melinda and Jonathon remained.

"I don't know about you, but I'm going home to pour myself a large sherry." Melinda sighed. "If you get a moment tomorrow, go for a walk along Turnbull Lane. You'll spot the houses Brian Calder built. You won't be able to miss them. It might give you a point of reference for what you just heard." She accompanied him to the door, and once outside, she locked it. "Are you heading back to the manor now?"

Jonathon shook his head. "I told Mike I'd pop into the pub when the meeting was over. I left the car in his car park and walked here." He held out his arm. "And seeing as you're going in the same direction…."

Melinda hooked her arm through his. "Seeing me to my door. Well, almost. Chivalry is *not* dead in Merrychurch after all, it seems."

They walked in silence along the edge of the village green, Jonathon deep in thought. The heated discussion had been unexpected, but what surprised him was that Grant had been on his own against the rest of the council. Was it *that* divisive an issue?

"Penny for them," Melinda said after the silence had continued for several minutes. There was no one in sight, undoubtedly a result of the cold night air. Ahead of them, the sign for the Hare and Hounds reflected the streetlight, promising warmth and alcohol and good company. The faint hint of music swelled as someone opened the pub door, and figures hurried away to escape the cold.

"I doubt my thoughts are worth that much."

"Let me be the judge of that."

Jonathon came to a halt. "I didn't expect Grant to have no support from the council. Everyone seemed against him. Is it usually like that?"

Melinda shook her head. "Not at all. This is why you need to look for yourself. Once you've seen, you'll understand the level of feeling you experienced in that meeting." She covered Jonathon's hand with hers. "Persevere? Don't give up on us at the first hurdle."

He smiled, leaned in, and kissed her cheek. "I'm not about to quit. We de Mountfords haven't managed to keep going this long without developing a lot of stamina."

She laughed. "You do remind me of your uncle."

It was the nicest thing she could have said.

Jonathon walked Melinda to the vicarage, then retraced his steps to the pub and the warmth it promised. It was pleasant to walk into the bar area and be greeted by villagers he'd come to know.

It feels as if I'm starting to fit in around here.

Mike beamed as Jonathon approached the bar. "Hey. You look frozen. D'you want a beer or a coffee? If it's the latter, go into the kitchen and help yourself. You know where everything is."

At the bar, Paul Drake snorted. "I should think he could make a cuppa blindfolded by now, the number of times he's here."

Jonathon grinned. "Yup. Just like you could find that stool if the lights were out."

Paul cackled. "You got me there, nipper. I'm thinkin' of 'avin' me name engraved on it. Or a plaque at least."

Jonathon walked through into the kitchen and found a fresh pot of coffee waiting for him. Mike usually drank water when he worked behind the bar. *He did that for me.*

The man was definitely a keeper.

CHAPTER TWENTY-ONE

Wednesday, November 15

JONATHON MADE a noise of sheer contentment as the aroma of freshly brewed coffee tickled his nostrils. "Even Janet doesn't bring me coffee in bed. Maybe I should ask her to start doing that."

Mike's snort made him jump. "Only if I'm not around. Talk about living dangerously."

Jonathon opened his eyes and grinned at Mike, who sat on the edge of the bed. "I don't know what you're complaining about. You certainly weren't complaining yesterday when I—"

Mike launched across the bed and covered Jonathon's mouth with his hand. "*You* have a wicked mouth," he whispered. Then he leaned in closer and kissed him.

When he pulled back, Jonathon chuckled. "Yep. You said *that* yesterday too." He sat up and took the mug Mike offered him. "Do you have anything urgent planned for this morning? Because if not, there's something I'd like to do. Two things, actually."

Mike arched his eyebrows. "Might these two somethings be connected to a certain murder? It's just occurred to me that she died ten days ago, and we still have no firm idea as to who killed her."

"Which is why I want to look into that leather treatment." Jonathon took a long, welcome drink of coffee. "But also… something happened last night at the council meeting, and I'm really confused about it. What do you know about a housing development on Turnbull Lane?"

Mike frowned. "Nothing."

"Or a property developer called Brian Calder?"

His eyes widened. "Now him, I know. I've seen him in the pub a few times. Quiet guy, keeps to himself."

Quickly, Jonathon gave him a précis of the fracas of the previous night. "I know it's nothing to do with the murder, but…."

"But you're intrigued."

Jonathon nodded. "It was just the level of… animosity that came out of nowhere. I want to know more."

"Fine. Let's get up, have some breakfast, and then we'll go for a little drive and check out these houses. After, we can check out places where they might use that leather treatment." Mike paused. "This wasn't quite what I had planned for this morning."

Jonathon stilled. "Oh? Am I interfering with your plans? You should have said something."

Mike waved a hand. "Wait a minute. I brought you coffee with the intention of getting back into bed for a cuddle, then casually asking you if… you'd like to spend the weekend in London with me. To celebrate your birthday."

"Oh." Warmth coursed through Jonathon.

"It *is* on Saturday, right?" Mike peered at him anxiously. "Abi's agreed to cover me, and I've booked us two nights in a hotel—hopefully a really nice one—plus we've got tickets to see a show Saturday night."

"You've gone to an awful lot of trouble, haven't you?" Jonathon had never had a boyfriend exhibit such thoughtfulness. His exes had all appeared to assume Jonathon would be the one to organize such things.

"Look, if you don't want to—"

It was Jonathon's turn to cut off Mike's words with a gentle hand. "Who in their right mind would say no to such a lovely, thoughtful gesture? I love it. And I like the idea of cuddling in bed too. Breakfast can wait a while." He smiled. "You can never have too many cuddles."

In a heartbeat, he lay in Mike's arms, snuggled up against him, his head on Mike's chest, feeling the reassuring thump of his heart beneath his ribs.

Mike kissed his head. "I'm so glad you like it. I wanted it to be a surprise, but then I realized there might be conflicts. You're a busy man, after all."

Jonathon sighed contentedly. "Never too busy to be whisked away for a weekend. Although, I am intrigued as to what show we're going to see. *Wicked*? *Phantom*? *Les Mis*?"

Mike chuckled. "None of those. Something much more… appropriate." When Jonathon craned his neck to peer at him, Mike grinned. "*The Mousetrap* by Agatha Christie."

Jonathon snuggled closer. "Just what we need. Inspiration."

THE MORNING air was crisp, and Jonathon slipped his arm through Mike's as they walked along the lane. A simple act, but it meant a lot that they could do it without fear of confrontation.

At least, he *assumed* there'd be no confrontation. Merrychurch had to have its share of haters, like everywhere else. But so far, they hadn't crawled out of the woodwork.

"I love this village," he murmured as they strolled. "This stone you see everywhere, the thatched roofs, the quaint gardens.... It's like Merrychurch has been suspended in some kind of time bubble, untouched by the modern world."

Mike chuckled. "Speaking of bubbles... I hate to burst yours, but even here, the modern world creeps in. The old-fashioned streetlamps are being replaced by these LED versions, which give out a cold white light that's nothing like the warm glow of their predecessors. Not to mention the houses that have been sold, then demolished to make way for a new, more modern house that's all glass and angles."

"Aw, don't." Jonathon wanted Merrychurch to retain its charm as long as possible. "There are things we can do, surely, to help keep the village looking the way it does?"

Mike came to a stop. "In theory. But then you get people who apparently don't feel the same way." He sighed. "No wonder I've never seen this. I have no cause to drive this way. But I've lived here over a year now. How could I have missed this?"

In front of them, the street turned into an obviously new estate, a collection of maybe twenty houses. What was immediately noticeable was that they all looked the same. Red brick, double-glazed windows, tile roofs—all with identical postage-stamp lawns in front and a garage built as part of the house.

Jonathon sighed. "Now I understand. That planning officer—Grant Spencer—said they weren't an eyesore, which they're not. They're houses like you'd see anywhere in the country. But Josh was right too. They're—"

"Oh, it's *Josh*, is it now?" Mike smirked.

Jonathon gave him a whack on the arm. "Listen. He said they weren't designed sympathetically, that they had nothing in common with the look of the village." He surveyed the development. "They could have done so much more."

"Like what?"

"You see it all the time, where buildings are added that maintain the *feel* of a place. They didn't have to design a set of twenty boxes with little or no soul. The mayor got that part right too. He said they'd look fine elsewhere, but not here. Not in Merrychurch." Jonathon broke free of Mike's arm and walked over to the road that cut through the estate. *It's just... wrong.*

Mike's hand was at his back. "It's called progress, I suppose."

Now Jonathon understood the comments from the meeting. "So Brian Calder applied for planning permission for these, and it was approved. I can see why a lot of people would wonder how he managed that. Now he's going to build *more* houses, and it looks like his plans have been rubber-stamped. Again."

"Where?"

Jonathon turned to face Mike. "At the end of Mill Lane, apparently."

Mike's mouth fell open. "How the fu—hell did he get *that* approved? Mill Lane is one of the oldest parts of the village. That water mill dates back to before the Domesday Book. And he wants to build these… *boxes* there? Over my dead body."

Jonathon had to smile. "Look at you. I can see you standing up at the public meeting and giving someone a piece of your mind."

"Too right, you can!" Mike's eyes flared.

Jonathon took hold of his hand. "And I'll be standing next to you," he said quietly. "At least now I know what's at stake." What still puzzled him was why planning permission had been granted in the first place.

It made no sense.

AS THEY entered the pub, Mike's phone buzzed.

"You take care of that—I'll make coffee," Jonathon told him before heading for the kitchen. He quickly set up the coffee machine, then noticed a white box in the middle of the table. "Mike?" he yelled. "What's in the box?"

"What box?" Mike came into the kitchen and halted at the table. "Oh." He lifted the lid, peered inside, and grinned. "Aw. She's a sweetheart." He flipped it open to reveal two slices of apple pie. Attached to the lid was a yellow Post-it.

I baked. And yes, it is edible. LOL. Enjoy. Sue.

Jonathon grabbed two side plates from the cupboard. "Apple pie for elevenses. Excellent."

"Elevenses? Are we hobbits now?" Mike sat at the table.

Jonathon laughed. "Never mind the hobbits—my grandfather used to talk about having elevenses. A cup of tea or coffee, plus a snack." He glanced at the wall clock. "Perfect timing too." Carefully, he placed the slices onto the plates, then went to pour the coffee. "What was the text?"

"That was Melinda," Mike said, between mouthfuls of pie.

"Good Lord. Does she want *you* to join the council now?" Jonathon put the mugs on the table, then joined Mike.

Mike laughed. "Nope. Not that I'd say yes if she did. I have enough to do, thank you very much. She wanted to let me know that we have an appointment at eleven o'clock tomorrow morning at the Cedars."

Jonathon beamed. "Lily's agreed to meet us." At last. Now maybe they could crack that code. He pulled a plate to him and forked off a piece of the pie, relishing the tartness of the apple combined with the sweet pastry.

"Needs cream," Mike commented. "But damn, she can bake. So, what are you going to be doing while I'm working my fingers to the bones this afternoon?"

Jonathon leveled an incredulous gaze at him. "Pulling pints hardly constitutes manual labor. And you know what I'm doing. I'm going to check out this leather treatment."

"Where will you start?"

Jonathon had already given that question some consideration. "Eddie Prowse. He's the guy who valets the Jag, as well as the rest of Dominic's cars. He might have some idea who would use this stuff."

Mike grinned. "Here's a thought. If he uses it on your Jag, does that mean both of you are suspects?"

Jonathon rolled his eyes. "*He* might be—*I* have an alibi." He smiled sweetly. "You. Now stop coming out with inane comments and eat your pie."

"What pie?" Mike's plate looked pristine.

Jonathon snickered. "I'd better eat mine quickly, before you decide you've not had enough."

Possession might be nine-tenths, but Mike was sneaky—and fast.

JONATHON LOCKED the Jag and walked along the drive to where Eddie was wiping down a Mercedes, with a deep toolbox at his side from which he took fresh rags.

He glanced up as Jonathon approached. "Hey. Don't tell me the old girl needs some TLC. She 'ad plenty less than two weeks ago." He narrowed his gaze. "You bin drivin' 'er through all them muddy country lanes? I keep tellin' ya—she's for lookin' at, not drivin'."

Jonathon laughed. "And where's the fun in that? No, the Jag's fine."

Eddie gave the Merc one last polish. "Class. Real class." He put down the rag and turned to Jonathon. "When you called an' said you needed to talk, I assumed it was the car. Whass' up?"

Jonathon took the Post-it from his wallet, where he'd written the brand of leather treatment. "Do you use this?" He handed it to Eddie.

He peered at it closely. "Sure. I tend to use it on the more high-end cars, or the older ones that need to keep their looks. Everyone else gets the bog-standard version."

"How many cars do you treat with this in Merrychurch? And more importantly, when did you last treat them?"

Eddie grinned. "Oh God. You're at it again, ain'tcha? Tryin' a bit of the old Poirot, are we? Or is

Father Brown more your speed?" He reached into the back pocket of his overalls and pulled out a village shop diary. "Okay. Let's see. You after cars that 'ave been done recently? 'Ow recent are we talkin'?"

"The weekend of the bonfire party, possibly. Maybe just before." It couldn't be much earlier than that for there still to be residue.

Eddie flipped over the pages. "Then we're talkin' four cars—an' that includes your Jag."

"When did you valet the car?" Jonathon had lost all track of time.

"The morning after the party. I came up special, 'cause of all the soot an' shit that was flyin' about." He gave a wry smile. "You didn't even notice me up at the 'all? An' you call yourself a detective." He tut-tutted. "That gardener of yours even gave me some coffee from 'is flask. Nice ol' bloke."

Well, there was Eddie's alibi, if he'd even needed one. "Who do the other cars belong to?"

"That MP fella, for one. Drives a Range Rover. *Niiice*. He don't drive it much, only when he's down 'ere. But it always needs a good clean 'cause he takes that dog of 'is everywhere. Bloody paw prints." Eddie glanced at the page. "I did 'is car on Saturday afternoon. Then there's the mayor. He's got a lovely BMW. Beautiful car. I worked on that… late Saturday afternoon. Yeah, that's right. They all came to your party, but the wife drove in her Ford Focus."

"And the last car?"

Eddie sighed. "Cream of the crop. A lovely Rolls. It's the one the mayor uses for all his official visits. Gorgeous paint job. They don't make 'em like that anymore."

"But who owns that?"

Eddie laughed. "*He* does. The mayor. I thought it was owned by the village council, but nah. That's what 'appens when you work your way up through the ranks of a company. If you make it to the top, you get to buy the company."

"And when did you valet the Rolls?"

Eddie checked the diary. "Early Sunday. Yours and the Rolls were the only jobs I did that day." He closed the slim book and replaced it in his pocket. "That it, then? You worked out which of 'em did it?"

"Hardly," Jonathon said, laughing. "Thanks for your help, Eddie." He held out his hand, and Eddie shook it. "And the next time you're up at the manor, I'll make sure to say something."

"You do that." Eddie started packing up his toolbox.

Jonathon walked listlessly down the drive. *So that's two people who might have come into contact with that treatment.* And both of them happened to be Merrychurch's most influential citizens.

Very helpful indeed.

"Hey. Wait a sec!"

Jonathon turned at Eddie's shout. "Yes?"

"I just thought of somethin'. Doris has started stockin' that leather stuff in the shop. I saw it there recently. So there could be loads more people who use it in the village."

"Really?" Visiting the shop to check had been on his list of things to do. At least Eddie had saved him a trip.

Eddie regarded him with wide eyes. "I know. There's me, offerin' a mobile valetin' service, providin' five-star treatment an' only the best products—an' now

every Tom, Dick, or Harry can get their 'ands on 'em."
He huffed. "Bleedin' liberty."

Jonathon resumed his walk to the Jag. Now that
Eddie had confirmed the ease of availability of the
leather treatment, it seemed as though they were no
better off.

Okay, not as helpful as I thought.

CHAPTER TWENTY-TWO

Thursday, November 16

MIKE HAD driven past the Cedars Retirement Home on many occasions, but this was the first time he'd visited it. The house was a Tudor-style construction with exposed beams and cream-colored plaster, and all the window frames were a light brown hue. Gardens surrounded it, and to the side of the house were french doors that led to a lawn where chairs had been set up to take advantage of the sun or shade. Not that anyone was out there, but Mike imagined it would be very pleasant when the weather allowed. Huge old trees cast long shadows over the grass, which would be welcome in the summer months, and the house had a peaceful ambiance.

"It's a beautiful place to live," Jonathon commented as Mike drove up to the gravel parking space at the front.

"Depends what it's like on the inside." Mike gazed at the windows, where faces could be seen. "Even a mink-lined prison is still a prison if you're stuck in there." His only experience with care homes had not been good. His granddad had ended up in one in North London, and while it had looked pleasant from the outside, the reality of living there had been entirely different.

"Let's wait and see." Jonathon patted his knee.

Mike switched off the engine, they got out, and he locked the 4x4. Inside the house, the hallway had a high ceiling, and thick dark blue carpet lay everywhere. Music played unobtrusively. Behind a desk sat a middle-aged woman in a dark blue dress suit so similar to the carpet that she was almost camouflaged. Mike wondered if it was intentional.

She greeted them with a smile. "Good morning, and welcome to the Cedars. How can I help you?"

"We have an appointment with one of your residents." Mike returned her smile. "Lily Rossiter."

The woman gave a nod of recognition. "I'll take you to her. She's expecting you." She came out from behind the desk and gestured toward the rear of the property. "She's in our sunroom." They followed her and entered a large room that looked out over the gardens. Several couches and chairs filled the light, airy space, and she led them to a high-backed chair near the window. On it sat a small elderly woman, gazing through the window, lost in thought, her white hair pulled back into a bun, wisps of it escaping and framing her head in a sort of halo. She wore a pink blouse, cream slacks, and a long cream cardigan, on which was attached a gold brooch. A pair of glasses rested on her lap, with her fingers curled around them. Beside her was a small table, barely visible beneath a stack of books.

As they approached, she turned her head carefully, and just like that, her air of introspection vanished. She smiled broadly at them. "Good morning. You must be Jonathon and Mike. Melinda has described you so well that I know who is who. Please forgive me if I don't stand to greet you. My legs are not what they used to be." She held out a wrinkled hand. "I'm Lily Rossiter. I don't get many visitors these days, except for Melinda, of course. Such a lovely woman."

Jonathon shook her hand, and then Mike did. The woman from reception indicated a small couch nearby, and between them, Mike and Jonathon shifted it closer to Lily's chair. Then the receptionist left them alone, after promising to provide them with tea.

"It's good of you to see us." Mike settled back on the couch, with Jonathon beside him.

"Nonsense. You're here for my totally selfish reasons. As soon as Melinda told me about you, I knew I had to get you here." Lily smiled. "My days are spent in reading and contemplation, so the chance to do a little code breaking? Heaven."

"It sounds like it was a fascinating life," Jonathon admitted.

Lily laughed. "Dear boy, Bletchley Park was merely the start. I was simply a cypher clerk there. *After* the war was when things got really… interesting." She gazed out the window. "One of these days, I should seriously consider writing my memoirs—not that I'd be allowed to, in all probability. Some of the events concerned have been sealed. I'll be long gone by the time *they* see the light of day."

Mike stared at her. "You worked in intelligence?"

She turned her head to face him, her eyes bright. "I couldn't possibly comment." They all laughed. "Seriously, though, I've had a wonderfully varied life, Mike. I've met so many fascinating people. Of course, I seem to have outlasted most of them." Lily looked up, then placed her glasses in their case. "Ah. Tea."

Once the tray had been left with them and Mike had poured out three cups, Lily relaxed into her chair. "Now. Tell me all about this code."

"Actually, we think there are two separate codes," Jonathon informed her. "One for numbers and another for letters."

"And how far have you got?"

"We've kind of cracked the letter code," Mike said hesitantly.

Lily arched her almost nonexistent eyebrows. "What does 'kind of' mean? Either you've decrypted it or you haven't."

"We matched up the code with amounts deposited in her account, after comparing one month's entries." Jonathon pulled his notebook from his pocket.

Lily sighed. "Then you haven't decrypted it, not fully. Show me what you have."

Jonathon opened the notebook and handed it over. On one page he'd written all the numbers, and above them the letters they knew so far.

R J O   W

0 1 2 3 4 5 6 7 8 9

Lily perused the two lines. "And this is based on…"

"Five different codes, with various combinations of letters. For example, where she'd written WRR, that day there was a payment for £500, and so on."

She held the notebook in both hands. "What you have here is a basic substitution cypher. You substitute numbers for a fixed set of letters. Obviously it's not the entire alphabet—you only need so many letters. This could be a word, a phrase, the first letter of each word in a line of poetry, Biblical text, a song...." Lily studied the page again. "If I could say something here? Zero *can* be zero—it can also be ten." She took a pen from the nearby table. "If I may?"

"Oh, please." Jonathon flashed Mike a grin. This was clearly fun.

Lily crossed out the zero and added it to the end of the line. "Now, let's write out those letters again."

1 2 3 4 5 6 7 8 9 0
J O   W   R

She gazed at it in satisfaction. "That's better. That RJ was bothering me. I think we're looking for a word, and no words begin with RJ. Moreover, a lot of words end in R. What are the most common letters before an R?"

Mike thought for a moment. "E? A? It's got to be a vowel at least."

"I agree." Lily gave the letters her full attention for a moment, and Mike found he was holding his breath. Lily tilted her head to one side. "Was she a whiskey drinker, perhaps?"

Jonathon blinked. "Yes. Whiskey and champagne. There were bottles of each at the cottage."

"And did she drink a particular brand?"

"Yes. Johnnie Walker Black Label."

Lily smiled before handing the notebook back to Jonathon. She sat back in her chair and finished her tea, her eyes focused on them, as though she was waiting for something.

Jonathon stared at the sheet, with Mike peering over his shoulder. Then Mike grinned.

"Got it." He was about to ask Jonathon for a pen, but Lily held one out to him. Mike scribbled in letters below the numbers.

1 2 3 4 5 67 8 9 0

J O H N W A L K E R

Lily's smile spoke of approval. "It had to be something she was familiar with. Maybe something she saw every day. Now... let's look at the second cypher."

"You're thinking she'll have used the same method? Substituting a letter for a number?" Jonathon opened the notebook to the next page, where he'd noted the numbers.

Lily nodded. "Of course, the easiest substitution is A equals one, B equals two and so forth."

"It can't be that," Jonathon argued. "One of the figures is thirty-one."

Lily beamed at him. "We'll make a cypher clerk out of you yet, my boy."

Jonathon's flush was adorable. "Then how do we decrypt it?"

"That's simple. Somewhere in her cottage is a key. As I said before, it could be lines from a song, a text from the Bible.... The most important thing to remember is that it will contain all the letters of the alphabet."

"How would a text work?"

"The first figure in the code would be the number of lines down, the second would be the number of letters across. What did *your* figures look like?" When Jonathon showed her the page, she frowned. "No. You're not looking for a large text. Maybe something a lot simpler." She flashed Mike a smile. "Would you pour me another cup of tea, please? I find tea helps me think."

Mike obliged, then handed her the cup.

"Now, on a different matter.... She wasn't demanding all her victims pay her the same amount. That points to one of three factors. One, how awful their secret was. Two, their social standing. And three, their ability to pay. Did any of the amounts change at all?"

Mike thought quickly. "One person was paying £250, but that was increased to £500. There could be more examples, but we didn't get a lot of time to look before the DI showed up and kicked us out."

Lily took a sip of tea before speaking. "Then something changed in that person's circumstances. We can discount the secret, so that leaves two and three. Did they come into more money? Did their social standing change, meaning they would pay more to keep this secret in the dark?" She stilled. "You say the police removed you from the premises? Oh dear. That won't do. You need to get back in there if you're to find that key."

"That could be... tricky," Mike admitted.

"You can do it. I'm sure," Lily said with fervor. "And now... tell me what you've discovered so far. I was most impressed by your efforts this summer, I must admit. Melinda told me everything." Her eyes twinkled. "Including the fact that you two are... how do they say it nowadays? An item?" She shook her head. "I am both heartened and disillusioned by what I see in the media. There appears to be progress and great steps toward a better future, and then... society goes out of its way to prove that there are just as many people out there filled with hatred and fear of what they do not understand."

"I keep telling Mike things *will* get better," Jonathon said in a low voice.

"That's because you're young. You see with eyes filled with optimism, whereas people of my generation tend to view the world more cynically." Lily smiled. "I like your way better."

Mike glanced at his watch. "Much as I would love to stay and talk, I have a pub to open."

"And it looks like I have to work out how to get us back into the cottage." Jonathon didn't look hopeful.

"I wish you both all the best for your endeavors. Please, come back and visit an old lady again? It's been delightful to share your company."

Mike got to his feet, leaned over, and kissed Lily's cheek. "We'll be back. Now we know *you're* here."

They said their goodbyes and left her in the sunroom, finishing her tea.

"What a lovely lady," Jonathon said as he fastened his seat belt.

Mike was in total agreement. "I'd bet that Lily was a real character when she was younger."

"She still is." Jonathon snickered. He mimicked her voice. "'Either you've decrypted it or you haven't.' I think she's fierce."

Mike wouldn't argue with that assessment either.

CHAPTER TWENTY-THREE

JONATHON LEFT Mike to open up the bar, then hurried out of the pub, his phone in hand.

Graham answered after a couple of rings. "What's up?"

"You know that DI said we can't go back to the cottage unless a police officer accompanies us?"

There was silence for a moment. "What are you looking for? And it had better not be those diaries, because they're all here at the station."

"No, not the diaries. By the way, have you cracked the codes yet?"

Graham snorted. "Like hell we have. We've got as far as you did. We matched up the deposits in her bank account with the entries in the diaries. So we know how much and when, but no idea who. Oh, and I checked with her bank. All the deposits were made in cash."

Jonathon had assumed that would be the case. "They're not going to leave a trail, are they? The thing is, Mike and I have an idea how to work out the second code. But to do that, we need to take another look at the cottage." He waited, hoping Graham would be reasonable.

"Assuming you do find whatever it is you're looking for… you would of course be sharing that information?" Before Jonathon could respond, Graham forged ahead. "Stupid question. Of course you would. Okay. Right now I'm up to my eyeballs in it, so there's no way I can go with you to the cottage. But the DI has had to go to Winchester, so the coast is clear if you wanna take a look. Just don't make it obvious you've been there, all right?"

"I think Mike's going to owe you several pints at this rate." Jonathon was buzzing.

"And I intend supping every last one of them." Graham sighed. "I must be nuts, letting you do this."

"It'll be worth it when you crack the case before the DI does."

Graham chuckled. "Oh God, I'd love to see his face if I did. Okay. Go do your thing, Sherlock. Will Watson be going with you?"

"He's behind the bar right now."

"Then be careful, please. You've heard about murderers returning to the scene of a crime? Don't end up being the second body in this case. One is more than enough, thank you very much."

"I'll be careful." Jonathon thanked him and disconnected the call, then quickly composed a text to Mike. *Going to the cottage with Graham's permission. Gonna find that key.*

Seconds later, Mike's reply pinged back. *Be careful.*

Jonathon smiled. He could take care of himself.

THERE WAS no one in sight as Jonathon parked the Jag in the lay-by. *Probably because it's too cold to be out here.* He locked the car and continued along the lane that led into the forest. Yellow-and-black police tape cordoned off the house, stretched between poles that surrounded the cottage. Jonathon ducked under it and approached the back door. The jam table was still there, but had been cleared of its contents. He peered at the ground—several large paw prints were still in evidence, although some had been obliterated by boot prints. *Coppers. Couldn't they see this is evidence?*

Then he noticed something else. The legs of the table were painted white, but in a few places the paint had been scratched off, revealing metal beneath. The markings appeared to follow a line, as though something had been dragged over them.

For the life of him, Jonathon couldn't remember if the table had been in that state before.

He pushed the door open, ducking beneath the tape yet again to gain entry. Little had changed inside since their last visit, except there appeared to be more light. Then he realized the afternoon sun was filtering through the side window, catching the motes of dust that danced lazily in its beams.

Jonathon went over to the empty chair and sat in it, peering below to see if there was a drawer. When he found one, he yanked it open, looking for the elusive key. What he found was another book of remedies. Useless.

Sunlight hit the jars and bottles on the shelves to his right, and he gazed at row upon row of herbs, plants, powders, and whatever else she kept up there. Each jar or bottle was labeled clearly, and for one moment,

Jonathon thought he was on to something. *Maybe the labels are the key?* He scanned them, mentally ticking off letters of the alphabet—until he recalled what Lily had said.

No. He was looking for something simpler.

Jonathon relaxed into the chair and let his attention drift around the room. *Something she'd be familiar with. Every letter of the alphabet. Something simple.*

Her block of knives sat empty, the knives clearly removed by the police. The work surfaces had been cleared too, as well as the kitchen table, except for the jars of ginger jam that still sat at one end of it. *Never mind the jam. Where's that key?*

He stared at the wall of shelves, interrupted only by a section of plain brick, where the cross-stitch hung in its frame. Sunlight played over the glass that covered it, and Jonathon could see where the surface was marred by fingerprints. *SOCO and their fingerprinting dust.* Then he looked again. The fingerprints followed two lines.

Two perfectly straight lines of distinct fingerprints.

Jonathon got up and walked over to the framed cross-stitch. A red fox, leaping over a snoozing beagle. Then he read the two lines stitched beneath.

The Quick Brown Fox Jumps Over The Lazy Dog.

Memories of his mother trying to teach him to type. Making him type that line over and over again, covering his hands so he couldn't see the keys. Insisting he practice, because that phrase contained every letter in the....

Jonathon grinned. He was looking at the key.

He fumbled in his jacket pocket for his notebook, the pages falling open to where he'd written down the codes.

35/21. Jonathon counted along each letter, until he reached the last one. 35 = G. He counted again, until he reached the twenty-first letter. 21 = S. Hastily he scribbled them down, until he had four sets of initials.

GS

DB

JB

BC

Jonathon stared at them, still grinning. *Gotcha.*

Finally he knew who Naomi Teedle had been blackmailing—well, her most recent victims, at any rate. All they had to do now was work out *why*.

He stuffed the notebook back into his jacket pocket and stood. There were a couple more hours before the pub would shut and he could talk to Mike, affording him time to go home and do some thinking. Jonathon opened the door and stepped out into the afternoon sun, being careful not to disturb the police tape.

He did *not* need DI Mablethorpe on his back.

Jonathon walked to the edge of the property, ducked beneath the tape, and stood there, gazing back at the cottage. *Why would someone returning to the UK rent a house in such an isolated location?* It was on the outer edge of the village, cut off from neighbors and amenities. Maybe, many years ago, a poacher had resided here, living off the land, staying out of the eagle eye of the manor house's occupant.

She obviously saw something about this place. But still... why hide away out here?

Then it came to him. Maybe Naomi Teedle had secrets of her own.

Jonathon shivered. The sun had disappeared behind a bank of cloud, and a chill had descended. He hurried back to the Jag, pulled out of the lay-by, and rejoined the road that skirted the village, heading home.

As he approached the lane that led to the manor house, a car coming in the other direction flashed its headlights. Jonathon pulled over to the side of the road as a Range Rover did the same.

Josh Brent wound down his window and leaned out, waving a gloved hand. "Have you recovered from the other night?"

It took Jonathon a moment to fathom his meaning. Then it became clear. The council meeting. "Yes. And I did as you suggested. I took a look at the houses on Turnbull Lane." He tried not to stare. Josh was wearing a thick roll-neck sweater in white, with a leather jacket over it.

Jonathon was doing his best not to drool.

Josh gave a satisfied smile. "*Now* you see why we were so frustrated. He can't be allowed to do that again." From beside him, a furry head popped up and a short bark rang out. Josh laughed. "Yes, Toby, we *are* going for that walk, I promise."

"Are you going to the forest?" Jonathon asked impulsively.

Josh shook his head. "I don't think I'll be taking that route again. It still gives me the creeps." He shuddered. "To think, when I stopped to buy that jar of jam, she could have been lying in there... dead."

It was on the tip of Jonathon's tongue to say *Sitting. She was* sitting *in there.* Then he remembered that not all the details of the crime scene had been made public.

"No, it's not a nice thought, is it?"

Josh's gaze met Jonathon's. "No, and it's not a nice place either. I wouldn't go there again, if I were you."

The hairs on Jonathon's arms prickled. "Unfortunately, I don't have much choice."

"And why is that?"

Jonathon gave him a polite smile. "I own it." And with that, he wound up the window, pulled away from the roadside, and turned left into the lane that eventually became his driveway.

He wanted to get into a warm interior and try to rid himself of the chill that was giving him goose bumps.

MIKE PUNCHED in the key code Jonathon had given him for the main door and stepped into the house. Everywhere was quiet—not really surprising, as it was gone midnight.

What *was* surprising was the lack of communication. He hadn't heard a peep from Jonathon since lunchtime, except for a brief text to inform him that Jonathon was home. Mike appreciated that. During the rest of the evening, he'd cast longing glances at his phone, debating whether to send a text, but had reasoned against it. *How does that look? Like I can't cope with not hearing from him? Like I'm worried about him?*

Mike let out a quiet laugh. Yeah, he had it bad, because it was all true.

He walked quietly through the house to Jonathon's bedroom. Janet's rooms were at the farthest point of the house, affording her some privacy. *Us, too, if it comes to that.* Light showed from under the bedroom door, and Mike opened it to find—

"What are you doing?"

Jonathon sat in the middle of the bed, papers spread out in a semicircle in front of him. He glanced up and grinned. "Wow. Is it that time already?"

Mike narrowed his gaze. "Tell me you did remember to eat something."

"Janet brought me sandwiches at…. Oh, I forget what time." Jonathon beckoned him over, still grinning. "Guess what I did today?"

Suddenly it all became clear. "You found the key, didn't you?" Mike shrugged off his jacket, placed it over the back of a chair, and climbed onto the bed. "So? Don't keep me in suspense. Who was she blackmailing?"

"Well, based only on people whose initials I know—and we'll have to consult the electoral roll if we're going to make sure this is accurate—I *think* we're looking at Grant Spencer, Debra Barton, Brian Calder and—this is where it gets tricky—either John Barton or Josh Brent. JB was all I had to go on."

Mike gaped at him. "The mayor's wife? What could Naomi possibly have on her? Or her husband? Or the MP?" He paused. "Grant Spencer. Isn't he the planning officer you met at the council meeting?"

Jonathon's eyes gleamed. "And Brian Calder is the developer who built those houses. Put those two names together and what have you got?"

"Possibly a dirty deal between the two. Calder pays Spencer to make sure the planning permission gets through?"

Jonathon gave an enthusiastic nod. "Only somehow Naomi gets wind of this and demands money to keep it quiet. From both of them."

"Did they pay her the same amount?"

"No. Calder was paying more. Remember what Lily said? Maybe the difference was based on their ability to pay. A planning officer can't make *that* much, surely."

Mike smiled. "Whereas a property developer?" Then he had another thought. "If it *is* Josh Brent, and not the mayor, that also means two blackmail victims were seen near the cottage the day of the murder."

Jonathon collected up the papers. "We still need to check the registers for anyone else with those initials before we take another step."

"And you're not going to have time for any of that," Mike announced. "Because tomorrow we're heading to London for your birthday weekend."

Jonathon blinked. "Oh. I'd forgotten all about that." His smile lit up his eyes. "So much to look forward to." He held the sheets of paper against his chest. "There are so many things buzzing through my head right now."

Mike stretched out a hand, took the papers from him, and placed them on the bedside cabinet. "Enough. You need to switch your brain off for a while."

Jonathon laughed. "But I'm too excited to sleep."

Mike crawled over to where he sat, leaned in, and nuzzled Jonathon's neck with his beard. "Who said anything about sleeping?" he murmured.

CHAPTER TWENTY-FOUR

Friday, November 17

MIKE WATCHED anxiously as Jonathon gazed at their hotel room. This was decidedly new territory. Going away for a weekend? Couples did that, right? Mike had spent hours online trying to find the perfect hotel, one that would capture the essence of what he wanted out of the weekend. Now that they were standing in a beautiful room, with an amazingly huge bed—and yes, there were chocolates on the pillows—he hoped he'd got it right.

Because the whole room spelled *Romance*.

"Well?"

Jonathon turned to him, beaming. "It's wonderful." He went over to the door that led to their bathroom and peered inside. "Oh, nice. There's a freestanding bath that's more than big enough, and a walk-in shower."

Mike arched his eyebrows. "Big enough for what?" Like he had to ask.

Jonathon laughed. "Yeah, right." He gazed around their room once more. "I have to admit, when you told the taxi driver to take us to the Soho hotel, this was not what I imagined." His eyes twinkled. "Soho conjures up memories of gay bars and clubs in an area a whole lot less swanky. This is gorgeous." He walked up to Mike, locked his arms around his neck, and kissed him, taking his time.

"So, what do you want to do next?" Mike said as they broke the kiss. "There's plenty of time before dinner to go for a walk or do some sightseeing or shopping."

"I had something different in mind," Jonathon murmured before pressing his lips to Mike's neck and gently sucking the skin.

"Oh? And what was that?" Concentrating while Jonathon did that was next to impossible. How Mike even managed to form words was a miracle.

Jonathon locked gazes with him. "Christening the bed." He chuckled. "After the bath. Or the shower. I'm easy."

Mike snickered. "I'm saying nothing." He caught his breath as Jonathon unhurriedly slid to his knees and unbuttoned Mike's jeans. "Did you ever stop... and think that we do this... a lot?"

Jonathon stared up at him, grinning. "And your point is?"

When he put it like that....

MIKE TOOK a long drink from his pint and let out a sigh of contentment. "I miss London. More specifically, I miss *this*." He gestured to the gay bar, packed to the rafters with men of all ages and sizes. The music was loud, but it hadn't reached earsplitting volume, so that was fine. Everywhere he looked, guys were chatting, laughing, drinking cocktails, kissing....

Yeah. That was what he missed. The freedom to be himself.

"We're a long way from Merrychurch," he murmured.

"Like we said, the chances of someone opening a gay bar in Merrychurch are about as likely as a Jewish Pope." Jonathon smiled. "I know what you mean, though. Canal Street in Manchester is like this." He sipped his strawberry mojito, then grinned. "Maybe we need to do this on a regular basis. Find ourselves a cheap hotel—"

"In London?" Mike snorted.

"—or an Airbnb for the weekend," Jonathon continued. "Then we spend a couple of nights just... having a good time."

It was a tempting thought. "I used to love Friday nights in Soho," Mike confessed. "There was always something going on. You never knew what would happen from one weekend to the next."

"Or who you'd meet." Jonathon nudged him with his elbow. "Look. That booth in the far corner."

Mike followed his gaze, squinting. "Who? The guy sitting on his own? Do you know—?" The rest of his sentence died in his throat. "Isn't that—?"

"Grant Spencer, Merrychurch planning officer," Jonathon whispered, barely audible above the music.

Grant didn't appear happy to be there. He was staring into his pint, his shoulders hunched.

"What is he doing here?" Mike gazed at Grant in consternation. "I had no idea he was gay."

"I was thinking more along the lines that he's bi, seeing as he's married."

Mike blinked. "Oh." Then he froze as a guy emerged from the toilets and joined Grant, sitting beside him. "Well, now. The plot has truly thickened." The two men appeared to be in deep discussion about something, and judging from their expressions, it wasn't good.

"Who is that? Do you know him?"

Mike sighed. "*That* is Brian Calder." He turned to face Jonathon. "Oh boy."

"Oh my." Jonathon frowned. "Why do you—?" His mouth fell open, and Mike jerked his head to see what he was missing.

Brian and Grant were apparently on very good terms, judging by the way Brian had his arm around Grant's shoulders. The kiss they shared spoke even louder, however.

"I think I'm moving those two to the top of the list," Jonathon murmured.

"Ben didn't see either of them near the cottage," Mike reminded him.

"And Ben himself admitted he didn't see *everyone* that morning." Jonathon seemed unable to tear his gaze away from the couple. "He did, however, mention a pair of walkers with their hoods up. That *could* have been those two. I mean, look at them. They're obviously upset about something. What if one of them committed the murder and the other found out?" He sagged against the padded back of the seat. "Think about it. They both have a lot to lose. Naomi could have been blackmailing them about the deal they pulled over on the housing development, or the fact that they're having an affair—because I think it's a pretty safe bet Grant's wife is clueless."

"There's another possibility. What if one of them decided to go ahead with the second development because she's dead, and the other thinks it's too soon? Or maybe hates the idea?" Mike watched the couple, noting how Grant had relaxed, with Brian's arm still around him. "This is not a new occurrence. Those two have been together for a while."

"How can you tell?"

Mike smiled at him. "Experience. But right now, I'm thinking we should get out of here before they spot us."

"Agreed." Jonathon drained the rest of his cocktail and stood.

Mike left what remained of his pint and joined him, casting a final glance toward the corner—

And met Grant's stricken gaze as he walked toward the bar.

Shit.

Mike put his arm around Jonathon's back and guided him out of the bar. "Oh, well. We'll deal with those two when we go home. Right now, I'm taking you to dinner."

Where I'll try my hardest not to think about what this all means.

JONATHON CLOSED his eyes and lost himself to his senses: the silky feel of the water against his skin; his head resting on Mike's shoulder; Mike's chest against his back, solid and comforting; and Mike's hand as he languidly rubbed a washcloth over Jonathon's belly and chest, the scent of lavender invading his nostrils.

"This is bliss," he murmured. "We need one of these at the manor."

Mike chuckled, and it reverberated through him. "We'd never get out of it."

"It's the perfect place for thinking."

"Oh, is that what we're doing? Thinking?" Mike kissed his temple. "Funny. I thought we were—"

"Hush. That comes later. Right now, I'm thinking." Jonathon was trying to work out what was eluding him. Because something was niggling away at him, the feeling that he'd missed something....

Something important.

But whatever it was remained annoyingly out of reach.

Jonathon sighed. "What's the plan for tomorrow?"

"It's your birthday, so whatever you wish. The only fixed point is the theater in the evening. Apart from that, you have a whole day in London." Mike's arms surrounded him, a cage of comforting flesh. "Is there anything you'd like to do? Some place you'd like to go?"

"Well...." Jonathon twisted to look at Mike. "There *is* the Photography Centre at the V&A Museum. I haven't been there for ages, and it's one of my favorite places. You don't have to come with me if you don't want." Jonathon knew from past experience how long he could spend wandering from exhibit to exhibit.

"Did you see there's an exhibition of Wim Wender's polaroids, at the Photographers' Gallery in Soho?" When Jonathon stared at him in surprise, Mike flushed. "I took a look online a few days ago to see what was on that might interest you."

The fact that he'd done that only confirmed what Jonathon knew with all his heart. "I love you," he said softly.

Mike cupped his cheek and kissed him, languidly and thoroughly, as they moved together, shifting positions, water spilling over the sides onto the tiled floor.

No more thinking.

Saturday, November 18

"WELL? DID you guess who the murderer was?" Jonathon demanded as they left the theater, the people around them discussing the play's ending. When Mike said nothing, Jonathon speared him with a look. "You did, didn't you?"

Mike laughed. "I hate to disillusion you, but I have a theory about that play. You know how they always ask you not to reveal the ending? I think that's because virtually every single one of them could be the murderer and they have several scripts to work with. Who it is depends on which performance you watch." Mike smirked. "Oh, come *on*. It's been running continuously since 1952. Do you *really* think every theatergoer who's ever seen the play has kept quiet about the murderer? Because if so, your faith in human nature is amazing."

"Well, my guess was totally wrong. Not that I'm surprised. You had that collection of people, all with evidence pointing against them, most with good motives…." Jonathon sighed. "Rather like what we have. Except the only motive I can see so far is that she was blackmailing them."

"How about we go grab a bite to eat and read through your notebook to see what we *do* have so far?" Mike's eyes sparkled. "You did bring it with you, didn't you?"

Jonathon bit his lip. "It's at the hotel. I brought it just in case."

"What—just in case we had a spare moment with nothing to do?" Mike chuckled. "Then here's Plan B. We go back to the hotel, order something from room service, and take it from there?"

Jonathon narrowed his gaze. "There's only one part of Plan B that worries me—the take-it-from-there part. Because I think we both know where that might lead."

They reached the main road, and Mike stuck out his hand to hail a taxi. "I tell you what. I promise not to start anything until we're in bed with the lights out."

Jonathon laughed. "I'll believe that when I see it."

A taxi pulled up to the curb, and they climbed in the back. Mike called out their destination, then settled against the leather seat and snickered. "Besides, that'll be quite novel for us. We've already christened the shower, the bath, the couch...."

Jonathon smacked him on the leg before sneaking a glance at the taxi driver in the rearview mirror. Fortunately he was concentrating on the traffic.

And Jonathon was thinking about that list of suspects.

JONATHON TOOK a sip of champagne. "This was a lovely idea," he confessed.

"We couldn't let your birthday pass without having a glass or two." Mike topped up his champagne flute, then held up his own. "Happy birthday, sweetheart."

Jonathon clinked their glasses. "Thank you. I don't think I've ever had such an enjoyable birthday."

Mike replaced the bottle in the ice bucket. "Now... where did we get up to?"

Jonathon leaned back against the mound of pillows and scanned his notes in his lap. "Of the five people

Ben recalls seeing near the cottage, three of them have a possible motive. Well, maybe two. I really can't see Nathan killing her."

"That doesn't mean we discount him."

Jonathon jerked his head up. "We discounted Rachel."

"Yeah, because... she's Rachel."

He had to admit, Mike had a point. Rachel had no motive, and more to the point, they knew her. "George Tyrell doesn't have a motive, but we can't cross him off the list. Of all the dogs we've encountered, Max comes closest to those paw prints."

"That leaves Debra Barton and either her husband or Josh Brent." Mike grinned. "You know what I'm thinking. Your father's face if it was Brent...."

Jonathon sighed. "Wishful thinking does *not* mean he did it. And his dog, Toby, has little paws, so the prints weren't his. But if Naomi *was* blackmailing them, that's a good motive for seeing her off. And don't forget what Jason said. The day after Naomi died, his mother was talking on the phone to someone, saying how it was a great weight off them. Plus that 'Ding, dong, the witch is dead' comment."

"Of course. That does sound like the reaction of someone whose blackmailer just died. And then there's the whole matter of whoever she was speaking to. That leaves Brian Calder and Grant Spencer, with more than one strong motive—but neither was sighted near the cottage, except if they turn out to be our mystery walkers."

"Not to mention that all those who *were* there deny going inside."

"Well, *somebody* did." Jonathon tapped his notes. "There are fingerprints, DNA, and residue. All we have to do is find out who they belong to." He huffed. "There must be *something* that shows one of our suspects went into that cottage. Having said that, even if they *did* go inside, it doesn't prove they killed her."

Mike chuckled. "Think again. They *all* denied doing that. Someone is lying."

Jonathon fell silent, mentally seeing the inside of the cottage. *What am I missing?* He closed his eyes and tried to picture the room exactly as it had been that morning.

He jumped when Mike gently touched his hand. "Bloody hell!" Jonathon opened his eyes and gave him a mock glare. "That could have been nasty. I might have spilled my champagne."

Mike snickered. "Heaven forbid. I only wanted to ask what you'd like to do tomorrow morning. We don't have to leave right after breakfast, and there are trains running frequently."

Jonathon had been thinking about this. "Would you mind if we checked out after breakfast?"

Mike smiled. "You want to go home and do a little investigating, don't you?"

"Am I that transparent?" Jonathon's chest tightened. It felt wrong, especially after Mike had gone to all the trouble of arranging the weekend.

Mike leaned in and kissed him softly on the lips. "Nope. You're adorable." He took Jonathon's notebook and placed it on the bedside cabinet.

"Are we done for the night?" Jonathon couldn't take his eyes off Mike's broad chest as he knelt up on the bed, casually unbuttoning his black shirt.

Mike dropped the shirt to the floor. "Sleuthing, yes. As for what's left of the night, it can last as long as we want." He shifted on the bed to straddle Jonathon as he undressed him.

A happy sigh slid from Jonathon's lips. "We can sleep on the train."

CHAPTER TWENTY-FIVE

Sunday, November 19

"BUT... YOU'RE not here. You're in London!" Abi stared at them, ignoring the pint she was pulling.

Mike laughed. "In that case, I'm a hologram, and you're about to pour most of Seth's pint down the drain."

"What? Shit." She let go of the pump and glared at the overflowing glass.

"Hey, it's fine." Seth held out his hand and took the glass.

Abi wiped her hands before folding her arms. "What are you guys doing here? I didn't expect you until this evening." She reached behind her to remove a Post-it from the wall. "You had a call from Constable Billings. He said he didn't want to disturb you while you were... away, but to tell you the daughter is arriving Monday. If that makes any sense."

"Naomi's daughter," Jonathon murmured from beside him.

"I suppose you'll want to get behind here now." Abi didn't look all that happy about the prospect.

Suddenly Mike realized he wasn't happy about it either.

"Well, to be honest, I was gonna ask you if you could carry on—"

"Sure, sure." Abi beamed. "I could do with the money, to be frank."

"Then you carry on, while I go and make us some lunch." Mike headed for the kitchen, with Jonathon following. Once inside, he closed the door behind them and went to the fridge. "There's some macaroni and cheese left over from yesterday, if you fancy that. I can shove it in the microwave."

"Sounds good." Jonathon sat at the table, his hands clasped. "Her poor daughter. A day of traveling to get here, and we still can't tell her who murdered her mother. After two weeks."

"Which means Graham will be getting it in the neck from the DI," Mike added gloomily as he placed the white earthenware dish into the microwave, after covering it with wrap.

The door opened and Abi stuck her head around it. "Er, Mike? Someone out here wants to talk to you. I told him you're not working today, but he's really insistent."

"Who is it?"

"Grant Spencer."

Mike flashed Jonathon a glance. "Tell him to come in here." When she frowned, he nodded reassuringly. "It'll be okay just this once. Let's not make a habit of it, all right?"

"Sure." Abi withdrew.

Mike didn't sit but waited, his body tense. He'd known Grant would be along at some point, but they'd barely been in the pub five minutes. *He must have been waiting for us to show up.*

A quiet knock at the door and Grant entered, his face pale. "Hey, Mike. Jonathon. Have you got a minute?"

Mike gestured to an empty chair. "Take a seat. I'm in the middle of rustling up some lunch. I don't need to ask why you're here, do I?"

Grant dropped into the chair, not meeting their gazes. "Not really. Got the shock of my life when I saw you in that bar. I… I came to ask you not to tell anyone." His breathing grew slightly erratic. "No one can know about this."

"How long has it been going on? You and Brian?"

Grant swallowed. "About four years. My… my wife has no idea."

"And which came first?" Jonathon asked. "The affair, or the deal where you agreed to approve the planning permission for Turnbull Lane, in spite of public feeling on the issue?"

There was no mistaking Grant's reaction. His face whitened. "I… I don't know what you're talking about."

Mike snorted. "Give it up, Grant. That approval has *dodgy* written all over it. *That's* why you don't want anyone to know about it. Yes, your marriage might be over, but people might also start to wonder about a development that no one ever believed would gain approval but which did, by some miracle. Now, if it turned out that the developer and the planning officer were in bed together—literally—questions would be asked." He shook his head. "It was just bad luck us seeing you both last night. Wasn't it? You'd managed to keep it under wraps this long. You must have thought you'd gotten away with it when Naomi Teedle died."

"What?" Grant's eyes widened.

"So how did she find out? More importantly, which secret was she blackmailing you for?" Mike leaned on the table, looking Grant in the eye. "Or was it both?"

"Blackmail?" Grant croaked.

Mike nodded. "We know you were paying her every month. Cash deposits, paid into her bank account." He glanced at Jonathon. "What date were Grant's payments due on?"

Jonathon pulled his notebook from his jacket and consulted it. "The twenty-fifth."

Grant sagged into the chair. "How the hell did you know that? She... she didn't write it down anywhere, did she?"

"Only in code." Jonathon put the notebook on the table. "Suppose you tell us how this all got started."

Mike took a glass from the cabinet, filled it with water, then placed it in front of Grant. "I think you might need this."

Grant huffed. "A whiskey is what I need." Nevertheless, he drank half of it. "You were right. We'd been... together about a year, when Brian came up with the idea. There was nothing wrong with the plans, nothing that would get them rejected. It was just that..."

"People didn't think they were quite... Merrychurch," Jonathon suggested.

"Exactly." Grant's expression grew gloomy. "There had already been a lot of objections. So... I agreed to approve them. When people started kicking up a fuss, I got a mate of mine at county level to look over the plans. He said he couldn't see any reason why county wouldn't approve them too, if it came to an appeal. It wasn't exactly an official statement, but I put the word around that an appeal would be a waste of time, and the development went ahead. We thought we'd gotten away with it. And then…." He took another drink of water. "Brian got a letter from Naomi Teedle. Saying she wanted to meet with him, and how it would be inadvisable to ignore her. So, he went to the cottage. Turns out, she'd been in London one weekend, shopping for her daughter's birthday present, and…."

"She saw you together," Mike concluded. "And then she put two and two together."

"Yeah." Grant wrapped his hands around the glass, his shoulders hunched over.

Mike went quiet for a moment, before shaking his head. "Nah. I don't buy it. The chances of her happening to be in the *exact* same spot as you two—and in London too—have to be astronomical. I mean, I know she said she was a jammy sod, but even so…."

"Well, how else do you account for her being there?" Jonathon demanded.

Mike rubbed his beard. "I think it's more likely that she'd already observed something in the village. Maybe you two weren't as discreet as you thought, and she caught a glimpse. Maybe it happened more than once, and it piqued her interest."

Grant jerked his head up. "Oh my God," he said softly.

"You think she followed them, don't you?" Jonathon stared at Mike.

Mike nodded. He addressed Grant. "Did you drive or go by train?"

"Train. I couldn't take my car, and it was too risky both of us going in his." His eyes widened. "The station. The bloody station! I *thought* I saw her there as I was getting on the train, but it was only a fleeting glance. And then I forgot all about her. I was too busy thinking about meeting Brian." His face was a picture of misery.

"So Brian goes to see her, and she demands money," Mike stated, getting the conversation back on track.

Grant nodded. "What we didn't expect was that she'd demand money from me too. Except *I* was paying so she wouldn't tell my wife about the affair. Bloody witch," he said bitterly. "Getting money out of both of us. I suppose I should have been relieved she didn't soak me for all that much. There was no way I could have afforded a huge sum anyway. But Brian? He got off worse than me."

"So when she was found dead, it must have been a huge relief. No more blackmail." Jonathon frowned. "Then what were you and Brian discussing on Friday night? Because it was obvious you weren't happy."

A sigh shuddered out of Grant. "As soon as we learned she was dead, Brian decided to go ahead with the second development. I felt it was too soon after the first one, that people would start talking again, but no, he said he was going for it. Now there was no one in our way." Grant swallowed hard. "About that—"

With a burst of clarity, Mike saw what lay at the root of Grant's unhappiness and desperation. "Does Brian have an alibi for that morning?" he asked quietly. "Do you know where he was? Because that's what you're afraid of, isn't it? You don't know for certain that he didn't kill her."

Grant stared at him with wide eyes, nodding sluggishly. "He said... he said he was at home. Only, I know he wasn't. I went for a jog that morning, except it was an excuse. I often ran past his place in the hopes I'd see him. Pathetic, isn't it?"

"Not really," Jonathon murmured. "I've been known to do the same thing myself. Love makes you do funny things."

"So you ran past Brian's place. And?"

"His car wasn't there. And he was nowhere to be seen. So I came home."

"This might sound like a funny question, but what car does Brian drive?" Jonathon asked.

"A Mercedes. He loves that car."

Mike gave an internal sigh. *So maybe Ben did miss someone after all.* "Did you tell Brian you'd been to his house?"

Grant swallowed. "I couldn't. All I kept thinking was, what if he *did* kill her?"

"Of course, the police might think *you've* got a pretty good motive for killing her too," Mike suggested. "And that you're merely shifting the blame onto Brian."

Grant froze. "God, no! I was home, with my wife... apart from that forty-five minutes when I went jogging."

"Did you see anyone while you were out who could corroborate that?"

Grant frowned, but then he nodded violently. "I saw Paul Drake. He was driving along the lane in that truck of his. He'd been to pick up pig feed. He asked if I wanted a lift. I laughed and said that rather defeated the purpose. Then he drove off."

"You haven't come right out and asked Brian if he killed her, have you?" Jonathon said quietly.

Grant gaped at him. "But… I mean… I love him, but… you never know what a person is capable of, do you? And besides, if I don't ask him, he doesn't have to deny it." He sighed. "Which made perfect sense to me at one time, but now? Not so much." He met Mike's gaze. "Should I tell the police?"

Mike considered the question. "Right now, the only evidence against him is the fact that she was blackmailing him. There's no evidence to put him at the crime scene…."

"Maybe, maybe not," Jonathon muttered.

Mike knew he was referring to the leather treatment. It was a possibility. "Tell Graham Billings," he said at last. "Tell him everything. And you'd better come clean about the dodgy dealings too." He gave Grant a frank stare. "You *do* realize your wife is going to find out at some point?"

"Yeah. I'll deal with that when it happens." Grant got to his feet and held out his hand. Mike rose and shook it. "Thanks, Mike. You too, Jonathon. I knew I had to say something. And now I've told someone, it'll get easier the second time." He drew in a deep breath. "I'll leave you to your lunch." And with that, he left the room.

"Lunch?" Mike groaned. "I didn't turn on the bloody microwave." He hit the buttons and the whirring started. Mike sank into his chair. "Well. At least that's one person we can cross off the list."

"You think he's telling the truth?"

Mike nodded. "Mind you, that's the ex-copper in me talking." Then he let out a wry chuckle. "The inhabitants of Merrychurch are going to have a field day with this. Another gay affair. Makes you wonder just how many people in this village are hiding their sexuality."

"Which is why I'm never going to hide," Jonathon announced quietly. "And why my father is *not* going to get his own way. Take me or leave me—this is me."

Which is why I love him.

Mike gazed at the kitchen table and sighed. "I wish Abi would tidy up after herself. I left this clear on Friday before we left." He picked up the empty toast rack and the butter knife, and placed them next to the sink. "Put the butter and jam in the fridge, would you?"

"That's it!"

Mike turned to find Jonathon staring at the jar of mango-and-peach jam. "Yes, that's jam," he said in amusement.

Jonathon let out an exasperated sigh. "You don't understand. I've been racking my brains for days now, trying to work out what has been puzzling me. And here it is." He held aloft the jar. "I know who was in that cottage," he announced triumphantly.

Mike arched his eyebrows. "And? Don't stop there. Who was it?"

"George Tyrell. Remember that ginger jam he said he bought from the table outside? Well, he couldn't have."

"Why not?"

"Because that variety was never outside, that's why. She'd only recently made it. In fact, it was so new, she hadn't even made up a fancy label to print out, like the others." Jonathon grinned. "The only way he could have taken a jar of that jam was if he was inside the cottage."

"She might have brought one out for him."

Jonathon arched his eyebrows. "Then why did he say he never saw her? He lied. And something else. He tied Max up outside so he could go in. I've just realized what those scratches were on the table legs. They were caused by that heavy chain leash of his, rubbing against them. I'll bet you anything you like that the police could find traces of that white paint in among the links." His eyes widened. "Oh. And another thing. He comes from the same city as Naomi. They both lived in Nottingham."

"Sure, but not at the same time. She had to have been immigrating to Australia by the time he was born."

"It's still something, right?" Jonathon pulled out his phone.

"What are you doing?"

"Calling Graham. Because there's one thing he can do to clear all this up, and that's take George down to the police station and take his fingerprints. If they match—bingo. And if I tell Graham everything I've come up with, he's got enough evidence to warrant taking George in." Jonathon scrolled through and dialed.

Mike's hunger was forgotten as he listened to Jonathon's animated conversation. It all made sense—except for one thing. When Jonathon finished and disconnected the call, Mike sighed.

"You do know it's only a theory, right?"

"Graham seemed happy with it."

"There's one thing you haven't considered." When Jonathon frowned, Mike rolled his eyes. "Motive? What's his motive? Why on earth should he want to kill her?"

Jonathon tucked his phone into his jacket pocket. "Let's go find out."

"What?" Mike gaped at him.

"I'm serious. We know he was inside that cottage. Let's go ask him why." Jonathon waved his hand. "Don't worry. I'll tell him we've informed the police, so he'll know it's only a matter of time before someone turns up to ask a few questions. That way, we won't be in any danger. That is, if he *is* the killer." He pulled on his jacket, then stared at Mike. "Well? What are you waiting for? Are you coming with me or not?"

Mike chuckled. "Oh, I'm coming with you, if only to stop you from doing anything stupid. But when we get there, why don't you let me ask the questions? I've had more experience than you, trying to get the truth out of people. It's not as if he's going to hold his hands up and say, 'It's a fair cop, guv. I done it. Bring on the handcuffs.'"

Jonathon huffed. "Fine." As they headed for the door, he muttered, "You always have to play the experience card, don't you?"

Mike laughed. "Trust me. If we're ever in a situation where a knowledge of photography, cameras, depth of field, et cetera, is required, *then* you can take the lead."

Jonathon snorted. "I can see it now. We're about to be battered to death by someone wielding a tripod."

Mike was still laughing as they left the pub.

JONATHON RANG the doorbell and stepped back. From within came a deep bark. "Well, Max is home."

Seconds later the door opened, and George stood there, holding a tea towel. He gave them a warm smile. "Well, hello again. Is it time for more cocktails?"

"Not exactly. Can we come in? There's something we'd like to talk to you about." Jonathon gestured to Mike. "You know Mike from the pub?"

"Our ex-policeman. Only by reputation." George frowned. "You both seem rather serious."

"That's because we're freezing," Mike offered.

George's eyes widened and he stood aside. "Of course. Come on in." Once inside, he closed the door behind them and led them into the cozy living room, where a fire was roaring in the hearth. Max lay on the rug, his paws crossed under his chin. He lifted his head and let out a soft woof when they entered.

"Sit down, please." George waited until they were on the couch before sitting in the armchair. "Now, what's this all about?"

Before Mike could say a word, Jonathon surged ahead. "I felt it only fair to give you a heads-up. The police will probably want to take your fingerprints."

George stilled. "My…. Why should they want to do that?"

"To eliminate you from their inquiries," Mike said calmly. "Now that they have reason to believe you were in Naomi Teedle's cottage the morning she died."

Jonathon watched George's face, noting the pallor that stole across his features, making his blue eyes appear all the more startling.

"But… I told you. I never went inside."

"Yes, I know," Jonathon said patiently, "but that jar of ginger jam says otherwise."

George frowned. "I bought it. From the table outside."

Jonathon let out a sigh of disappointment. "It was never outside. It wasn't even on the list on that clipboard. That was a new variety she'd only recently come up with. You took a jar in case you were seen near the cottage. There was no way you could have known that it would only serve to prove you went inside. And that's not the only evidence the police have."

George's face was like ash, and Jonathon's heart sank. *I hate being right.* What made his stomach clench was that he liked George.

"Didn't you think to wipe the doorknob as you left? The police have a couple of very good prints." Mike regarded him carefully. "Or maybe you weren't thinking clearly by that point. Not that it matters now. Once they can place you at the scene, it will all come out. Including… why."

George stared at them in silence, before nodding. "Oh, well, that's it, isn't it? How can I ever have thought for *one second* that I'd get away with it?" He put his head in his hands. "These last two weeks, I felt like I was going to explode. The effort it took to act normal that night you came here. When you'd gone, I had the worst migraine ever." He shuddered. "Thank God. Now I can breathe."

Jonathon couldn't believe how quickly George had caved. Then he reasoned that the pressure had to have been enormous.

George straightened and looked Mike in the eye. "You're right, of course. I never thought about prints. I mean, it's not as if I went there to kill her. I never meant for this to happen. And when it was all over, all I could think about was getting out of there." He bowed his head. "All I wanted from her was the truth," he said softly.

"About what?" Mike's tone was almost gentle.

George jerked his head up. "I just wanted to know why she killed my twin brother!"

CHAPTER TWENTY-SIX

JONATHON STARED at George, his mind still trying to process that statement.

Mike appeared to recover more quickly. "Okay," he said dazedly. "I think you'd better start at the beginning."

George barked out a nervous laugh. "I still can't believe she was right here, in Merrychurch. I mean, of all the places to end up…. And I wouldn't have known it was her for certain if it hadn't been for your bonfire party." His gaze flickered to the drinks cabinet. "Do you think…?"

Jonathon got up and went over to it. "In the circumstances? Yes, I think we could all do with a drink." He pulled down the flap, chose three glasses, and poured a small measure of brandy into each. Jonathon handed the glasses to Mike and George, then retook his seat.

George took a sip and shivered.

Jonathon regarded him thoughtfully. "When I asked you the other day if you were an only child, your answer puzzled me at the time. You said, 'Yeah, there's just me now.' Is that what you meant? That you had a twin?"

"Not exactly." George took another sip and sighed. "I really do need to start at the beginning, which for the purposes of this story, is when I was twenty-eight. Back then, I was working for the council and living in a flat in Nottingham, not that far from my parents. I had a sister, Marie, but... I'd grown up hardly ever seeing her. She'd been diagnosed with a severe mental disorder years before, and when it got too much to take care of her, Mum and Dad found this great place. She was well looked after, honestly, and it really was the best place for her."

Jonathon waited, sipping his brandy.

"Anyway, some of the guys from work decided to go on holiday to Spain and asked if I'd like to join them. I loved the idea because I'd never been abroad. Of course, I needed a passport, so I went to see my parents for my birth certificate. Funny thing, that. I'd had no need of it until then. Except when I asked them, they weren't happy. I soon found out why." George took another drink before continuing. "They weren't my parents at all. They were my grandparents, and my sister in that home? She was my mother. It turned out her mental health issues were related to drugs she'd used in her teens and early twenties. Then I got the whole story. How she'd run away from home when she was fourteen, when she discovered she was pregnant. How she'd moved into what they called 'student accommodation' but what sounded more like a squat. How she gave birth to me. That was when my grandparents stepped in. No way would they let her bring up a child, of course. But they couldn't bear the thought of giving me up for adoption, so they decided to bring me up themselves and tell me Marie was my sister."

"That sounds like a very traumatic discovery," Mike said quietly. "Basically, your whole life was turned upside down."

George nodded. "Of course, once I knew the truth, I had to see her. It was so weird, sitting with this forty-two-year-old... stranger I'd always thought of as my sister, and suddenly everything had changed."

"Was she pleased you knew the truth?"

George studied his glass. "It was hard to tell. Most of the time, what she said didn't make much sense. But there were a few things that kept recurring. She talked about the young midwife, Jane, who turned up to deliver me. Kept talking about being Mr. Spock's understudy, and of course, that sounded like sheer nonsense. Something else about fireworks. But then there was this one day when she looked me in the eye and said in a voice that turned my blood to ice, 'Look at me. That nurse ruined my life. I've never been the same since she killed my baby.'"

Jonathon leaned forward. "Could that have been her illness talking, do you think? Could she have imagined it?"

"That's what I thought, to be honest," George admitted, "but it was a story she kept repeating. What it boiled down to was this. Mum wasn't exactly in a good place the night I was born. She'd... taken something. To put it bluntly, I think she was off her head. My grandparents think she didn't even know she was going into labor, which sounds amazing, but you hear similar stories all the time, don't you? *But...* she swore she heard *two* babies crying. Definitely two. Then there was just one. This Jane hands her a baby all wrapped up. One baby." He shivered, then looked at Jonathon. "And before you ask, the first time I heard that? Yeah, I thought she'd imagined the whole thing."

"You obviously changed your mind," Mike remarked.

George sighed heavily. "Yeah, well, when she kept saying the same thing, over and over—that I'd had a twin, and that this midwife had… killed it somehow, whether by accident or on purpose…. Then yes, you start to wonder."

"You said your twin brother," Jonathon interjected. "How could you know it was a boy?"

"Just a feeling," George said with a shrug. Then he gave a nervous laugh. "My grandma told me when I was little, I used to have an imaginary friend. I called him my brother. Kinda spooky, right? Who knows? Maybe I did." He took another sip of brandy. "Anyway, after a few years of hearing this tale, I decided to see if there was any truth in it. I used my birth certificate to try to locate the cottage hospital in Nottingham where Jane would have worked, but it no longer existed. There was no one of Jane's description working as a nurse or a midwife in Nottingham—"

"Description?" Jonathon frowned. "How could you know what she looked like?"

George gave him a sheepish glance. "All I had to go on was that story Jane had told my mum, the one about the firework accident that had burnt her ear, and the bit about looking like Mr. Spock's understudy. It was a long shot, but I reasoned, if I was going to believe her story, I had to believe all of it. Then one day, I found someone who'd known Jane." A long breath shuddered out of him. "You can imagine how I felt. It was true. Jane was a real person. Only, that meant there was the possibility that the rest of Mum's story was true too. This lady was a former nurse who'd worked with Jane in the sixties. *Then* she told me Jane had gone to live in Australia."

"What did you do?" Jonathon asked.

"Do?" George stared at him incredulously. "There was *nothing* I could do. That was it, the end of the trail. And a dead end at that." He paused to draw a breath. "You know the rest. When I took early retirement, I came to live here. That was five years ago."

"When did you first realize who Naomi was?" Jonathon didn't doubt his story. He recalled the things Naomi had said at the bonfire party. Only now he was hearing them from George's point of view. *The emotions he must have gone through.*

"She didn't even come on my radar until a couple of years ago. She was just this old lady who lived out in the forest and made all kinds of remedies. But then...." George finished his brandy and placed the glass on the floor. "I'm not sure where I was at the time. I only remember overhearing the story of how she'd delivered a baby like it was nothing. So she delivered a baby. So what? But when I got to hear the story from different points of view, I heard that she'd told Mrs. Barton it wasn't the first baby she'd delivered."

Mike regarded him closely. "That wasn't enough to connect her to Jane, was it?"

George shook his head. "No. I thought it was a coincidence. I mean, as far as I knew, Jane was living in Australia. No, this was just a story—until the night of the bonfire party."

"You said you'd been trying to talk to me, but there was always a crowd," Jonathon said. "And that you were there when the mayor was with me. That meant you heard everything Naomi said."

"Yeah." The word came out like a sigh. "You want to know the first thing I noticed? Her speech. It was like being a kid again, back in Nottingham. I hadn't heard anyone say *ay-up mi-duck* in years. And *jammy sod*. My grandma used to say that to me. But Naomi didn't *sound* like she was from Nottingham. Then I learned why. Thirty years of living in Australia." He shivered. "I tell you, I went cold all over. It couldn't be her— could it? The name was different, for one thing. That meant nothing, of course. Anyone can change their name, right? And then she put all my doubts to bed."

Jonathon nodded. "When she showed us her ear, told us how it happened—and about how she used to tell people she was Mr. Spock's understudy."

"I watched her walk away, and all I could think of was that I'd come to Merrychurch for a reason—to be an instrument of justice."

"What do you mean—that you were going to kill her for killing your twin?" Mike's voice hardened. "Something you had no proof that she'd even done?"

"No!" George's eyes were wild. "Like I said, I never meant to kill her. I only wanted her to admit the truth—and *then* I'd see her brought to justice."

"Tell us what happened," Jonathon said gently.

George leaned forward, his elbows on his knees. "I went out that morning with the intention of confronting her and finally finding out what happened. When I got near the cottage, there was no one around, so I tied up Max to the table leg and knocked on the door. After a minute, she answered. I told her I needed to speak to her about something really important, and then I said, 'Of course, I really need to be saying all this to Jane.' She stared at me for a minute, but then let me in." George sat up. "I didn't bother wasting time. I told her who I was. How I knew who *she* was. She didn't say anything—like she could deny it—but then I just blurted it out. 'Why did you kill my twin?' She gaped at me like I'd gone mad. I told her not to bother denying that there were two babies born that night. That my mum had heard them."

"How did she react?" Mike asked in a calm voice.

"She stood there in front of the fire and told me that Mum was mistaken. There had only been me. But there was something about her that told me she was lying. This look of panic in her eyes. I told her that I didn't believe her and that I was going to the authorities to tell them everything. I was going to get her charged with manslaughter or murder. Then she changed her tune. She said okay, okay, so yeah, there was another baby, my twin—and then she looked me in the eye and said, 'But your twin is out there somewhere.' That was when I lost it." George covered his face with his hands.

Max got up from his place by the fire, wandered over to where George sat, and pushed his nose against George's knee with a soft woof.

"George? What did you do?" Jonathon had never felt so torn. He hadn't wanted George to be the killer, but now that he knew the truth….

Gently, George lowered his hands. "I saw red, that's what. I saw this person who'd destroyed my mum's life, who'd lied to me, who was *still* lying to save her own scrawny neck. I called her a lying bitch and I pushed her, hard." He gazed at his hands. "I always thought I had small hands for a bloke. I never thought they'd be strong enough to exert that much force. She went flying backward like she was nothing, and smashed her head into the fireplace. I stood over her as she lay there, not moving, and… that was when I panicked. I grabbed a jar of jam from the table and ran out of there. I didn't see a soul. By the time I got home, I went straight to the bathroom and threw up." He looked down at Max and smiled. "You trying to help me? It's a bit late for that, fella."

"What makes you think she was lying when she said your twin is still out there?" Jonathon wanted to know.

"It was just so obvious. If that were true, then why lie in the first place and say there was no baby? No, she thought if she convinced me I had a twin, I wouldn't take it any further. That panic I saw in her? *That* told me the truth."

The doorbell rang, and Mike held up his hands. "I'll get that. It's probably Constable Billings."

George sighed. "Yeah. That's okay." He gave Mike a shaky smile. "It's not like I'm gonna run off, am I? I've already told you two everything. Now I get to make it official."

Mike patted his shoulder and left the room. Seconds later came the low murmur of voices.

Jonathon couldn't stay quiet a moment longer. "Okay, I understand why you did it. I really do. I don't know how *I* would have reacted in your shoes. What I don't get is the whole ginger roots business."

George frowned. "What ginger roots? What are you talking about?" The door opened and Graham entered, with Mike following behind. George got to his feet. "Constable Billings. It's okay. I know why you're here. Ready when you are." He held out his arms, the wrists together.

Graham blinked. "Er… I don't think there's any need for cuffs. If you'd just get your coat, I'll take you down to the station."

"Okay." George turned to Jonathon. "Can I ask you a favor? Can you take care of Max for me? I'd ask Melinda, but Max would have Jinx for breakfast."

"Sure, I'll find someone to look after him." Jonathon's mind was in a whirl. Something didn't add up here. He followed them into the tiny hallway.

Graham waited while George put on a jacket. "I owe you, mate," he said quietly to Mike. "You too," he added, with a nod to Jonathon. "I'll be in the pub later." And with that, he escorted George out of the house to where a police car waited at the edge of the village green.

Mike heaved a sigh of relief. "Well, I didn't expect any of *that* when we arrived here." He peered at Jonathon. "You've gone very quiet. Was that something of an anticlimax?"

"Just a feeling I can't seem to shake." And a growing suspicion that Jonathon didn't like one bit.

"What kind of feeling?"

Jonathon met his concerned gaze. "I don't think George did it."

CHAPTER TWENTY-SEVEN

MIKE STARED at him. "But... he just told you he did it. You heard him admit it."

Jonathon shook his head haltingly. "We heard him admit to pushing her so she fell and smashed her head against the fireplace. But that wasn't what killed her, was it? He said nothing of strangling her. And a moment ago I mentioned the ginger roots. Mike, I swear he didn't have a clue what I was talking about."

Mike chuckled. "Listen to us."

"What?" Jonathon didn't think they'd said anything that strange.

"Anyone hearing this conversation would find it hard to believe that *I'm* the ex-cop, and *you're* the *amateur*," he said, air-quoting.

"You're obviously a good example to follow. And what if I'm right? What if he didn't do it?" Only, Jonathon thought there was no what-if about it.

"Well, you can't go charging down to the police station and tell DI Mablethorpe they've got the wrong man. Let them come to that conclusion for themselves."

Jonathon's stomach clenched. "But... we can't *leave* him there." When Mike gazed at him levelly, he sighed. "You're right, of course. Once they talk to him, they've got to see he didn't do it."

A soft whine reached his ears, and Max walked into the hallway, peering about him.

Mike reached down and stroked him behind the ears. "He's not here, boy," he said softly. Then he straightened and looked at Jonathon. "What are you going to do with Max?"

"He can't come to the manor. Janet would kill me." A lightbulb went on in his head. "But I know who *might* take him. Sue. She's got Sherlock, right? So she's used to big dogs. And they might get along. It would be a solution until they let George go."

Mike smiled. "You're certain that's going to happen, aren't you?"

"Yes. Once they realize he didn't strangle her, they'll know they've got the wrong man." The more Jonathon thought about it, the more convinced he became.

"A man who has admitted to causing her harm. They'll charge him, y'know." Mike sighed again. "You *do* know what we're suggesting, don't you? That after George left, someone else turned up and finished the job? What are the odds on that? And what will the police make of that theory?"

Jonathon walked back into the living room, Max at his side. "I know how it sounds, but think about it. The residue on her neck. Why would George have leather treatment in his house? He doesn't drive, for one thing.

Not if he's a narcoleptic. And it's not as if he'd use it around the home." He flung out his arm. "I mean, do you *see* any leather in here?" The couches and chairs were covered in a worn brown fabric. "Plus there's the bit about the knife. No mention of her going for him with a chopping knife, was there?"

"Okay. Let's say you're right. And I admit, it's looking that way. So who did it? Who stopped by and took advantage of the fact that she was in a bad way? Maybe George knocked her unconscious. He thinks she's dead and runs. But she comes round. She's groggy, with a head wound. And then someone else walks in and—"

"And strangles her, before stuffing her mouth full of ginger roots. Only, our killer wore gloves." Max whined, and Jonathon gave him a sympathetic glance. "Go on. Call Sue and see if she'll take him. Then we can go back to the pub and get something to eat. I'm starving."

Mike chuckled. "I did promise you macaroni and cheese, didn't I? Sure." He paused. "You know, word *will* get around about this."

Jonathon nodded. "And the only people who know George isn't the killer will be us, the police—and the murderer."

And now he was more determined than ever to get to the bottom of it.

LUNCH WAS over, and the pub was closed until six. Jonathon was glad of the respite. A little peace and quiet was exactly what they needed after the day they'd had so far. First Grant, then George....

Mike brought coffee into the bar where they were sitting, and Jonathon beamed. "Just what I need. I've

had enough drama for one day." Then his phone warbled, and one glance at the screen told him he'd spoken
too soon. "Oh hell."

"That can only mean one thing. It's your father."

It wasn't a question.

Jonathon sighed heavily before connecting the
call. "Good afternoon, Father. To what do I owe the
pleasure of this call?"

"I thought I'd made myself clear," his father began in his usual abrupt manner, "but apparently I need
to repeat myself. All this running around the village,
questioning people… it has got to *stop*. For the last
time, Jonathon, you are *not* a detective. Leave it to the
professionals, is that clear? Although I suppose my ad-
monishment is akin to closing the barn door after the
horse has bolted, seeing as they now have a suspect in
custody. At least that puts paid to any future 'investigations.' And as a former detective, Mike should know
better than to let you get involved like this."

For a moment Jonathon was too stunned to reply.
Then he found his voice. "Father, how did you find
out that I've been asking questions? And about the
suspect?"

"Brent called me, if you must know."

A suspicion began to form. "When, exactly, did he
call?"

"About an hour ago." There was a pause. "Why do
you ask?"

"Oh, I just find it interesting that he should be the
one to call you, when the evidence against him is looking more and more damning."

"Brent? A murderer?" A loud, explosive snort
filled his ears. "The man's an MP, for Christ's sake. He
has the ear of the prime minister."

"An MP whose initials are on a list of people who were being blackmailed by the deceased. Who was seen near the crime scene that morning. Who wears gloves. Who drives a car that had been recently valeted using a leather treatment of which traces were found on the victim."

Another pause. "All circumstantial." But the fire had died in his father's voice. "Doesn't prove anything."

"Maybe, maybe not. But let me put it another way. The police have got the wrong man, but that's not common knowledge. And then a prominent MP calls a High Court judge, basically to get him to warn his son off, an hour *after* the police arrest someone. Does that suggest to you that the MP might be afraid of something?"

This time the silence was deafening. After a moment, his father cleared his throat. "I think, in those circumstances, you have enough evidence to present to the proper authorities. And I advise you to do just that. Let the police handle it."

"I think that's a good idea. Now, if you'll excuse me, I have things to do. Enjoy the rest of your day." Jonathon disconnected before his father could move on to other subjects.

Mike folded his arms. "Seriously? He tried to get your father to tell you to back off?"

Jonathon picked up his mug. "You know what? I think it's time we paid Mr. Brent a visit."

Mike laughed. "Okay, so George admitted everything, I'll give you that. But don't think for one minute that you're going to confront Brent with our evidence and *he's* going to confess too. Especially if he knows the police have someone for this. The man's a politician."

"Which means what?"

Mike grinned. "Which means, he's a slippery customer."

"I just want to rattle him," Jonathon admitted. "Plus, I don't want him to think that all he has to do is go running to my father and I'll back down like a good little boy." He set his jaw. That really pissed him off.

"Finish your coffee, then, and we'll go see him." Mike drained his own mug. "This is going to be interesting."

"In what way?"

Mike grinned again. "In a David-versus-Goliath kind of way. The skinny, five-feet-six amateur detective meets the dashing, rising-star politician who, up until a few days ago, made him speechless with lust."

Jonathon gaped at him. "I was *not* speechless."

"Mm-hmm. Well, just check your chin for drool before we go in there." Mike smirked before taking his mug into the kitchen.

"So what if he's gorgeous?" Jonathon called out after him. "That doesn't mean he can get away with murder." Except he knew his father was right. All their evidence was circumstantial.

They needed something more.

MIKE PARKED the 4x4 in front of Brent's house. "Very pretty."

Jonathon agreed. The thatch on the roof had recently been redone, and the gardens in front were immaculate. In spite of the weather, however, the windows were open. "It must be freezing in there."

They got out, strolled up the tidy little path that led to the front door, and knocked. From inside came raised voices.

"I don't care what it *isn't*, just find out what's causing it." The door was flung open and Josh Brent stood there, his hair slightly unkempt, his red tie loosened from around the neck of his white shirt, his dark blue suit elegant and expensive-looking. He blinked. "Something I can do for you? Only, now is *not* the best time. I've returned home to find my brand-new boiler has gone on the fritz and every radiator in the house is scalding hot. We can't seem to bring the temperature down."

"I'm doing me best" came a gruff voice from inside.

Josh rolled his eyes. "*And* charging me an exorbitant rate for doing it. All because it's a Sunday." He sighed. "Gentlemen. What is the purpose of your visit, and can it wait?"

"Not really." Jonathon raised his chin and looked Josh in the eye. "We wanted to speak with you before we pass on what we know to the police. A courtesy, really."

Josh bit his lip, his eyes bright with amusement. "What you *know*? How very mysterious. Well, you'd better come in." He led them into the hallway, then through into a neat drawing room. Shiny brown leather couches formed a U-shape around the fire, and a thick rug filled the floor space between them. "Please, take a seat." He closed the door behind them, then sat on the couch facing them, his arm along the back, his legs crossed—a picture of relaxation. "My apologies for the heat, but there really is nothing I can do about that. Now, I admit to being intrigued. What could you possibly want to tell the police that involves me?"

"You seem like the sort of person who likes to come straight to the point," Mike said with a smile, "so we won't waste your time. We know you were being blackmailed by Naomi Teedle."

Josh opened his eyes wide. "I was? Well, that's certainly news to me. Wherever did you get that idea?"

"You were in her diaries. She kept records of all payments made." Jonathon watched him carefully.

"Really? My name was in there?"

"Your initials, actually." Simply *saying* it sent ribbons of unease unfolding in Jonathon's belly. *What if we've got it wrong?*

Josh arched his eyebrows. "That's it? That's all you have? And how many other people have the same initials as me? I can think of two others in this village alone, and that's before you even consider the rest of the population." He tilted his head to one side. "That's unless you have evidence that her blackmailing activities were limited to Merrychurch alone."

More tendrils of disquiet crept through Jonathon. *We* had *assumed her blackmail activities were confined to the village.* Which was a dumb supposition when he thought about it.

"Except those initials carry more weight when we add in the fact that you were seen near her cottage the morning she died," Mike added.

Josh made an impatient noise. "A fact that I have not denied. I told you. I stopped by on my walk and bought a jar of jam. And if that is the extent of your evidence, I rather think the police will be less than impressed. Indeed, I'm pretty certain the phrase 'wasting police time' will crop up at some point in the proceedings. Especially as they now have a man in custody."

God, he's smooth. All Jonathon wanted to do in that moment was ruffle Josh's feathers, make even one small chink in his armor of cool assurance. "Actually?

I think they'll be very interested in the fact that your car was recently valeted using a product that was found on the victim."

A faint frown creased Josh's brow. "Really? And my car is the only one in the village to have benefited from such a product?"

For a moment Jonathon was speechless. The only other car they knew about was John Barton's. *Oh God. What if it's him and not Josh?* His stomach roiled again, and he felt a flash of alarm. "I'm really sorry, but... could I use your bathroom?"

"My—?" Irritation flickered in Josh's eyes. "Very well, if you must. Upstairs. The first door on the landing."

Jonathon thanked him, rose to his feet hurriedly, and left the room. He took the stairs two at a time, found the bathroom, and bolted the door behind him. Inside, he took a moment to breathe, which helped to quell his earlier flare of panic. Jonathon gripped the cool porcelain sink and stared at his reflection in the mirror, while from below him came the sound of banging pipes and muted swearing.

Have we got this all wrong? The more he thought about it, the more Jonathon realized there was nothing concrete to tie Josh to the murder. He bowed his head, not daring to imagine his father's reaction when he got wind of this.

Then he stilled. Next to the sink was a white cabinet with open shelves, and on one sat a tube of cream. A very familiar tube. Alongside it were unopened packs of surgical dressings and a roll of white tape. Jonathon looked around the bathroom. At his feet was a small pedal-operated rubbish bin. On an impulse, he depressed the pedal and peered inside. Used dressings

filled it, their white surfaces marred by disgusting-look-
ing gunk.

Jonathon smiled. A coincidence? Perhaps, but if he
was right, then his wish for something concrete had just
been realized.

Let him argue his way out of that.

Jonathon pulled out his phone and scrolled through
his contacts. It was time to bring in the big guns.

CHAPTER TWENTY-EIGHT

MIKE HOPED Jonathon was all right. He'd looked a little pale as he'd left the room in such a hurry. Jonathon's exit seemed to have created an awkward vacuum. Josh appeared impatient, checking the time on the small clock above the fireplace. Mike took advantage of the situation to take a good look around.

A dresser stood against one wall, its shelves adorned with brasses and framed photographs, of which there were a great many. It seemed Josh had been a keen horse rider in his youth. There were photos of him receiving ribbons, photos of him with various horses, and a photo of him dressed in red, obviously taken at a hunt. This last image fascinated Mike, and he had no idea why.

"Do you still ride?" Mike asked, indicating the photos.

Josh gave a heavy sigh. "I fell from a horse when I was in my early twenties. It caused a bunch of nerves in my hip to knot. I get around fine, but now and again, it's agony. Haven't been able to ride since." He gazed fondly at the frames. "Those were good times." Josh pointed to the one of him in red. "I was seventeen in that one. My first ride with the hunt. Of course, that's all gone now."

Mike looked closely at the photo, trying to decide why it should be of such interest to him. Until the reason struck him so forcibly that he caught his breath.

Oh my God. How could I not have seen that?

The door opened and Jonathon entered. Before he could say a word, Mike beckoned him over to the dresser. "I was just admiring these photos." He said nothing as Jonathon joined him, but pointed to the hunt image. *Go on*, he urged Jonathon silently. *Tell me you see it too.*

The hitch in Jonathon's breathing was answer enough.

"Gentlemen, if you are done with presenting your *evidence*, then I really must ask you to leave." Josh scraped his hand through his hair. "I have quite enough to cope with this afternoon without your amateur imaginings." He stood to remove his jacket and placed it over the back of the couch. "Really, this heat is intolerable."

Beside him, Jonathon smiled. "Oh, I don't think we're done. In fact, I think we're only getting started." He sat down, and Mike joined him. Jonathon flashed him a grin. "You saw it first. Be my guest."

Mike cleared his throat. "I hear you've set your sights on one day becoming prime minister."

Josh gave another superior eye-roll. "That isn't exactly a secret. I've often spoken of my political ambitions."

Mike nodded. "Which explains why you paid Naomi Teedle whatever she wanted. It wouldn't do for it to come out at some point that a prominent politician had an affair with the mayor's wife—though from what *we've* gleaned, the affair is still ongoing, isn't it? That *was* you she was talking to on the phone, the morning after Naomi was killed? 'Ding, dong, the witch is dead.' Does that ring a bell?" Mike gave Josh a cool, calm smile. "And think of the scandal if it became known that you're the father of her child."

Josh gaped at him. "I'm the—Now you really *are* indulging in fantasy."

Jonathon's eyes blazed. "One—Jason Barton is the spitting image of you when you were younger. And two? I'll share with you something I learned in school. I always found biology to be a fascinating subject. Genes, chromosomes…. Did you know, for instance, that the probability of two blue-eyed parents producing a child with green eyes is 1 percent? But if *one* of the parents has green eyes, that probability rises to 50 percent." He smiled. "Debra and John Barton both have blue eyes. Jason, however, has beautiful green eyes— just like you."

Josh gave him an incredulous stare. "One percent… that's what, one child in one hundred? Those odds aren't so great when you put it like that."

This is getting us nowhere. Josh seemed impervious to everything they slung at him. If it wasn't for every instinct Mike possessed telling him Josh was their man, he'd have succumbed to doubts by now. Then it came to him. *Take aim at someone he cares about.* If they were correct and the affair was still going on, that was more than seventeen years of secret assignations. Maybe even love. *How far would he go to protect her?*

Mike smacked himself on the forehead. "Jonathon. Maybe we're looking at this from the wrong angle. In fact, maybe we're talking to the wrong person. After all, Debra's initials were on the blackmail list too. What if *she's* the one Naomi was blackmailing? I mean, she wouldn't want her husband finding out about Jason. *And* she was seen near the cottage too."

Josh became very still. "Leave her out of this. She had nothing to do with that woman's death. The very idea is preposterous."

Josh's phone rang, and Mike silently cursed the caller. *Talk about bad timing.* There had been no mistaking that first genuine flicker of emotion. When Josh's face lit up in a broad, triumphant smile, Mike's heart sank. *This is not good.*

"Thomas. So good to hear from you again. And by the way, excellent timing. I was about to call *you*." Another smile, only this one was aimed right at Jonathon. "Ah, I see. Coincidentally, that was exactly what I want to discuss with you."

Jonathon jerked his head to stare at Mike, his eyes wide. Then it occurred to Mike that silence had fallen. One glance at Josh made it apparent that his call was not going as he'd expected.

"Yes... well, yes, I see what you mean. ... Yes, I do understand. ... Of course, I know that *you* can't. ... Surely, there's someone you can recommend? ... I see...." Then his face paled. "I thought as we're friends, you might. ... Oh. ... Very well... if you're sure.... ... Thank you. Goodbye." He disconnected, then sank back against the cushions, staring at the phone screen.

"A word of advice," Jonathon said quietly. "I'd take my father off speed dial if I were you."

"Your father and I are friends," Josh replied stiffly.

Jonathon speared him with an intense look. "And who do you suppose told me to take my evidence to the police?"

Josh stared at him, then drew in a deep breath. "Fine. I might as well tell the truth. She *was* blackmailing me. And yes, you're quite right. I am Jason's father. And this situation might have gone on for years but for a remark she made at your bonfire party." He sighed. "I got a call from Debra. Apparently Naomi had said something to Jason about how handsome he was—just like his father. Debra knew that remark for what it was—the prelude to another demand for more money. She was warning us. Sooner or later she'd say that and someone might actually pay attention to it. Debra was in a state. I told her not to worry about it, that we'd wait and see what Naomi came up with."

"And then?" Mike studied Josh carefully.

"The next morning, I went to see Naomi, with the intention of making her a substantial offer that she couldn't refuse. I wanted to call an end to it. But when I got there... she was lying on the floor, already dead." Josh's expression was grave.

"On the floor," Jonathon repeated deliberately.

"Yes, that's what I said, on the floor."

"So what did you do?"

Josh frowned. "Do?"

Mike coughed. "If *I* found a dead body, I'd notify the police."

"Perhaps *you* would," Josh remarked dryly, "but look at it from my perspective. I was being black-mailed, and the blackmailer was now dead. I did what anyone would have done in those circumstances. I got out of there."

"I do have one small problem with your version of events." Jonathon cleared his throat. "As far as I'm aware, dead people tend to stay dead. They don't suddenly come back to life and slash people with a chopping knife."

Josh snorted. "What are you talking about?" His earlier tenacity was back in full force.

Jonathon pointed to his forearm, where Mike could make out what looked like a bandage beneath Josh's shirt. "If she was dead, how did you get that cut?"

Josh glanced at his arm. "This? This is not a cut. I grazed my arm on some rosebushes when I was pruning them. I was doing some clearing up in the garden. Sweeping up leaves, burning them, making the place look tidier."

Mike might almost have believed him if not for the flicker of fear that crossed his face.

"So you were pruning rose bushes in a T-shirt? In November?" Jonathon smiled. "Let me tell you what *I* think happened. I think you went there, just like you said, to pay her off. But when you got there, you found she'd been attacked. She was groggy, disorientated…. You helped her into a chair—and then you thought this was too good a chance to miss. You put your hands around her throat and you strangled her. Except she fought back. Not excessively—she was in too bad a state for that—but she reached for the nearest implement she could find and sliced at you with a knife. It probably cut through your coat and shirt, but I'm willing to bet it came into contact with your skin. You probably didn't even feel it at the time. When you were sure she was dead, you stuffed her mouth full of ginger roots. A nasty touch. And as for you clearing up your garden, I don't think you were burning leaves that day—I think you were burning your clothes."

"More fantasy," Josh said with a sneer.

"Actually, I prefer Jonathon's version of events," Mike commented.

"Thankfully the police will want something a little more substantial than his fairy stories." Josh gave him a superior smile. "They require proof."

Jonathon gave him a thoughtful look. "But they've already got it." He pointed to Josh's arm again. "They're not getting any better, are they? The blisters? In fact, they're getting worse."

A little pallor crept over Josh's face. "How did you—" He snapped his mouth shut.

"But you haven't been to see a doctor about them because then questions might be asked. You went to the chemist's and bought a cream instead. I know, because my doctor prescribed one for me, but it was also available over the counter." Jonathon held up his hand. "Did it look like this when it started out? A few blisters?" His voice took on a kind, soothing tone. "You don't have a clue, do you? How much of it did you get on your skin? More than the slight brush that *I* had with the stuff, I'll bet. You'll be lucky to keep your arm."

Josh became so still. "What do you mean?"

"That stuff she was chopping? It's called hogweed. Last year, a man came into contact with it in his garden and almost lost his leg."

Mike quickly pulled up the photo he'd saved and showed it to Josh. "Look familiar?"

Josh regarded the stark image with eyes filled with horror. "But… she was cutting that stuff?"

"We have no idea what she intended doing with it."

Josh's eyes widened. "I do. I'd called her Saturday night, telling her I was coming to see her, that this had to end. And I... I bluffed. I said I wasn't the only one with secrets, and I was sure she wouldn't want hers getting out. It was just a stab in the dark, but I guess I hit home." He stared at them, aghast. "I turned up earlier than I'd anticipated. That stuff... it was intended for me. She was going to kill me!" His indignant tone would have been amusing in other circumstances.

"That, or blind you," Jonathon said quietly. "Hogweed sap in the eyes?" He paused. "By the way, where are your gloves?"

"Gloves?" Josh said with a frown, then swallowed. Mike chalked up another direct hit.

Jonathon nodded. "The leather ones you wear to drive. I noticed them the other day when you stopped me on the road. I imagine they're in your car. I daresay the police will find them very interesting. Never mind the traces of leather treatment—there could be skin cells, blood.... After all, there was a lot of blood resulting from that head wound, and if you put your hands around her throat, you probably came into contact with some of it." He glanced at Josh's hands. "What do you think, Mike? How easy will it be to match up the marks left on Naomi's skin with those hands?"

Mike turned his head at the sound of a car pulling up outside. He peered through the window and smiled. "I think Josh has more visitors. We might leave such things up to them." Mike narrowed his gaze. "This isn't a coincidence, is it? When did you call the police?"

Jonathon smiled. "When I was in the bathroom. I saw the cream I've been using on my hand, along with a lot of surgical dressings, and I put two and two together. Especially when I saw the discarded dressings in your bathroom rubbish basket." He gave a thin smile. "I have similar ones in my trash at home."

"Hey, nice work," Mike said approvingly. Then he grimaced. "You looked in his rubbish basket? Ew."

Jonathon fixed him with a hard stare. "What does that matter? At least I found the evidence."

"When you've quite finished congratulating each other," Josh said suddenly, "you might like to think about one thing. I haven't confessed to killing her."

Mike gave him a pitying glance. "With your DNA on the knife and wherever else it turns up, you won't need to," he said quietly. "If you simply walk through a room, you leave your DNA behind you."

The door opened, and a tall guy in overalls stood there, holding a spanner. "Sorry to disturb you, but there are some coppers 'ere who want to talk to Mr. Brent. I let 'em in. Was that all right?"

"That's fine, Bill," Mike told him. "You go back to your plumbing."

"Gotcha." Bill left after firing an inquiring glance in Josh's direction.

DI Mablethorpe stepped into the room, followed by Graham. "Mr. Brent? I wonder if you'd accompany us to the police station to answer a few questions." He gave Mike a curt nod. "I was told we'd find you here."

"And you'll find evidence in the bathroom, and his gloves in the car. Jonathon and I will follow you to the station to tell you everything we know."

The DI arched his eyebrows. "Indeed. And following that, we might have a little conversation about sticking your noses into police business. It appears you need a reminder." He gestured with his arm. "This way if you please, Mr. Brent." He led Josh from the room.

Jonathon glared at the door where the DI had stood. "How d'you like that? He's more polite with the murder suspect than he is with us, and we just handed him the case on a platter. If I hadn't phoned...."

Graham snickered. "Thanks for that, by the way. Most of it made sense."

"I was in a hurry," Jonathon remonstrated. "And then we kept him talking to give you time to get here." He paused. "How is George, by the way?"

"He's in the cells, and he's okay. You can drop by tomorrow and see him. Looks like we'll be charging him with causing actual bodily harm." Graham smiled. "But I'll keep an eye on him, don't you worry. Now I'd best be on my way, before the DI complains. Again." He gave them a nod. "See you at the pub later, though."

Mike grinned. "Where there'll be a pint with your name on it."

"*One* pint?" Graham looked wounded.

Mike laughed. "As many pints as you can drink before someone has to carry you home."

Graham rubbed his hands together energetically. "*Now* you're talking." He left them and headed for the street.

Mike held out his hand. "Home?"

"Whose home?"

"Doesn't matter. Wherever you are is home." It sounded corny, but it had to be said. And judging from the way Jonathon's face glowed, it was exactly the right thing to say too.

CHAPTER TWENTY-NINE

Monday, November 20

"THANKS, GUYS. I think that's everything." Graham signed their statements and placed them in a folder. He beamed at them. "I like this. You two do all the work and I get the credit." He winked. "Only kidding. But the DI had to admit, you came up trumps."

"*Eventually*, he admitted it," Mike said with a chuckle. "But it didn't stop him from giving us a lecture about *interfering*."

"Did it have any effect?" Graham asked with a twinkle in his eye.

"None whatsoever."

Graham burst out laughing. "Thank God for that."

"Has Brent changed his tune yet? Or does he still think he can get away with it?"

"He keeps talking about his friends in high places." Graham snorted. "Funny thing is, most of those *friends* seem to be keeping a distance. Word has gotten around. Now, I wonder how that happened." His eyes gleamed.

"Nothing to do with us," Jonathon said innocently.

Graham merely arched his eyebrows. "I dare say he'll change his tune when the forensic report gets in. That'll be a while yet, though." Graham smiled. "Pity he'll have to stay in custody until then." He walked away, whistling.

Jonathon leaned in to Mike and lowered his voice. "I suspect word getting around has a lot to do with my father. Not a man to cross."

"Good for him. Now, if he could only let you get on with your own life, I might actually like the man." Mike sighed. "But I suppose that's too much to ask."

"Excuse me?" They turned to find a woman, her blond hair streaked with white and tied back, wearing a pair of sweats and a baggy sweater, a bag slung over her shoulder. At her feet sat a suitcase. "Hi. I'd like to talk to someone about Jane Teedle?" There were dark shadows under her blue eyes.

Mike shook her hand. "Hello. You must be Gabriela, Naomi's—Jane's—daughter. The accent was a bit of a giveaway." He frowned. "Have you come straight from Heathrow?"

Gabriela smiled. "It's not as bad as it sounds. I had a layover in Singapore, and I managed to sleep on the flight." She squinted at him. "And who might you be?"

"Sorry. I'm Mike Tattersall. I run the village pub."

Her face lit up. "You don't have a room going, do you? I didn't book any accommodation before I left. I was in too much of a hurry to get here. My husband got back from his trip, and I booked the first available flight out."

"I think we can do better than a room at the pub," Jonathon said with a smile. He held out his hand. "I'm Jonathon de Mountford."

Gabriela's eyes widened. "The photographer? Do you live around here?" Then she rolled her eyes. "I am such a drongo. Of *course* you do. You live in the manor house. Mum told me about you in her last letter." Her face tightened. "Are the police any closer to finding out who did this?"

"As a matter of fact, yes, but…." Whichever way Mike looked at it, Gabriela was in for a shock. "Tell you what. Let's find a couple of chairs, I'll get my constable friend to provide us with tea or coffee, and we'll tell you what we know. Except…. This is not going to be easy."

"Is that your nice way of preparing me for a few nasty surprises?" Gabriela sighed. "Mum always said she didn't get on with some people in Merrychurch. When I heard she'd been murdered, I didn't imagine this was gonna be pleasant." She squared her shoulders. "Let's get it over with."

Mike gave her a warm smile before addressing Jonathon. "I'll go find Graham. Can you ask someone if we can use an interview room? I don't suppose anyone will mind. They've got enough on their plate with George and Brent in custody."

Jonathon nodded. "Sure."

Mike went in search of Graham, his heart going out to Gabriela. *Poor woman. Fancy finding out that your mother was a blackmailer?*

They'd break it to her as gently as possible.

GRAHAM CLOSED the folder. The four of them were seated around a table in the interview room.

"That's all I can tell you, I'm afraid. We're following a few lines of inquiry, and once we get some results back from forensics, we should be able to make an arrest." He put the folder aside on the table.

Gabriela sighed wearily. "Thanks. And thank you for not sugarcoating it. I needed to know what Mum had been up to." She shivered. "Though I don't think I'll be sharing that with the kids. They don't need to know."

"Will you be staying in the UK long?" Jonathon asked. He couldn't imagine she'd want to, especially after learning the truth about her mother's death.

"Long enough to get a better look at Merrychurch," she said with a tired smile. "I only saw a bit of it from the taxi as we drove here. It looks gorgeous. Reminds me of this TV show where there were all these murders in sleepy little villages. I guess this is life imitating art." She let out a sigh. "I've lived 99 percent of my life in Oz. Five minutes in this place, and yeah, I could live here. In a heartbeat. Who'd have thought it?"

Jonathon frowned. "Ninety-nine percent?"

She chuckled. "Not sure what the actual percentage is. I'm not sure how old I was when we moved to Australia. I mean, it's not like I remember traveling there. I was only little, not even a toddler."

"But you were born in Australia," Mike said.

It was Gabriela's turn to frown. "Er, sorry, but you've got that wrong. I was born in the UK." She smiled. "And I can prove it." She opened the bag she'd slung over the back of the chair and pulled out a brown envelope. "I brought this with me in case I had to prove who I was." Gabriela removed a folded square of paper. "There you go. My birth certificate." She handed it to

Mike, who opened it up and stared at it for the longest time.

The hair on the back of Jonathon's neck prickled. "Mike? What is it?"

In silence, Mike got out his phone and scrolled across the screen. "This is the email Keith sent me, with the birth and death certificates attached." He tapped the screen, then handed it to Jonathon. "Take a look at this. Then look at the certificate."

Jonathon took the phone and the certificate, holding them a distance apart. At first he couldn't see anything wrong, but then—

"Oh my God," he said softly.

"What? What's wrong?" Gabriela's voice held a note of panic. "Tell me what's wrong."

Jonathon met Mike's gaze. "Are you thinking what I'm thinking?"

"It's the only explanation that makes any sense."

"Well, will one of you tell me?" Gabriela demanded, sounding exasperated.

"Yeah, and then let *me* in on it?" Graham asked. "'Cause I'm lost here."

Jonathon handed her the phone. "Your mother had a child, a boy, Gabriel. Born in 1968. But he died when he was a few months old. This is his death certificate."

She studied it carefully. "Oh wow. Born the same year as me. She never said a thing. Come to think of it, how is that possible?" Then she paused. "He was called Gabriel?"

Jonathon nodded. "We'd assumed she named you Gabriela as a reminder of him. Now scroll left. This is his birth certificate. What you have there is a copy of the original. They tend to be smaller."

Gabriela peered at the screen, frowning. Then her breath caught, and she jerked her head to stare at her birth certificate. "But… this means we were born on the same day."

"No, you weren't. It's just the same birth certificate." Mike gently took it from her and pointed to the column headed Sex. "Take a closer look. She added FE to change it from male to female. Then she added an *a* to change Gabriel into Gabriela."

She stared at them, blinking. "I don't understand."

Jonathon took hold of her hand. "We have a story to tell you that might clear things up."

Gabriela glanced at his hand. "I'm not gonna like this, am I?"

Jonathon said nothing but held on tight as Mike told her the story George had related. He didn't leave out anything, and Gabriela gripped Jonathon's hand tightly when Mike got to the part about hearing two babies crying. When Mike finished, she stared at the tabletop in silence for a minute, Jonathon's hand still curled around hers.

Finally she raised her head. "She wasn't my mother, was she? I was only a baby that she stole." She appeared dazed, shaking her head every now and then.

"That's what it looks like," Jonathon admitted.

"Back in a minute." Graham got up and left the room.

"Maybe she was suffering from depression after his death," Mike suggested. "She wasn't thinking clearly. All she could see was a young girl who was so off her head, she didn't even know she was in labor—and then she had twins. Maybe Naomi thought no one would believe the girl if she ever said anything. After all, it was just the two of them."

"And it does explain why she took that passage to Australia so quickly. She wanted to get away—to get *you* away."

The door opened, and Graham entered. "I think there's someone you should meet," he said softly. Then he gave a nod toward the door, and George came in. His face lit up when he saw Mike and Jonathon.

"Hey. Have they told you? It wasn't me. I didn't do it. I didn't kill her."

"We know, George." Jonathon gestured to the chair Graham had vacated. "Sit down, please."

George sat before giving Gabriela a polite nod. "It seems so crazy that someone else would walk in there after me and…." Gradually, his gaze came back to her, and he stared, his mouth falling slightly open.

Gabriela was staring too. "Why do I feel like I know you from somewhere?"

Mike patted George on the shoulder. "Looks like your mum didn't imagine what she heard that night after all."

George flashed him a confused glance before bringing his attention back to Gabriela.

Jonathon was buzzing. "George… this is your twin, Gabriela."

The shared looks of dawning realization, followed by soft cries of wonder and joy, left Jonathon feeling so light that he was giddy with it.

He gestured to Mike, and the three men crept out of the room where none of them were needed right then.

"I DID offer to put Gabriela up here," Jonathon murmured against Mike's back. He was warm and drowsy, in that pleasant state just before sleep takes over. "But she's staying at George's place." His hand was on Mike's chest, and he was sleepily rubbing it.

"Mm-hmm."

"She says she's going to spend a few weeks here, getting to know him."

"Mm-hmm."

Jonathon chuckled. "Are you even listening to me?"

Mike rolled over and kissed him on the lips. "Yes, dear. Now go to sleep." Then he turned back onto his side.

Jonathon snuggled against his back. "Love you," he whispered.

"Love you too. Now go to sleep."

Jonathon's last thought before sleep claimed him was that if this was what married life was like, he couldn't wait.

EPILOGUE

Saturday, December 23

JONATHON STEPPED back and surveyed the entrance hall. The Christmas tree stood at the foot of the stairs, all fifteen feet of it. It had taken him, Mike, Sue, Andrew, and Janet more than five hours to cover all its branches with baubles and tinsel. The overall effect was so magical, he was lost for words. It reminded him strongly of Christmases past, when all the family had descended upon the manor house to celebrate the season.

Those days are gone. Time for a change.

"Admiring our handiwork?" Mike asked as he came up from the kitchen, carrying two mugs of steaming hot chocolate.

Jonathon laughed. "Why not? We did a fantastic job." He wrapped his hands around the offered mug. "Just what I need."

Mike jerked his head in the direction of the stairs. "I took a look in the fridges. Are you expecting an army for Christmas? There's a hell of a lot of food down there." He snickered. "Ivy must be having kittens at the thought of cooking all that."

"She isn't, because she's not the one who'll be cooking it." Jonathon had been waiting all morning to reveal his plans, and once he'd received the text, it was finally official.

Mike narrowed his gaze. "What's going on?"

"It's going to be a different sort of Christmas here this year. I've given Ivy the time off so she can be with her family. Janet is staying, however. Apparently we're her only family now." If he could only get her to call him Jonathon, that would be the best present she could give him.

"So who's doing the cooking?"

"Anyone who happens to be around. Although I should add that I'm expecting guests. They'll be joining in too. It's going to be an all-hands-to-the-pump kind of Christmas." Mike looked so stricken that Jonathon laughed. "Relax. It'll be fun. I am quite capable of roasting a turkey and whatever comes with it. And whenever you can tear yourself away from the pub, you're more than welcome to join us."

Mike gazed at him thoughtfully. "You said nothing about guests. I had no idea."

Jonathon knew Mike well enough by now to guess what was on his mind. "Just because there will be people staying does *not* mean you and I will not have time to be together. Trust me. They'll have other activities planned, rather than demanding all my attention." He held out his hand, and Mike took it. "And they're the sort of guests who wouldn't blink if we disappeared to my bedroom now and again," Jonathon added with a grin.

"Now you're *really* intriguing me. When do they get here?"

"Oh, not long now." When the doorbell rang, he laughed. "But not *that* soon." Before he could get to the front door, Janet was there first.

"Mr. Barton, sir," she announced.

Jonathon stilled. He hadn't seen much of John Barton in recent weeks, following the revelations about Josh Brent. John had resigned his seat on the council and had made no public appearances. There were rumors, of course, about him and Debra splitting up, but Jonathon tried not to listen. He genuinely liked the mayor, and this had to be an awful time for him.

I wonder why he wants to see me? Jonathon's stomach clenched. *Stupid question. I helped bring this whole sorry mess to light.* The least he could do was be there if the man needed help.

"Let him in, Janet. And then you can call it a day, if the room is ready for my guests. As of now, you're off for Christmas."

She beamed. "Thank you, sir." Then she stood aside, and Jonathon did a double take as not *John* Barton entered the hallway, but Jason, bundled up in a thick coat.

"Is… is it okay for me to call round?" There was an air of such dejection about him that Jonathon's heart went out to him.

"Of course it is," he said warmly. "In fact, you're just in time for some hot chocolate."

Mike took the hint and came over, holding out the mug. "Here. You take that. It looks like you need to warm up. Is it snowing yet?"

"Not yet, but it definitely feels cold enough for it." Jason took the mug. "Thanks."

"Now, why don't you and Jonathon go into the drawing room and have a talk? There's a fire going." Mike caught Jonathon's gaze. "I'll be in there once I've made some more hot chocolate."

Which was Mike shorthand for "I'll give you two time to talk."

Not for the first time, Jonathon was thankful for having Mike in his life.

"Let's go," he told Jason, leading him through the house. Once they were inside the warm drawing room, Jonathon took his coat and placed it over a chair back. They sat on the couch in front of the fire, the only sound the crackling and spitting of the logs.

After a moment, Jonathon made the first move. "How are things?" He kept his tone soft.

Jason sighed. "A mess, if you really want to know. Mum's in a state. She keeps repeating that she had no idea Josh Brent could do such a thing. Imagine how that makes me feel. In the space of one day, I found out that my dad isn't my dad, and that the guy who is? Killed someone." He swallowed. "It doesn't matter how many different ways I look at this, I keep coming back to the same thing. My dad's a murderer."

Jonathon sighed. "Okay. You want to hear my take on this?"

"Please." Jason sat on the edge of the seat, hunched over, his hands around his mug.

"The only thing that makes Josh Brent your dad is that you share a few genes and chromosomes. That's it. Throughout your life, has he ever made any attempt to get to know you? Be friendly toward you?"

Jason considered the question for a second or two before sighing. "It was like I didn't exist."

"Exactly. You were the secret he didn't want getting out. And then we have John Barton. A man who has cared for you all your life. Who cares what you do in the future." Jonathon smiled. "There's a saying that you don't get to choose your family. Well, I have news for you. Yes, you do. And that works doubly if you're LGBT. Family are those who love and accept you because of who you are. I'd be willing to bet that John loves you. Will *still* love you when you're out. And if you want to keep thinking of him as your father, then you bloody well do it."

Jason sighed before settling back against the cushions. "Thanks."

"For what?"

He smiled. "Speaking your mind." He drank a little hot chocolate. "And giving me a moment to breathe."

Jonathon patted his knee. "Any time you need to breathe, decompress, whatever, you're welcome to come here." His phone vibrated, and he squirmed to remove it from his jeans pocket. When he saw the text, he sighed. "I wish my father was more like John. It would make my life a whole lot easier."

"Problems?"

Jonathon pasted on a bright smile. "Nothing I can't handle." He reached over and squeezed Jason's hand. "You'll have to excuse me. I have some guests arriving soon. Stay here, relax, enjoy the fire, drink your hot chocolate, and I'll be back." He smiled. "Then you get to meet some more family."

He got up from the couch, left the room, and hurried through the house, looking for Mike. He found him coming up from the kitchen, carrying another mug.

Mike gave him an inquiring glance. "What's up?"

"Remember I told you to trust me, because I had a plan to deal with my father?"

A flash of comprehension crossed Mike's face. "I take it these guests have something to do with that."

"They do. And I was going to explain it all to you before they arrived, but then Jason appeared. So explanations will have to wait." The doorbell rang, and Jonathon grinned. "And as usual, she's early." He hurried over to answer it.

"She?"

Jonathon opened the door. "Ruth Ainsworth." He barely had time to get the words out before Ruth launched herself at him in her usual exuberant manner, her long black coat dusted with a light sprinkling of snow, a few flakes caught in her black hair.

"About bloody time! It's freezing out here." She gave him a huge hug. "You haven't changed a bit." She released him and took a step back, gazing at him critically. "Well, maybe a bit less skinny."

Jonathon frowned. "Okay, what have you done with her?"

"She's bringing the bags. I drove." Ruth grinned. "That was the deal."

"How much stuff have you brought?"

Ruth snorted. "We are not all like *you*, y'know, Mr. Backpacker-in-the-arse-end-of-nowhere. Some of us simply don't *do* traveling light." Her gaze alighted on Mike, and she smiled. "Wow. You must be the man."

Mike blinked. "I'm not sure how to take that."

"Trust me, it's a compliment." Ruth shook his hand. "I'm delighted to finally meet you. And this is Clare." She peered behind her, frowning. "Where the bloody hell has she got to?"

"Who's she, the cat's mother?" Clare rolled her eyes before proffering her cheek to Jonathon to be kissed. "Hi. Nice to see you again. Now someone take these cases off me before I fall over."

Jonathon laughed and relieved her of some of her burden before finally closing the front door. Then he gave Ruth a mock glare. "*You* are early."

She gave him a bright smile. "Aren't I always?"

"Yes, but you only sent me the text this morning to say you were definitely coming today. It was a bit of a rush to get your room ready."

"Ooh. Tell me we've got a huge bouncy four-poster bed." Ruth's eyes sparkled. "I've always wanted to sleep in a four-poster."

Clare snickered. "Ha. You mean, you've always wanted to get kinky in a four-poster. And it's not like Jonathon doesn't already know that." Then she saw Mike and stilled. "Ah. Hello."

Mike looked from Clare to Ruth and finally to Jonathon. "Okay. Does someone wanna tell me what the situation is here? And by someone, I mean you."

Ruth rolled her eyes. "Only if he does it while making toasted tea cakes or crumpets, or something else equally delicious. I'm starving."

Jonathon laughed and pointed. "Down those stairs. And yes, there are crumpets." He led the way down to the kitchen, with Mike at his side. In no time at all, Clare was dropping crumpets into the toaster, and Ruth was busy buttering them as fast as they came out.

Jonathon put the kettle on. "Okay, introductions. This is Mike Tattersall, the—"

"Who is exactly as you described him." Ruth winked. "You always did have a thing for beards."

"That's rich coming from you," Jonathon retorted, "seeing as I was *your* beard on quite a few occasions."

"And vice versa," she flung back at him.

Jonathon rolled his eyes, then turned to face Mike—who was staring at Ruth.

"Something wrong?" she asked sweetly.

"You're a—"

"Lesbian, yes." Her eyes twinkled. "There's no fooling this one, is there?"

"As opposed to most of your family, apparently," Jonathon muttered. He sighed and addressed Mike. "Ruth is not out to her family. At least, she wasn't the last time we spoke. I had to check with her first before I told you about my plan, because—"

"Because no one has the right to out anyone against their wishes," Mike said, nodding. "And Clare is—"

"My bit of stuff, for the last five years," Ruth said, grinning. Then she gazed fondly at Clare. "I call her the wife. Because one day, she bloody well will be."

Clare took Ruth's hand and kissed it.

Jonathon gazed at her in frank astonishment. "I thought you didn't believe in marriage."

There was that sweet smile again. "I didn't. I do now. People change." She leaned across the kitchen table. "I never thought I'd find you planning to thwart your father. The Jonathon *I* first met wouldn't have dared."

"That's because I was ten years old," he fired back.

Suddenly Mike started laughing. "I can't wait to hear this plan of yours."

Jonathon met Ruth's gaze. "Right now, we haven't discussed it much, beyond buying us some time. If Father—and Ruth's family—think Ruth and I are in a relationship, then maybe they'll ease up on pressuring us to find a partner."

"My parents have talked of nothing else ever since I broke off the engagement to Rod back when I was twenty. Of course, *I* knew there was no way I could go through with it. Rod didn't have a clue. He just thought I'd got cold feet and called it off." Ruth leaned into Clare, her dark head a sharp contrast to Clare's blond hair. "When Jonathon called me, wanting to talk about his father's plans, I jumped at the idea. We haven't come to any firm decisions—that's what this visit is for—but the chance to spend Christmas with friends and family, where we could be ourselves and no one would give a damn? That's priceless."

"Not that we could decide anything without talking to you," Jonathon added, reaching for Mike's hand. He fell silent, letting Mike take it all in.

Mike lifted Jonathon's hand to his lips and kissed it. "I think it's going to be a very interesting Christmas."

"Hello?" Jason's voice filtered down the stairs. "I wondered where you'd got to and—do I smell crumpets?"

They burst out laughing.

"Come on down," Jonathon called up to him. When Ruth looked at him questioningly, he smiled. "It's okay. Jason is family."

"Why do I get the feeling this little family is going to get bigger?" Mike said with a sigh.

"Because you know me. You know *us*."

Jonathon had no idea where this new step would take them, but putting down roots in Merrychurch seemed like a great way to start.

READ HOW JONATHON'S STORY STARTS

TRUTH WILL OUT

K.C. WELLS

A Merrychurch Mysteries case

Jonathon de Mountford's visit to Merrychurch village to stay with his uncle Dominic gets off to a bad start when Dominic fails to appear at the railway station. But when Jonathon finds him dead in his study, apparently as the result of a fall, everything changes. For one thing, Jonathon is the next in line to inherit the manor house. For another, he's not so sure it was an accident, and with the help of Mike Tattersall, the owner of the village pub, Jonathon sets out to prove his theory—if he can concentrate long enough without getting distracted by the handsome Mike.

They discover an increasingly long list of people who had reason to want Dominic dead. And when events take an unexpected turn, the amateur sleuths are left bewildered. It doesn't help that the police inspector brought in to solve the case is the last person Mike wants to see, especially when they are told to keep their noses out of police business.

In Jonathon's case, that's like a red rag to a bull....

www.dreamspinnerpress.com

CHAPTER ONE

JONATHON DE Mountford had forgotten how charming Merrychurch railway station was. From its quaint black-and-white mock wattle and daub exterior, to the colorful bunting decorating the arch above the door, to the troughs, pots, and hanging baskets filled with flowers everywhere he looked. The yellow-painted warning line toward the edge of the platform was bright, as if freshly done, and the station sign, with its white lettering on a dark blue background, was free from the graffiti Jonathon had seen in such plentiful supply only a short time ago in Winchester.

Only one thing was missing: there was no sign of his uncle, Dominic.

Jonathon checked the time on his phone. Ten minutes had elapsed since he'd gotten off the train, and the platform was deserted. The station guard had disappeared into his office, but Jonathon could hear him whistling cheerily. Then his mind snapped back to Dominic. Okay, it had been a very early train, but Dominic had assured Jonathon that he was still a habitual early riser and that collecting him from the station would be no trouble at all.

Maybe he's waiting outside.

Jonathon adjusted the strap of the backpack slung over his shoulder, grasped the pull-up handle of his suitcase, and trundled through the open doorway into the station, with its ticket counter and bright posters. The only incongruity was the self-service ticket machine, but he assumed even Merrychurch had had to succumb to some of the demands of the twenty-first century.

Passing through the wide wooden door onto the pavement beyond, Jonathon found himself standing alone, a car park to his left, surrounded by a picket fence. Nothing else to be seen but the lane, with tall trees on both sides. No traffic. No noise, except for the birds chirping away.

And still no sign of Dominic.

Jonathon checked his texts, but there was nothing. Sighing, he scrolled through to find Dominic's number. When all he got was his uncle's recorded message, the first tendrils of unease began to snake through his belly. This really wasn't like Dominic.

A glance up the empty country lane, a glance down, and he made his mind up. There seemed little point in waiting any longer. The best thing to do would be to make his own way into the village and then on to the manor house. He knew that Merrychurch was only a mile or so away, and, based on experience, it wasn't worth waiting for the local bus, which only ran once an hour. With the happy chirping of birds in the trees to accompany him, Jonathon headed toward the village, pulling his suitcase behind him.

It was a beautiful late-July day, just the right temperature that he didn't need a jacket. As he walked along, he recollected the recent emails and conversations he'd had with Dominic. There was nothing he could put his finger on, but Jonathon had gotten the definite impression that all was not well. The speed with which Dominic had agreed to Jonathon coming to stay had been enough of an indication.

So why isn't he here to meet me like he said?

Jonathon cast his mind back to their last conversation, a week ago. They'd spoken about the village fete, due to take place on the grounds of the house in early August. Dominic loved doing his Lord-of-the-Manor routine, and from what Jonathon could recall from past visits, it was usually a fun day. They'd also talked about Jonathon's latest book, a collection of photographs taken on a recent trip to India. More than once, Dominic had expressed his pride in Jonathon's work.

Maybe we should have discussed what was bothering him. Because it had been plain to Jonathon that something was definitely on Dominic's mind.

From behind came the sound of a vehicle, and Jonathon squeezed himself into the hedge, pulling in the case to stand it beside him. It surprised him when the car came to a stop in the road next to him.

"Do you need a lift?" The voice was male, deep, and cheerful.

Jonathon regarded the driver of the 4x4. He was in his late thirties, maybe early forties, with dark brown hair cut short and neat. Warm brown eyes peered at Jonathon from behind a pair of rimless glasses. "If you're going to Merrychurch, then yes."

The driver smiled. "I didn't think you'd be walking any farther. The next village after Merrychurch is

Lower Pinton, and that's four miles from here." He nodded to the seat beside him. "Hop in. There's room in the back for your case."

"Thanks." Jonathon crossed to the passenger's side, stowed the case, then clambered into the front seat. "It was nice of you to stop." He clasped the backpack to him, his precious camera safely protected within it.

"I figured you'd missed the bus. Easily done, now they've reduced the timetable." He waited until Jonathon had fastened his seat belt before moving off. "Where are you staying in the village?"

"Excuse me?" Jonathon arched his eyebrows.

The driver laughed. "Okay, yeah, that was presumptuous of me, but the suitcase was a bit of a giveaway. And I'm only asking because if you don't have anywhere to stay, I own the local pub, and there are rooms if you need one."

"Ah." Jonathon kept his gaze focused on the passing landscape. "I'm staying with my uncle, but thanks all the same."

The lane leading to Merrychurch hadn't changed in all the years Jonathon had been visiting his uncle: trees met in a leafy arch over the road, the odd house here and there....

"Have you been to Merrychurch before?"

Jonathon smiled to himself. "A few times, yes."

"You probably know the place better than I do, then. I've only lived here for the past eleven months."

Just then a rabbit darted out from the hedgerow, and the driver swerved the car violently to avoid it. Jonathon found himself holding his breath, but fortunately the rabbit escaped injury and reached the other side of the road.

The driver expelled a low growl, then glanced across at Jonathon. "I hate it when the little buggers do that. One of these days, I'm not gonna be able to stop in time."

The fact that he'd swerved at all was a plus in Jonathon's book.

A minute later they were in the heart of the village. The driver stopped the car in front of the charming, picturesque pub, leaving the engine running. "So, can I drop you someplace? Where does your uncle live?"

Jonathon was overcome with an unexpected rush of nerves. He knew there were those in the village who resented his uncle—Dominic had intimated as much on several occasions—and he didn't want to say something, only to find his Good Samaritan harbored a grudge and turned out to be a psychopath. Then he pulled himself together. The stranger had already admitted he was a recent addition to the village population, so it was highly unlikely that he bore Dominic any ill will.

"My uncle had agreed to meet me," Jonathon explained, "but—"

"But he wasn't there when you arrived," the man concluded. When Jonathon lifted his eyebrows once more, he smiled. "That much was obvious, or you wouldn't have been walking into the village. Has he messaged you to say he was delayed?"

Jonathon shook his head. "Which is… weird."

The man gave an emphatic nod. "Right. In that case, I'll take you to him. That way, if he's not there, I'll bring you back here and you can wait in the pub until he surfaces. What do you think?"

Jonathon thought it was about time he knew the name of his Good Samaritan. "Sounds great to me." He extended a hand. "Jonathon de Mountford."

The man shook it. "Mike Tattersall. Pleased to meet you." His eyes widened. "Ah. I guess I don't have to ask who your uncle is, then."

Jonathon had suspected that might be the case. Even if Mike was a recent addition to Merrychurch, he would have known about de Mountford Hall, the imposing manor house on the outskirts of the village.

Mike's face clouded over, and he switched off the engine. "Your uncle is a sore point at the moment."

Jonathon stilled. "Why?"

"My sister, Sue, is his cleaner. She's worked up at the house for the past three years. Everything was fine, until last month."

Jonathon had the impression that Mike's sudden change of mood was more to do with his sister than Dominic. "What happened?"

Mike sighed. "Sue's a member of an animal rights activist group. I try not to get involved, partly because it gives me the willies to hear she's off on some protest. What I don't know can't keep me awake at night." When Jonathon frowned, he gave a shrug. "Comes with the territory. I'm an ex-copper. I've tried telling her to stay on the right side of the law, but it's not easy. She can be bloody stubborn when she wants to be. Anyway, last month she got wind of something and went charging off to the manor to see your uncle. Turns out he's given permission for the local hunt to go across his land, which also means they'll be close to the village."

"But… didn't they ban fox hunting? It's just hunting with dogs now, isn't it?"

Mike nodded. "Sue has got it into her head that the local hunt bigwigs will be ignoring that part. No idea where she's getting her information from. But yeah, things got a bit... ugly."

That fitted in with Jonathon's uneasy feelings. Something *had* been wrong after all. "I think I'd like to go to the manor, please."

Mike appeared to shrug off his mood. He straightened in the driver's seat and nodded briskly. "Sure thing. Let's get you up there." He switched on the engine and pulled away from the curb.

Jonathon gazed at his surroundings. The village seemed as it always had: a few shops huddled together, the pub, and the post office. Then there were the houses, many of them thatched. The church tower rose above the trees, square and solid. The river still wound its way through the village, dipping below the picturesque stone bridge with its graceful arch. Ducks squatted along its banks, heads tucked under their wings, while others swam in the slow-moving, clear water, bobbing their heads below the surface, their rear ends stuck up in the air, as comical as Jonathon remembered from his childhood.

"Merrychurch hasn't changed," he murmured as they sped through the narrow, leafy lanes.

Mike chuckled. "Oh, you think so? I've learned from experience that things are seldom as they appear. You have no clue what's lurking below the seemingly tranquil surface." He snorted. "Yeah, there speaks an ex-policeman, always expecting the worst."

Jonathon studied him carefully. Mike was obviously too young to have retired. "How come you left the force? Where did you work?"

"London Met. And I was invalided out when I lost my foot in a raid."

Jonathon couldn't help the automatic glance toward Mike's feet.

Mike obviously caught the movement. "I have a prosthetic foot now. You'd never know it wasn't real if you saw it." Then he sighed. "At least that's what I tell myself every night when the shoes come off. Anyhow, as I was saying… when they gave me my compensation, I was at a loss. I'd been a copper since I was nineteen, and there I was, nearly forty, with no clue what I was going to do for the rest of my life."

"So you bought a village pub. Quite a change of pace from London, I imagine."

Mike laughed. "You have no idea. The pub was Sue's brainchild. She'd moved here with her husband, Dan, but things didn't work out for them. When he left, she stayed, although that meant finding work. The pub came up for sale, and she thought of me. I did suggest that she could work there if she wanted, but she soon scuppered that idea." He gave a wry chuckle. "She had a point. We'd have been at each other's throats within minutes. Chalk and cheese, us two." Mike nodded toward the windscreen. "There you are."

Jonathon followed his gaze. On either side of the lane stood the old stone gateposts that he recalled from his childhood, the ones that bore the family crest. Except the crest had worn away during the two centuries or so that the family had owned the manor house, and the gateposts were beginning to crumble too. They marked the boundaries of the original estate. Subsequent members of the de Mountford family had sold off parts of it, and now all that remained were the one hundred or so acres that surrounded de Mountford Hall.

"And there it is," Jonathon said softly. The manor house was just visible above the tree line, perched on top of a gently sloping hill, its white facade standing out against the green, glowing in the early-morning sunshine. As Mike passed through the gateposts and followed the gravel-covered lane, Jonathon peered up at the hall. "I can't imagine what he finds to do all day in that place. He must really rattle around in there." Dominic was a confirmed bachelor and had lived alone since he'd inherited the house. Up until fifteen years ago, he'd worked in London, in the family law firm, but he had surprised everyone by announcing his retirement at the age of forty-five.

Mike took a left turn, and the gravel lane became a driveway that looped in front of the house, circling a grassy knoll where an ornate fountain stood, its wells dry. He pulled up in front of the wide arched entrance. "Delivered to the door. How's that for service?"

Jonathon smiled and held out his hand again. "Thanks, Mike." He glanced around. There were no cars in sight, but that might simply have meant they were in the garage.

"It's very quiet. Mind you, it *is* still early. Maybe he overslept."

Jonathon cocked his head and listened. Even the birds seemed to have ceased their happy song. That only served to add to his returning unease. He put down his backpack, got out of the car, and walked toward the heavy oak door, darkened by the shadow of the stone arch above it. Jonathon pulled on the central knob of the brass door bell, hearing the clang within the house. He took a step back and waited, his gaze fixed on the door.

After a minute of silence, he turned to Mike. "Looks like he's gone out."

"He has servants, right? At least that's what Sue says."

Jonathon tried to recall. "He used to, but that was a few years ago. I haven't been here for two years, so I don't know. He certainly didn't mention getting rid of them." In which case it either appeared to be their day off, or they hadn't arrived yet, which seemed unlikely.

"Try the door. Maybe he left it unlocked." When Jonathon stared at him, Mike snickered. "Yeah, I know. Since when does anyone go out and leave a place like this unlocked these days? It was just a suggestion."

Nevertheless, Jonathon felt compelled to try. He grasped the heavy doorknob and turned....

The door swung open with a creak.

"Uh-oh," he whispered.

Mike was out of the car and at his side in an instant. "That's a bit odd. Want me to go in there with you?" he asked in a low voice. "Just in case there are...."

"What? Just in case there are what?" Icy fingers traced over Jonathon's skin.

"Burglars, maybe?" Mike peered at the door. "Look, it could just be me with my overactive imagination. Or it could be something as simple as your uncle forgot to lock the door when he went out."

Jonathon was praying for the latter. "Okay, you can come with me."

Mike puffed out his broad chest. "And stay behind me. If there's anyone in here, let me deal with them, okay?"

It took a moment or two to realize Mike was acting with such bravado to ease Jonathon's nerves. He gave a mock sigh of relief. "Absolutely." Not that he was afraid of taking on a few bad guys, but they'd have to be smaller than him, and since he was five feet six and as skinny as a rake, he thought that extremely unlikely.

Mike stepped into the cool interior, the white marble floor reflecting the sunlight that spilled in through the open door. He crept forward, his boots squeaking slightly against the tiles, his head to one side as he listened.

The house was as silent as the grave, and Jonathon ceased to see the funny side. "I don't think he's here."

Mike came to a stop and peered up the staircase. "Well, if there are burglars, they're quiet as bloody mice," he whispered. "I'm going to check upstairs, but I don't think there's anyone here."

Jonathon nodded. "I'll take a look around too." There was no way he was going to wait there, feeling as useful as an inflatable dartboard.

Mike narrowed his gaze. "Be careful."

It was rather sweet, Jonathon thought, considering Mike had known him for all of five minutes. Well, he could be sweet too. "I will if you will." Without waiting for Mike's reply, Jonathon crept over to the sitting room door. One glance around it convinced him that room was empty. He moved from room to room, the soles of his trainers making the same squeaky noises as Mike's boots.

No signs of disturbance. No signs of a break-in. Nothing.

When he reached the door of his uncle's study, he paused. As a child, this room had always been off-limits. Dominic's refuge for when visitors became too much, his sanctuary. Finding the door ajar only added to the panic fluttering in his belly.

"Dominic?" He pushed it cautiously, took two steps into the room—and froze.

"What's wrong?" Mike hissed from behind him.

Jonathon swallowed hard. "I think we need to call the police. And an ambulance." He tried to take another step, but his legs were like lead.

Mike pushed past him and came to a halt. "Oh, Christ."

Uncle Dominic lay in a heap on the floor by the fireplace, the harsh red of the blood pooled around his head stark against the white marble. Jonathon could only watch as Mike hurried over to the prone form and bent over to place two fingers against Dominic's neck. The silence stretched as Jonathon waited, unable to tear his gaze from the sight.

Finally Mike straightened and looked Jonathon in the eye. "I'm so sorry. He's dead."

His words didn't compute. Dominic couldn't be dead.

Mike walked over to him and grasped his upper arm. "Okay," he began, his voice calm and even. "I'm going to take you out to the car, and then I'll call the local police." When Jonathon gazed at him, blinking, Mike patted his arm. "You can't stay in here, Jonathon. This could be a crime scene."

That was when the shivers set in.

K.C. WELLS started writing in 2012, although the idea of writing a novel had been in her head since she was a child. But after reading that first gay romance in 2009, she was hooked.

She now writes full-time, and the line of men in her head clamoring to tell their story is getting longer and longer. If the frequent visits by plot bunnies are anything to go by, that's not about to change anytime soon.

K.C. loves to hear from readers.

Email: k.c.wells@btinternet.com

Facebook: www.facebook.com/KCWellsWorld

Blog: kcwellsworld.blogspot.co.uk

Twitter: @K_C_Wells

Website: www.kcwellsworld.com

Instagram: www.instagram.com/k.c.wells

BFF

K.C. WELLS

I'm about to do something huge, and it could change… everything.

I met Matt in second grade, and we've been inseparable ever since. We went to the same schools, studied at the same college. When we both got jobs in the same town, we shared an apartment. And when my life took an unexpected turn, Matt was there for me. Every milestone in my life, he was there to share it. And what's really amazing? After all these years, we're still the best of friends.

Which brings me to this fragile, heart-stopping moment: I want to tell him I love him, really love him, but I'm scared to death of what he'll say. If I've got this all wrong, I'll lose him—forever.

www.dreamspinnerpress.com